LEGEND

NATE TEMPLE SERIES BOOK 11

SHAYNE SILVERS

ARGENTO
PUBLISHING

CONTENTS

Shayne Silvers

Legend

Nate Temple Series Book 11

A TempleVerse Series

Formerly published as The Temple Chronicles Series

ISBN: 978-1-947709-20-1

© 2018, Shayne Silvers / Argento Publishing, LLC

info@shaynesilvers.com

THE NATE TEMPLE SERIES—A WARNING

Nate Temple starts out with everything most people could ever wish for—money, magic, and notoriety. He's a local celebrity in St. Louis, Missouri—even if the fact that he's a wizard is still a secret to the world at large.

Nate is also a bit of a...well, let's call a spade a spade. He can be a mouthy, smart-assed jerk. Like the infamous Sherlock Holmes, I specifically chose to give Nate glaring character flaws to overcome rather than making him a chivalrous Good Samaritan. He's a black hat wizard, an anti-hero—and you are now his partner in crime. He is going to make a *ton* of mistakes. And like a buddy cop movie, you are more than welcome to yell, laugh and curse at your new partner as you ride along together through the deadly streets of St. Louis.

Despite Nate's flaws, there's also something *endearing* about him...You soon catch whispers of a firm moral code buried deep under all his snark and arrogance. A diamond waiting to be polished. And you, the esteemed reader, will soon find yourself laughing at things you really shouldn't be laughing at. It's part of Nate's charm. Call it his magic...

So don't take yourself, or any of the characters in my world, too seriously. Life is too short for that nonsense.

Get ready to cringe, cackle, cry, curse, and—ultimately—*cheer* on this snarky wizard as he battles or befriends angels, demons, myths, gods, shifters, vampires and many other flavors of dangerous supernatural beings.

DON'T FORGET!

VIP's get early access to all sorts of book goodies, including signed copies, private giveaways, and advance notice of future projects. AND A FREE NOVELLA! Click the image or join here:
www.shaynesilvers.com/l/219800

FOLLOW AND LIKE:

Shayne's FACEBOOK PAGE:

www.shaynesilvers.com/l/38602

I try to respond to all messages, so don't hesitate to drop me a line. Not interacting with readers is the biggest travesty that most authors can make. Let me fix that.

1

I clinked glasses with Achilles, wishing I had some Macallan rather than beer.

"Alcohol. Because no great story ever started with anyone eating a salad," I told him.

Achilles chuckled, his eyes trained on the next group of men teaming up against Alex. The Minotaur was absent since this was just some unscheduled light training for Alex, who had wanted to work out. He'd asked me to join him, but I had politely declined. I didn't want to risk having a mental breakdown in the middle of the fight if something reminded me of Fae.

"Cocky little shit. Five?" Achilles gasped. "Wait. That's Leonidas! When did he arrive?" Achilles pointed out a bandana-clad fighter in the huddle against Alex. Achilles leaned forward on the new bench that had been installed. The rest of the bleachers had been burned, shattered, or otherwise obliterated in my fight with Mordred.

I watched as Alex stood facing his opponents—all hardened warriors who had been kicking ass since before the Trojan War. Alex breathed evenly, his muscles entirely relaxed, his feet positioned lightly to react quickly rather than planted firmly as one might do against a single opponent to hold their ground. He didn't even seem to be breathing hard—like a marathon racer stretching for a warmup 5k.

I watched Leonidas—almost hard to make him out since he wore a bandana over his face like a Wild West train robber. Was he trying to disguise himself, so Alex would underestimate him? Alex held two long sticks at his side—escrimas—but his opponents all had staffs taller than their own bodies. Smart on Alex's part. Speed, not power, was the best course against so many opponents. They moved forward in unison, and I realized I was gripping the bleachers, leaning forward as I held my breath.

Staffs swung with great whooshing noises towards Alex from multiple directions.

Alex began playing the drums.

The *rat-a-tat* sound filled the ring like automatic gunfire—Alex peppering both his attackers and their staffs with his escrimas in a blur that was almost too fast for me to follow. And through it all, he was pivoting and twisting, even angling two of his opponents to take each other out with a double knock-out blow when he ducked at the last moment.

The two opponents stared at each other, dazed, and then collapsed to the ground.

Two other opponents spent too long staring at the friendly fire and received a dozen welts each for their trouble. One particularly angry-looking guy lowered his staff across his chest in an attempt to block Alex's barrage. Alex reared back and kicked him hard enough to snap the staff in half and send the man slamming into his teammate.

Like a struck bowling pin, the unlucky teammate flew out of the ring, landing in a pile of debris beside the sleeping Talon. My cat warrior was on his feet with a piercing hiss almost like he had anticipated it, his tail all bushed up and twitching violently. His spear was pressed against the Myrmidon's throat before the man could even move. Talon quickly gauged the level of threat to me by risking a quick glance my way. Seeing I was safe, he glanced over to see Alex squaring off with the bandana-clad Leonidas. Talon snarled down at his victim. "I was napping. Never, *ever* disturb me when I am napping."

Then the spear evaporated, and Talon resumed his nap with a yawn that revealed wicked fangs long and sharp enough to shred flesh to ribbons. The Myrmidon looked properly chastised but didn't apologize to Talon—likely for fear of disturbing him since his eyes were again closed.

Achilles laughed—but muffled it with his fist so as not to disturb my cat.

Bandana-clad Leonidas dove forward with his staff, lunging it forward like a spear towards Alex's unprotected throat. Alex spun, barely moving out of the way in time, and the staff stabbed empty air but so close that the wood rested against the side of his neck as he continued spinning towards Leonidas.

Leonidas wisely dropped the staff and began swinging a fist at Alex.

Who had anticipated it.

He struck Leonidas' knuckles with a solid *thwack* of his escrima—the immediate crack was loud enough to signal a broken bone. Except Leonidas didn't let out that he'd felt it, already swinging his other fist.

But Alex struck that one down, too, with an even sharper cracking sound.

Then something very strange happened. Alex twirled his stick around Leonidas' forearm, and swung his arm in an exaggerated circular motion, turning the knuckle blow into...an elbow trap. Leonidas strained against it, grunting and dancing about, but couldn't get free. Alex's face was entirely calm as he let Leonidas wear himself out, dancing about the clearing while holding Leonidas in the trap.

Alex wasn't gloating, and he wasn't showboating. His face was as calm as a block of ice.

Then he grabbed the bottom of the bandana in his fist and yanked down, introducing Leonidas' face to his knee. Once. Twice. Three times.

Leonidas stumbled as Alex let him go, and then made a drunken lurch for Alex with his purple, bruised fists, swinging wildly. Alex dipped, rolled, and then kicked out Leonidas' legs hard enough to send him up into the air, horizontal to the ground. Then Alex hammer-fisted him down to the dirt, making Leonidas grunt twice—once at the initial blow, and again as he hit the earth.

Alex crouched down over Leonidas, staring him right in the eyes with his too-calm face. Leonidas gave a very slight nod.

That's when I saw the guy Alex had drop-kicked into his pal suddenly racing towards Alex with one half of the splintered staff couched against his hip like he intended to joust Alex—but from behind, while Alex wasn't looking.

Alex cocked his head right before I opened my mouth to shout out a warning, and I gasped as Alex leaned slightly to the side, blindly reached out to grab the end of the splintered staff. He used the man's momentum to stab it into the ground about two inches from Leonidas' ear. Alex held the staff in the ground with the one hand—like a fulcrum—as he grabbed the middle of the staff with the other and pulled, turning his attacker into a virginal pole-vaulter.

The Myrmidon went flying over both Alex and Leonidas—who had probably soiled himself when Alex slammed the splintered staff into the dirt near his face. Alex was chasing after the attacker before he'd had time to land and think about what he'd done wrong.

The moment he landed—on his face—and bounced, Alex pounced on top of him and punched him one time in each ear, dazing the Myrmidon without killing him—as the bastard really deserved for trying to stab Alex in the back.

Alex's calm voice rang out. "If you're going to stab a man in the back, don't fuck it up. Because you're gambling away your honor in hopes of a victory. If it doesn't pan out, there are no refunds, and everyone will know your only remaining currency is cowardice," Alex said coldly.

Achilles let out a slow, malevolent whistle.

"This is...*sparring!*" the Myrmidon mumbled woozily, but still managed to sound angry—like everyone's least favorite drunk uncle around the holidays. "It's all about expecting the unexpect—"

"No," Alex interrupted in a harsh tone—not cruelly, but definitively. "It was about your injured pride. And you tried to buy that back by cashing in your honor. Now, you're destitute. I no longer *see* you, vagrant. Come back when you have the funds to buy back some dignity."

And then Alex climbed to his feet, not sparing the Myrmidon a backwards glance. He didn't even look angry. Just...disinterested.

The ring was silent. Even the injured Myrmidons had quit groaning to listen in.

Alex helped Leonidas to his feet, lifted the king's knuckles to his face to inspect them, and then called out to one of the other Myrmidons for an ice pack. Leonidas stared back at Alex, speechless and obedient. Alex accepted an ice pack from a swift Myrmidon with a murmured thanks, wrapped it delicately around Leonidas' hands, and then guided him towards the bleachers to sit beside us.

Leonidas sat down wordlessly, and we all watched Alex in silence.

"My king," he said, lowering his eyes. Then he turned away and walked briskly back to the center of the ring, resuming his place. "Next," he called out in a crisp tone. The Myrmidons in line for the next bout looked decidedly uneasy about how to proceed, as if it was their first day in the yard.

Leonidas slowly turned to glance back at us, and it was more the whites of his eyes than the blood on his face that kept me from teasing him. "Where did you *find* him?" he asked in a whisper, slowly shaking his head.

I smiled, hiding my own astonishment like my father had taught me. "Fleeing the Wild Hunt in Fae. All by himself. And he was in his early teens."

Leonidas studied me, repeating my words silently. Then he turned back to the fight, muttering under his breath.

"And he did it with class," I added, smiling proudly. "I did a good job training him, but I don't want to take all the credit. You helped in some small way, I'm sure."

Achilles growled something unpleasant, but I wasn't even sure Leonidas had heard me.

2

Achilles motioned to two of his Myrmidons and then pointed at the backstabber. He made a flurry of hand gestures, and the Myrmidons nodded in understanding, setting their jaws as they approached their disgraced compatriot. I was betting he was on unpaid leave, to say the least.

Achilles nodded satisfactorily. "I don't know if you realize what he just did or not, but it was far more serious than fighting a good fight. He dispensed justice, honored a king, defeated impossible odds, and became a general to every soldier watching. He just won an impossible bout on four different fronts."

Leonidas climbed to his feet and walked away, keeping a critical eye on Alex, who was already sparring his new opponents, but in a more educational way—calling out suggestions and critiques to each fallen foe—all while he continued fighting those still standing.

And he *still* wasn't breathing heavily.

"I think you just pissed him off," I told Achilles, jerking my chin at Leonidas.

"No. He can't sit still for very long if he's watching a sparring match. Gets restless leg syndrome. That guy lives on adrenaline. Strangely enough, he's also very antisocial. Not much room for any of the extras in life. Only wants to do one thing at a time and do it well." Achilles arched a brow. "He's *Spartan*, in every definition of the word, not just the nationality."

I nodded thoughtfully, watching the Spartan King. I really hadn't spent much time around him at all since meeting him. I'd tried a few times, but he was a hard one to pin down. He had also spent a lot of time training Alex, and I'd been pretty busy with Hell and Mordred.

Still, it was hard not to fanboy. One of these days, I'd have a sit down with him. Maybe ask why he had come to St. Louis.

"That man is a monster," Achilles murmured reverently, staring back at Alex.

I shook my head, dismissing thoughts of Leonidas for the time being. "No. That man is my son," I corrected, smiling to myself.

Talon peered over at me, his tail flicking back and forth absently as he checked to make sure I was doing alright. It had been a week since I'd had any meltdowns, but I'd almost killed a friend by accident, thinking he was a pirate from Neverland.

So...yeah. I was under a close watch. By Talon. Because he had been the only one able to calm me down. Unfortunately for us, he was also at risk of having these flashbacks, so we were both being very careful not to think about our Fae childhood while experiencing strong emotions at the same time. I could talk clinically about things from my past but combine those conversations with any strong emotions and I was liable to have a meltdown.

Those flashbacks were debilitating, leaving me in a fog of confusion where I quite literally couldn't discern reality from memory. Luckily, I hadn't suffered any since my fight with Mordred. In a way, that was good. But in another way, it made me feel like a ticking bomb.

Even thinking about it now was increasing my heart rate, so I held my breath and began thinking of random book quotes. I took careful, calming breaths, and focused on the relaxing sound of manly love—fists kissing faces, boots embracing ribs, and the resulting groans of pain and merciful cries.

I smiled, feeling much better.

That alone probably said quite a bit about me, if one put stock in that mystical foo-fah known as human psychology. But as a card-carrying man, I was immune to such trivial weaknesses.

"Still freaking the fuck out for no apparent reason?" Achilles asked with all the empathy of a guillotine. "My king," he added almost offhandedly.

I narrowed my eyes at him. "Maybe you should train your men better," I muttered. "My boy is kicking their asses. Repeatedly." I pointed at Alex currently extracting his fist from a much larger man's nose. "One of these days, he's going to hit so hard his fist gets stuck. That's going to be messy."

Achilles grunted. "I helped train him, so all that can be said is that he took my lessons better than any of my own men," he argued, not putting much emotion into his response. Because we weren't really fighting. More like two angry old men in the sunset of our lives bickering back and forth on the front porch as we watched the sunrise of the new generation with ample disdain, bitching about *kids these days.*

Also, as deadly as Achilles was with a blade, it was accurate to say that he was understandably terrified of me. He admitted his fear by poking fun at me as a defensive mechanism—poking the bear. Because lately, when I had flexed on things that really mattered to me, well...

The target usually ended up broken.

As did anyone or anything in the nearby vicinity.

That's not bragging. That's admitting a fault with a smug grin—arrogant humility.

Like seven days ago when I had fought Mordred here at the Dueling Grounds—a place where no one could truly get hurt. You could kill someone here and the dearly departed would wake up in bed, none the worse for wear. Except, with Mordred, it had been his...

Heh. His Achilles' heel.

Because he'd harbored the stolen Nine Souls from Hell—the souls of dead gods, and probably not the good ones. Like Lord Voldemort, they were simply referred to as *those who shall not be named.* And I'd tried very hard to learn some of those names.

The Dueling Grounds worked on a very basic principle. Each person had one soul and one body, so when your body and soul died at the Dueling Grounds, your soul was sent back home with your body rather than the person actually dying.

But Mordred had an excess of Souls on him when he stepped into the ring.

So, each time we had killed him here, one of those Souls didn't have a body to ride back home to—because the other Souls kept his body locked down at the Dueling Grounds, refusing to let go. As a result, the safest place for everyone in the world to take a chance at having a near-death experience, ended up being the most dangerous place to one specific, real specimen of a bastard.

Mordred. King Arthur's illegitimate son.

Ultimately, we had whittled him down to one last Soul, which he had somehow managed to consume for himself, bonding it with his own soul like an extra battery.

I had managed to steal three of his Nine Souls.

He had fled to Fae to recover and we were a couple weeks away from a supposed meeting about a bullshit charity he had established—the Round Table Initiative—a charity designed to openly discuss magic with the public. With humans.

Which I knew would cause a panic, likely starting a war with Regulars against Freaks.

My plan was simple. Kill him before that appointment.

Coincidentally, that probably meant heading to Fae to dig him out of Camelot. And I needed to go to Fae to come to grips with my Fae childhood. I had a block as a result of dabbling in too many magic buckets and needed to go take a walk on the wild side. That was the theory, anyway. But it was the only one I had.

A nice little banished Fae woman named Alvara had suckered me into buying that theory by telling me she might be able to help me, and that she had friends who might have answers on me being a Catalyst. Something I'd heard quite a few people call me, but had found no solid information on what it meant.

All I knew was that the Catalyst had something to do with a world-ending war heading our way. Since so many entities from different pantheons seemed to agree, I had admitted that it was probably legitimate. And with so many Freaks, Legends, Gods, Monsters, and other powerful beings suddenly choosing to move to Missouri—the Gateway to the West—the facts lined up.

I just didn't know whether being the Catalyst was a good thing—to end the war—or a bad thing—to start the war. And that was a pretty important question to learn the answer to.

I felt my shoulders tightening again, so I counted to ten, took calming breaths, and thought of more random book quotes.

The price for answers on the Catalyst—and hopefully my flashbacks—was to take Alvara, and her daughter Alice, with us to Fae—let them see home again. And since I needed her help, I couldn't just take off for Fae without her, or I might risk the flashbacks hitting me right when I faced off with Mordred.

Simple as that. Quick road trip, get some answers, kill Mordred. Two weeks at the most.

Even I didn't buy that, but I was trying to stay positive. It was more productive than sobbing in a corner and clutching a teddy bear. Because when you're knee-deep in shit, there's no use standing still and complaining about it. Just start walking out of the shit. Obviously.

I had a few things to take care of here, before gallivanting off to Fae. The very real risk of time-slippage while I was away made it very important that I lined up my ducks in a row before leaving St. Louis. What if a year or two passed while I was in Fae for a few days?

I had an Hourglass artifact that would easily fix this problem but using it would draw the Fae armies on top of me like a swarm of flies to shit. I'd checked around, even asking my definitely insane ancestor Matthias for several other ideas to reduce that time-slippage, but we hadn't come up with anything reliable.

The only sure way to make sure that the world didn't burn in my absence was to move quickly while in Fae. A day, tops. Hopefully find Mordred the moment I wrapped up my business with Alvara and Alice and then kill him. If he was in Fae, St. Louis was probably fine. It was if he disappeared that I needed to seriously consider getting back out—to make sure he didn't destroy St. Louis while I was traipsing about with fairies.

3

Achilles let out a loud breath, snapping me out of my daze. "You know, I used to like war, fighting, chaos..." he said, trailing off to watch Alex whoop the shit out of his veteran Myrmidons. It was a testament to Alex's skill that Achilles wasn't chastising his men for repeatedly losing. "Then I met you. Watched you play at war," he said soberly, shaking his head. "Ruined it for me."

I winced. "Sorry, man."

He shrugged. "It is what it is. I learned war with bronze blades and chariots. But you guys are fucking insane with your fancy outfits, wings, murder-corns, and death-clouds."

I couldn't help it. I burst out laughing at his description, causing Talon to look up and check on me. Achilles scowled, thinking I was laughing at him, so I waved a hand good-naturedly. "You're not wrong, Achilles. Myself, I try not to think too hard about those aspects."

"Well, for what it's worth, I think I'll just stick to training Alex. If I could find a dozen men like him..." he said wondrously to himself, shaking his head at the idea.

It would be both terrifying and amazing.

We were silent for a time. "Anyway, I'm trying to say that everyone is having nightmares about what went down that night with Mordred," he muttered. "Like that Soul business. It rubbed everyone the wrong way. Midas is still hesitant to host the next Fight Night. Just in case..." He pointed at the men sparring with Alex. "You'll notice they aren't using blades. And Alex hasn't killed everyone here. Just in case. No one wants to be the first to test their bravery to see if the sanctity of the Dueling Grounds still works. After what you did."

I sighed. "But there were absolutely no fatalities. Everyone survived, right?"

Achilles snorted. "Sure. But what if next time it doesn't work? You could have at least warned us ahead of time," he added in a low growl. "Scared the living hell out of every powerful person in town. If this All War ever does happen, I'm sure you'll have no shortage of Freaks rallying to your cause after that terrifying display of power." And I could tell he wasn't being sarcastic. He truly believed that every major player in town was likely now on Team Temple.

Since he ran the most dangerous bar in town for Freaks—a Kill, as they were known—he heard all the gossip. Achilles Heel was where the nightmares of the supernatural world went to kick their boots up after a long day of mayhem. So...it was probably not far off base.

I shrugged. "If I had known ahead of time how it would all play out, I would have warned you. It was a last-minute idea. A sliver of a hope."

"Hope," Achilles grunted, arching a brow. "Speaking of, have you talked to Anubis about...you know. Feeding *his* Souls to your new Masks?"

I shook my head. "Not yet. Soon."

Achilles leaned back, laughing nervously. "Your funeral, man. Your fucking funeral," he said, holding up his hands in an innocent gesture.

The math came down to this. Of the original Nine Souls I had promised to return to Anubis, the King of Hell, I had used three to power my new Horseman Masks, Ruin—formerly known as Baby B— had eaten one, Mordred had consumed one, and the rest had been returned to Hell. If we were grading a school paper, I had earned forty-percent—a solid *F*.

And me officially becoming the Horseman of Hope had almost killed the Biblical Four Horsemen, for some still-unknown reason. The worst part was that, even though the Souls I had fed my Masks had calmed them down somewhat, I was on a timetable to find three new Riders for them.

Or things would get dicey, and the Biblical Four Horsemen might not survive the cosmic tension I had accidentally caused.

So, although that night felt like a victory...tallying up the actual score didn't make me feel very good about it all. I had solidly earned a participation trophy for not dying. That was it.

And now I needed to talk to my coach, Anubis.

I glanced over at Talon. His white spear –his Eyeless—wasn't in sight, but I knew he could call it into existence with a thought. Anubis had told me I would need to find Talon a blue Devourer—a stone able to eat Souls —in order to help me stand against Mordred. But that had been before I tricked Mordred into fighting me at the Dueling Grounds where we succeeded in taking eight of his precious souls away.

So...was a Devourer still important?

Odin had one in his legendry Spear, Gungnir—and he'd told me, *all the big kids have them.*

Unfortunately, mine had been destroyed in the fight with Mordred and by powering my Masks. I still had the black blade—which I had dubbed the *Feather*—but it didn't have a haft or a Devourer anymore. Just a blade with two feathers hanging from the tang—unicorn feathers identical to Grimm, hence the nickname.

But when I put on my Horseman Mask, a white chain with black thorns appeared, allowing me to use it similar to a bladed whip.

Except my Mask had also been damaged in the fighting, and I didn't dare put it back on until I knew how to fix it.

Achilles was shaking his head at something Alex had done. "It's almost like he was perfectly designed to murder people in combat. Like, oh, I don't know, a *Horseman.*" Then Achilles shot me a very, very dry look. "It would be ironic if a Horseman happened to save his life, earn his trust, and basically put him back on his own two feet. Hypothetically speaking. Almost like a storybook ending. A happily ever after."

I grunted, folding my arms. "It's not easy being this great, Achilles. I mean, I know I make it look very easy, but it's a hard job being a Horseman. I've got to pick out my socks—every morning, I might add. And then the day really gets challenging."

Achilles rolled his eyes. "You have a butler. I win."

I held up a finger. "My butler is a closet sociopath. Did I tell you what he did after the Mordred fight? When I returned home, panicked out of my mind?"

He smirked, his interest piqued. "No."

So, I told him the full story about the Airsoft assault as I ran for my life clad in a tiger-skin rug through the halls of Chateau Falco, sparing not a single embarrassing detail.

It felt nice. It hadn't then, but I had recovered from my welts a week later, so I could smile about it now. Dean and his stupid rules. Break them at your peril.

4

Achilles burst out laughing as I finished the story. "Okay, yeah. That's tough love for you." His laughter trailed off, and he was silent for a time. "All kidding aside, you're pretty lucky to have Dean. Kind of like a stand-in dad, or a godfather, maybe. Just like you stepped up to become a dad for Alex."

I thought about that for a moment, nodding absently. He had a good point. "And you think the icing on the cake is to hand Alex a Mask—to become one of this new herd of Horsemen? A job that is pretty much guaranteed to pit the world against him?" I shook my head. "I don't know, man."

"Well, who else are you considering?" Achilles finally said, leaning back in defeat.

"Matthias told me to pick my best friends."

Achilles snapped his fingers eagerly. "Yes. Do that—"

"Or," I interrupted, holding up a finger. "Pick my worst *enemies*."

His excitement deflated. "Oh. Well, don't go asking me, man. I hate you and everything, but I'm allergic to the crazy shit you get into."

"Achilles," I said in a serious tone, "I can honestly say that the thought never crossed my mind." I enjoyed the stark frown on his face. "Anyway,

I'm pretty sure you have to be mortal. The Biblical Horsemen were mortal."

Achilles glanced over at me. "Is that a guess or did someone tell you that?" He seemed genuinely curious, not hinting at some secret answer he knew.

"Not in the slightest. Even Matthias has very little idea of what he did—what impacts it will have. The Biblical Four Horsemen are equally stumped," I muttered, letting out a breath.

Achilles grunted. "They still recovering in Bali?" he asked.

I nodded, crossing my ankles. "Yeah. Othello wanted to get them as far away from me as possible. Just in case Mordred returns. *When* Mordred returns. Can't risk them dying from a cold, or Mordred killing them because they're weakened by a cold." I waved a hand. "Matthias joined them to see if he can learn anything useful for me. How their Masks work, or how it all ties together."

Achilles folded his muscular arms, pursing his lips thoughtfully. "Still no idea how it's all related?" he asked. "Why your Masks are making them sick?"

I shook my head. "No idea. Which is why I'm hesitant to involve any of my friends in this mess. Even though I'll have to involve three unfortunate souls eventually."

"I think *eventually* means *pronto*, judging by what you've told me." I grunted my agreement. "Yours is still damaged?" he asked. I nodded, touching the coin on my necklace. "Can I see it?"

I thought about it for a moment, and finally shrugged. I touched it and the Mask detached, no longer a coin. I set it on the bench beside me, remembering how it occasionally zapped people if they touched it. It hadn't zapped Callie, though...hmm. I hadn't thought about that in a while.

Too bad Callie was away on mysterious business of some kind. Everyone was being rather tight-lipped about it, probably assuming I would rush off to Kansas City if I heard something as mundane as a rainstorm was rolling in. But Alucard had received a call from Roland, Callie's old mentor, and had decided to pay the City of Fountains a visit. I'd ask him when he got back.

Callie had made it very obvious she didn't want any handholding. She had some demon problems to deal with, and I had this...well, a freaking buffet table of drama to deal with...

Holding tryouts for my Varsity Team of Horsemen.

Mordred and his Round Table Initiative.

Carl disappearing to bring his people back to St. Louis—when the Elders had been unilaterally banished from Earth long ago for some scary reason. And he wanted them to swear allegiance to me...

Being King of St. Louis and keeping an eye on the various supernatural families in town.

My Fae flashbacks and how it tied into the Catalyst thing.

The Knight of the Round Table I had stashed in Fae—who I had yet to actually meet.

And perhaps the three powerful artifacts my parents had left me: the Hand of God, the Hourglass, and the War Hammer.

Anubis had told me I still had godly ichor in my veins, and he probably had an opinion on how I had managed returning—or *not* returning, as the case may be—the stolen Souls. Because we had made a deal. I get him the Souls back, and I no longer have to be the Guide to Hell, and I get two get-out-of-Hell—or death—free cards.

Which meant...I might be able to bring my parents back.

So, I could ask them some very pointed questions before murdering them again for lying to me—even if only by omission—about so many things.

I let out a breath, once more forcefully calming myself. I didn't really want to kill them, I just didn't understand why everything they had done had been so secretive. My life—and my battles—would have been a whole lot easier if I had known what they had set up. And why.

Achilles was leaning over the Mask, murmuring to himself as he studied it.

The golden line down the center of the Mask seemed to shift like flowing metal—because I had used Merlin's ichor—stolen from the Round Table—to hold it together; I had been fresh out of extra souls after feeding the other Masks. In retrospect, I wasn't entirely sure that had been a good idea, but that was the story of my life, and there was no use crying over spilt milk.

Achilles let out a long whistle, leaning closer to inspect the crack down the center. "That's hardcore, man. I once saw War shoot Death in the face with a 44 Magnum." He met my eyes. "Point blank."

My eyes widened. "Oh?"

Achilles nodded. "Just a slight puff of dust. No mark at all."

Damn. I'd hoped to finally hear the cause of the impact craters I had seen on Death's bone Mask. If not a point-blank shot from a horse pistol, what the hell else could have done it?

"And that's Merlin's blood holding it together?" Achilles asked, sounding amazed.

"I think so." I admitted. Because that was really just a strong hypothesis. I had no way to verify if it really was Merlin's blood or if it was something else entirely. "I'm not sure it's holding it together, but rather strengthening it. It never fully broke, to get technical."

"How do you *permanently* fix it?"

"I think it needs a family," I admitted tiredly. "They seem to function best as a team. And in pairs, to balance each other."

Achilles gave me a meaningful look. "Back to the original question, then." I nodded. "Hope..." Achilles said pointing at the dark gray, quartz-like Mask before him. He trailed off meaningfully, glancing over at the Darling and Dear satchel by my feet. With a tired sigh, I reached inside and pulled out three more Masks, also all made of some kind of stone or quartz. They didn't vibrate this time, which was a relief. I pointed to the white one, first. "Despair, to balance Hope." Next, I pointed at the green and then gold Masks. "Absolution to balance Justice."

Achilles' mouth hung open as he studied them. "That's curious. The Biblical Riders are named after more tangible things—actions or events: Death, War, Conquest, and Famine. But yours are more..." he waved a hand, grasping for the right word. "Concepts? Ideals? Creeds?"

I shrugged, not having an answer. I had named them on a whim, but it had felt like the names had been pulled from me. I put the Masks away to signal the end of discussion, since Alex was shaking hands with his sparring partners. I couldn't help but notice the impressed, respectful looks on these hardened warriors' faces. Then he was walking towards us.

"I'm starving," he told me, trading grips with Achilles. "Let's go eat."

Achilles grunted. "We still on for Buddy Hatchet later?" Talon perked up, noticed the sparring was over, and climbed to his feet with a stretch that almost made me pull a groin muscle by observing it. Then he walked over in silence, eyes darting about the area like a security detail.

I smiled at the name of the bar he wanted us to attend. A Valkyrie he knew had set up shop recently—a bar where the patrons could throw all manner of blades at targets while drinking pitchers of mead, but the place was not limited to Freaks like Achilles' Heel.

"We'll see you there later, Achilles. Oh, and Anubis is joining us." Achilles sputtered incredulously, cursing up a storm, since he knew my talk was likely not going to go well. I had chosen the location because a lot of Regulars would be around us, hopefully making it a tiny bit safer for me.

I turned to Alex, guiding him towards the exit, ignoring Achilles scathing comments. "I'm famished. Hope Dean cooked something good or we're ordering pizza." Talon sniffed waspishly.

Alex gave me a very strange look but masked it quickly.

5

We strolled up to the front door of Chateau Falco, my ancestral home, and I couldn't help but smile. It was a beautiful old girl and had been a haven for the Temple family for generations. With over seventeen-thousand square feet and more rooms and sections than I properly knew what to do with, it was easy for visitors to get lost inside. Sometimes I just walked through it, reliving memories of my childhood, recalling things I had forgotten, and checking up on hiding places I had used to avoid Dean or my parents when I had done something particularly troublesome.

But Dean had almost always been able to find me, the posh bastard.

"I want to go check the tree for any sign of Carl's return," Talon said, glancing over at the massive, scaled, white tree nearby. Like a giant, reptilian, lawn ornament with leaves. From far away, it looked like a white tree, but there was no mistaking the oddities up close.

"You mean the D?" I asked him, biting back a grin. He ignored me and wandered away.

"He's very quiet lately," Alex said softly, so as not to be overheard.

I smiled. "Maybe he just misses Carl."

Alex rolled his eyes. "Pretty sure that's not it," he said, shaking his head at my obvious joke.

Because Talon and Carl were an odd pair and didn't easily get along. Talon was a very straight-laced, purpose-driven kind of creature, where Carl was...well, Carl was a fucking enigma.

He loved eating the flesh of the unborn—eggs.

He had a bizarre fascination with collecting high-heeled shoes—primarily red, if he could get his claws on them. I had even ordered him a custom pair designed to fit his velociraptor feet, and he frequently paraded around the house wearing them—and he was frighteningly nimble.

He used the bones of his enemies to make new swords and daggers and had been seen and heard speaking to them like a child would their toy dolls.

He had once complimented my vehicle by sniffing and licking the leather seats, informing me that he could almost hear the sounds of the slaughtered cows used to make the leather.

The best part, in my opinion, was that he was gullible enough to convince him of practically anything you wanted, since he had absolutely no understanding of social cues. We'd recently taken to playing Cards Against Humanity with him in an effort to teach him what was absolutely *not* acceptable in social conversation, because we had failed miserably with trying to teach him what *was* socially acceptable in social situations.

The only real similarity between Carl and Talon was that they could be incredibly violent.

But with Carl, the strangest things could turn him from a curious side-kick into a terrifying monster. I'd seen him go from calm to Apocalypse-level rage in the blink of an eye.

Carlageddon.

He was an Elder—a race of creatures who were feared by every single supernatural faction I had ever met. They had been so universally feared that the entire supernatural world had once teamed up to banish them from this world.

Carl was currently using the D as some kind of portal back to his realm —which was what Talon was checking on. Because Carl wanted to bring them back—to kneel to *me*. Carl had deemed me King in his eyes, and not just of St. Louis. In fact, I wasn't entirely sure what he thought I was actually King of. Or what he really thought of me as a person. It was obviously very positive, but I was nervous to ask what kind of expectations he had of me. Did he serve me thinking that I would lead his people to take over the known universe and enslave millions of people? Or something slightly less insane?

Long and short of it was that Carl was a psychopath with horrifying, inexplicable power, and no one quite knew what his intentions were. His people knew some kind of Song Magic, and after a recent vision I'd had, I was beginning to wonder just how close Carl and I were on the magical spectrum. Because in my vision, I had momentarily had access to Songs. Or at least been possessed by an entity that could use Songs as a weapon.

Talon didn't need to check on the tree, or Carl, since I had given Carl a bit of my blood before he left. He'd told me he could use it to track me across the cosmos or something similarly creepy. Right after he'd Sung a chilling, magical dirge of a prophecy that he'd self-admittedly *scraped from my mother's soul*, whatever that meant. He hadn't finished the Song before suddenly needing to leave.

Because he had thought he'd heard his mother calling out to him through the portal—which hadn't been functional up until he'd voiced his Song.

Since Ruin occupied the treehouse high up in the D, I knew he would let us know the moment a caravan of scaled, lizard warriors emerged from the trunk. Even thinking about that happening gave me chills. Because it was probably happening sooner than anyone wanted to admit.

I turned back to see Alex wearing a thoughtful frown as he watched Talon circle the tree. "This memory recall of our time in Fae is hitting us both pretty hard," I told Alex. "Talon remembers more than I do, and I think he's having a hard time dealing with it."

Alex grimaced. "Yeah, spending any time in Fae is hard to process," he agreed. Because he had once been a captive in Fae, too—before I saved him. But I couldn't risk thinking too hard about that in case it brought on a mental break.

Instead, I strolled up to the entrance of Chateau Falco and opened the front door.

And I was greeted by a line of neon pistols pointed at my face, held by a horde of demons grinning their wicked smiles.

Like a hive mind, they pulled their triggers in unison, and a swarm of

Nerf bullets zipped towards my face. I heard Dean shout, "No magic in the house, or you're on cleaning duty!"

But I wasn't *in* the house, so I threw up a hasty shield of magic, blocking all of the darts.

I was grinning triumphantly when I sensed a presence above me. I looked up to see a dark gray cloud hovering directly over my head. "Oh, come on!" And Ruin, the Baby Beast, unleashed his equivalent of a golden shower—primordial piss, since he was some kind of celestial being—all over me.

The army of demons had reloaded and proceeded to tag me with a second onslaught of Nerf bullets—this one I didn't block.

I ignored the chorus of laughter to shout at the top of my lungs. "Falco! Ruin is grounded!" I yelled at my house. Because my house was a sentient being, harboring a Beast within her walls.

And that Beast was Ruin's mother. She didn't reply, although she sometimes did.

Ruin shook his cloudy form like a wet dog, spraying me with more water, his shade of color lightening from gray to white as he emptied his reserves. He'd been storing it up for just this moment. Which pretty much told me who was behind it all. It really was water, not primordial piss. Well, technically, it was both. But scientifically, it was just water. Ruin really was a cloud of mist, not needing to eat any organic matter unless he wanted to take on a physical form, which he hadn't yet done. That being said, after he'd eaten one of the Nine Souls...

He definitely got soul poisoning, spraying torrents of water all over the place for a full day.

One of the gun-toting demons stepped out of the darkness to reveal his true form. Gunnar walked up to me, grinning from ear-to-ear. "Friendsgiving," he said. Then he gave me a playful, one-armed shove to jostle me.

But Alex—the weaselly little miscreant—had apparently crouched down onto all fours behind my knees so that Gunnar's playful shove sent me sprawling onto my ass into a pile of wet, cold, Nerf bullets. I cursed for about ten seconds, while reaching out to try and shove a fistful of muddy Nerf bullets into the back of his shirt, but Alex evaded me easily.

I finally let out a defeated laugh, shaking my head. Friendsgiving was months from now.

Alex and Gunnar helped me to my feet and plopped a plastic crown on my head. "Whose idea was this?" I asked, suspecting I already knew, but expecting others had been involved.

"His," Gunnar said, pointing to Alex.

I turned to him and dipped my head. "I think...yeah, I think I needed it. Thanks."

Alex shrugged. "We've had a dark run. You're usually the one to cheer us all up and make us laugh, but since you've been so busy lately, I figured it was time for me to strap on the boots. I wanted to bring everyone together for a reminder of what really matters."

Gunnar nodded approvingly, but something about his face looked tense—almost brittle—like he was pretending to be happy. Or his mind was elsewhere. I hadn't heard any bad news, and if there had been truly bad news—the imminent danger kind—he would have told me immediately, so it must have been pack business getting to him. The stress of being the Alpha.

Gunnar cleared his throat. "Dark stuff has happened and is going to happen again. Probably soon, knowing Mordred. But we still have to remember what we are fighting for." His face paled slightly at his own statement, and I wondered if he was coming down with a cold or something.

Alex was nodding. "Thought it would be fun to gather everyone together, even though I know it's way too early for Friendsgiving," he admitted, blushing slightly. "It sounds stupid when I say it out loud."

"Everything usually does," I teased him. "You didn't need to do all of this for me, Alex. Remember when I stabbed you in the heart? Good times."

"I do, as a matter of fact," he replied drily. "I remember every single minute of that hour-long torture, for some reason."

I winced. Then I caught a whiff of cooked food through the open doors, past the others who were scooping up all the Nerf darts—careful to take their shoes off before stepping back inside, or Dean would have murdered them all without even bothering to unbutton his dinner jacket.

I saw Alvara and her daughter Alice and managed to wave at the young girl, careful to keep the sudden apprehension from my face as I focused on my breathing. She waved back, and then skipped away, tugging Yahn along behind her. The Reds trailed like good ladies-in-waiting, smirking at Yahn's plight. *Dragons adoring a dangerous Fae child*, I thought to myself, shaking my head.

But I was also tense at the stark reminder that we were headed to Fae tomorrow. I turned to Alex. "Why did you invite them?"

He shrugged. "So you wouldn't have to pick them up in the morning, which might get people talking, if you know what I mean. Wondering what business you have at that time of morning, and where you are taking them. Thought it best to keep them off the radar. For all the world knows, you were at the Dueling Grounds having a little fun, went home for dinner, and then the bar with your friends. Nothing interesting." He met my eyes levelly. "In case Mordred has people watching."

Gunnar was studying Alex thoughtfully, not realizing he was nodding his head in approval. He didn't impress easily, much like Achilles. Yet here he was, being impressed and stuff.

Alex was the kind of guy you couldn't help but like, even if you hated yourself for standing in his shadow. And he cast a big fucking shadow. Worse, he was humble about it. Almost unaware. Except...I knew he was definitely aware of it. He just purposely chose not to relish in it.

Where was the fun in that? *Arrogance is bliss*, as the famous saying went.

Looking at him—reflected by Gunnar's opinion—I thought again on my Masks.

I saw Talon slinking our way, keeping his eyes to the skies, and I scowled. "You mangy bastard. *That's* why you wanted to check on the tree! You didn't want to get wet!"

"Who, me? I would never..." he said with faux innocence.

I heard a rustling of feathers and looked up to see Huginn and Muninn —Odin's Ravens—perched atop the door, cocking their heads as they stared at...

Talon.

"Here, kitty, kitty, kitty," they croaked in unison. Then they hopped in a half-circle to aim their rears at him, glancing over their shoulders to check their coverage of the entryway.

There was no way for Talon to walk through the door without them shitting on him, which was obviously their intent. One of their favorite games was chasing Talon around the grounds, trying to crap on him.

Talon looked crestfallen. "Make them stop. This is ridiculous," he pleaded to me.

I shrugged mercilessly. "Spare the water," I said, pointing up at Ruin, "Soil the kitty," I said, pointing at the large Ravens. "Now, let's go eat," I told Gunnar and Alex.

I tensed my shoulders as I walked through the door, fearing they would unload their Nordic bowels on me since Talon showed no signs of taking a gamble.

But I made it through unscathed and followed the delicious smells to the kitchen.

I even remembered to take off my boots first.

Dean was good at ingraining lessons into your cerebral cortex. And I'd suffered the loving bastard for thirty-odd years, now.

6

We sat around the table, chatting and drinking amicably and, like many times before, I found myself leaning back to observe in silence. No matter what Alex had said, this wasn't about me. It was about everyone else.

Alex was drifting around the table, speaking with each person directly, involving them individually in the Temple tradition of Friendsgiving. He was also serving them drinks, letting Dean focus on the last-minute meal preparations.

I had never in my life seen Dean let someone help him with something like this. Even with such simple assistance as serving drinks.

But maybe that was because I was Master Temple. The boss. Dean had a strange way of showing his respect at times. I had only just gotten rid of the welts from his gods-damned airsoft gun of corporal punishment.

Anyway, it meant something for Dean to let Alex help. Was it because Alex had orchestrated the dinner? Or was it because Dean was also impressed with Alex?

Alex poured a glass of wine for Gunnar, but Ashley declined, asking for some ice water instead. Alex happily provided it, then squatted down to talk to the two of them. Gunnar and Ashley both laughed, nodded along, and then Alex was off with a brilliant goodbye smile.

He flicked Alice's hair on the way by her chair and danced clear when she tried to grasp his hand. Then he curtsied to her from a safe distance before reaching Tory, the Headmistress of Shift—a school for wayward kids. At least, that was what the rest of the city thought. In reality, it was a school for orphan shifters, and in addition to traditional classes, she taught them how to control their flavors of monster. Because she was a Beast Master—able to control all shifters with her mind.

She was also incredibly strong, so she could bat around shifters with her pinky finger, before resorting to mind control on the harder cases.

She had recently been working with Raego, the King of the Dragons, to institute her graduate-level students into a kind of supernatural police force. They were still coming up with the name, but I'd heard a few creative ones already. I secretly funded the school, which had been built on the old Temple Industries property after it had been bulldozed and destroyed.

Tory had wanted a symbol for her students to wear, a badge of honor, for both the kids to hold dear and for the city to know that they were important—to be respected, trusted, and appreciated. The fact that Tory and her students were unaffiliated with any of the supernatural families was perhaps the biggest reason everyone was okay with the idea. The kids had been cast out or left abandoned by their original families, and Tory had grouped them into a new family.

An objective one.

I'd been carrying around a sack of Olympian Gold that I had won for defeating Athena—yes, her brothers and sisters had placed bets on the outcome of our knock-out, throw-down, hair-pulling bout. I'd come out with a healthy pile of coins for my efforts.

Since the gold had just been sitting around in my office collecting dust, I'd recently melted the coins down to make badges for Tory's Keepers—as they'd taken to calling themselves until an official name could be decided. Because names were important. Since I was the self-proclaimed King of St. Louis, I had made them in the form of the Temple Crest—the same symbol branded into my palm. The same one that adorned my front door. Because I was determined to make that symbol mean something more than just *those elitist wizards who lived in St. Louis.*

I wanted to put my Crest to good use. For the people of my city to see it and feel relief. Protection. Even pride, perhaps.

Not pride in me, necessarily, but in something bigger than me. People generally felt better when they had something to unite behind. And with this war that was supposedly coming, I figured it was best to get everyone behind a shield now, before it was too late.

Tory caught me watching her, smiled, and shifted her hair to show me the golden badge pinned to the shoulder of her dress. I smiled at it, as well as at the genuine excitement in her eyes. She had once been a helluva policewoman, but her association with me had gotten her fired—when dragons invaded St. Louis.

And now, to have her working with the dragons and me, back on her feet, with a cause of her own. Yeah. It felt pretty damned good. Especially since she had lost her lover, Misha. But she had adopted Misha's daughters —Sonya and Aria—or the Reds, as they were most often called due to their type of dragon. The Reds were currently nuzzled up against their glass-dragon, and still-undefined, love-interest, Yahn, at the end of the table. Even though Tory had lost Misha, she now had a bigger immediate family than anyone would have ever expected. The Reds, Yahn, and a whole army of wayward shifters who all looked up to her as their mother.

Alvara was sitting beside Tory, watching Alice. The young girl was busy serving a plastic teacup to Ashley—who took it with a graceful dip of her head. Alvara wore a faint smile, and I couldn't tell if it signified that she was dreading tomorrow or excited about it. I felt the same.

I had chosen Talon and Gunnar to come along with us.

I couldn't afford to take anyone else because one of the main points was to focus on my memories and having to babysit a battalion of newbies as they entered the bizarre world of Fae—complete with the effects it had on new visitors, transforming them into more primitive, savage forms of them-selves—was not conducive to me relaxing and trying to recall my past.

In all honesty, it was like I was going to a drug rehabilitation facility. Some peace and quiet in the chaotic mess of my life, hoping to find and establish some much-needed structure and order.

I left Alvara to her thoughts for now, promising myself I would talk to her after dinner. She was staying the night here, after all. I wanted to make sure she and Alice knew how to defend themselves. Because they were essentially fugitives in Fae, and if any natives found them there...I shuddered even thinking about it.

Gunnar and Talon would keep us safe as we stalked through Fae. As soon as I learned what I needed to know about being a Catalyst from Alvara's friends, I could whisk them back to the human realm and then return to finish out my rehabilitation—which would climax with me killing Mordred, in a best-case scenario.

Worst-case, at least get an eye on his activities in Camelot. At the supposed armies he was amassing to take over all of Fae. Because he didn't just want Camelot. He would come after St. Louis when he was finished digesting Fae.

I sighed, sipping my wine. *Not tonight*, I told myself. *Plenty of that tomorrow. Tonight is for relaxing.* Talon was likely still hiding, but Huginn and Muninn had given up and were now perched atop one of the china cabinets in the corner, watching us in silence with their beady, black eyes. I didn't dislike them, but I didn't quite trust them, either. Since they were Odin's Ravens, tasked with watching the world for the one-eyed bastard, I couldn't help but feel like we constantly had two drones hovering around, spying on us to report to Big Brother.

The two Ravens were depicted on my Crest and had informed me they were here for multiple reasons but hadn't ever clarified that vague statement. I'd met Odin a handful of times, and he hadn't clarified either. He'd also been a raging dick in the majority of those encounters, but insisted he was here to help me.

In the most infuriating ways possible.

Dean entered the room with a great big ham, setting it down on the center of the table. He nodded once at Alex, and the two began uncovering silver platters on the table, filling the room with steaming tendrils of both savory and sweet foods. A great feast. I marveled at how Dean managed it all, even now that I was used to it. He was no spring chicken.

The two of them filled up our plates, carrying the platters around the table for us to each choose what we wanted and didn't. Once we were all loaded up with brimming glasses and heaping plates, Dean tapped his glass with a fork in a light chiming sound and cleared his throat.

This was my favorite part. He was about to tell everyone how awesome I was.

I prepared myself to appear properly humble and gracious for the ocean of compliments soon coming my way...

7

Everyone settled into their chairs and waited for the chiming sound to fade away.

"Thank you for joining us," Dean began, smiling genially. "You have all faced incredible trials and tribulations in recent years, some more than others. What matters in times like these is that you rise to the occasion after. Every war is eternal, and every day could be your last. *Memento mori*, my friends, *memento mori*."

Like everyone else at the table, I found myself nodding my agreement, but I was slightly caught off-guard by the tone, topic, and insight Dean was preaching. *Memento mori* was a tribute to the Temple Crest, meaning *remember you will die*, so live life to the fullest—but it probably wasn't the best opening statement. In his defense, he wasn't much of a public speaker.

"Preparing this meal today brought back forgotten memories...of the laughter and celebration that often filled these halls. And the chaos," he added, pausing to look directly at me. Everyone laughed, but I couldn't tell if Dean smiled or not. He had an excellent poker face. "You have no room to laugh at Master Temple on that front, Gunnar," Dean added, making Gunnar choke on his wine.

I grinned at my one-eyed pal, but more in memory of the trouble we used to get into than at his discomfort.

"I say all of that to tell you this. I believe it is past time we brought back an old Temple tradition. In times of chaos, like now, one needs order. This home needs order. This...*family* needs order," he emphasized, smiling warmly.

I was still waiting on the heaps of praise part of the speech, but I was losing confidence as I picked up on Dean's not-so-subtle comparison between us needing *order* and the reference to me causing *chaos* as a child.

"We need order to balance the insanity outside Falco's arms. I know I'm ahead of the seasons, but I propose we bring back Yulemas—the celebration of the Winter Solstice. With Odin's Ravens on the Temple family Crest," he said, dipping his head politely at the bird brains, "it is no secret the Temple family has long respected a Norse tradition or two, even if they modified it slightly. I'm sure both Master Temple and Gunnar hold fond memories of past Yulemas holidays here at Chateau Falco," he said, smiling slightly—basically the Norse equivalent of a *Ho, Ho, Ho!* on Dean's usually stoic demeanor. "What I would like to do differently this year is open the doors to invite you to celebrate it with us."

The Ravens began cawing loud enough to make me cringe. "Yulemas! Yulemas! Yulemas!"

Everyone at the table was smiling broadly, bobbing their heads to their horrid chorus. Even as they cast wary glances up at Huginn and Muninn, likely reminded that they were the *actual* Ravens of Odin—and that maybe they should have been celebrating Yulemas for quite some time, what with the obvious proof before their eyes.

I was more interested in the fact that Dean seemed so adamant to bring it back. Well, not *back*, per se, but to make it a big event, especially given that late Spring was a little early to consider planning such a celebration. As I thought about it, I realized it had been quite a while since we'd put up our Yule Goat decorations all over the mansion. And with how many people we currently had shacking up here on most occasions, they practically *were* all family already.

And it...was kind of sad not to celebrate with such a big family.

"Think of how we could fill these halls with laughter, cheer, and song," Yahn said reverently, and...for the first time, I really thought about that.

It was...exciting.

Such a large home needed humans to fill it, and not just with their bodies, but with life. It was an utter waste to have such a vast, beautiful home and to only use it like a military barracks. I thought of Gunnar's pack of werewolves, Tory's students at Shift, and so many others attending a Yulemas party. And I began to stress right the hell out. That was a lot of fucking people.

Logistically, it was a nightmarish idea, but if we hired enough help...it would be the talk of the town. And a great opportunity to engage with all manner of people in hushed conversations. A way to bring the supernatural families together.

"There will be much to do," Dean said slowly. He sensed the sudden dip of excitement and waved a hand. "I will take care of the planning, but there are other opportunities available..."

He looked directly at me with a kind smile—nostalgia brimming in his eyes. This had been my mother's favorite time of year. After the family celebration, my father would always dress up like Odin—the Yule Father—and bestow presents upon us, as long as the naughty and nice list Huginn and Muninn had delivered to him included us in the appropriate column, of course.

Because Santa Claus had quite literally borrowed his holiday from the Norse.

Odin's Ravens would watch the world throughout the year, compiling their evidence to judge who had been naughty and who had been nice. Odin would then ride Sleipnir—his eight-legged horse, not eight reindeer—to each home to deliver presents.

Odin's elves and dwarves were straight outta Alfheim and Svartalfheim and ran the streets packing magical weapons and jewelry. Well, they *made* the magical, deadly weapons for the Norse gods and goddesses, but I had an overactive imagination as a child, connecting it with the infamous rap group, NWA—but changing the acronym to mean *Norse With Attitude*.

Look, Papa! I got an axe in my stocking! Time to kick those tights-clad pansies out of the Yule, fool! We rune these streets!

So, we had a blast pretending my father was the Yule Father—Odin—and he and my mother would play keep-away with the naughty and nice list that Huginn and Muninn had delivered to them. After, as Gunnar and I played with our new toys, my parents would sit down quietly by the fire, curled up on the couch, with Dean making sure we left them alone.

To think that I had now actually met Odin and his Ravens put a whole new perspective on the holiday. It made me wish I could tell my parents about it and watch my mother's eyes light up with sheer joy. But...

That may never happen. Unless I brought my parents back with Anubis' get-out-of-Hell-free cards—something I was seriously considering.

Dean had looked a little sad when he smiled at me. The same thought had probably crossed his mind, too—that my mother would have loved hearing about his plan.

It really was a great idea, though. I wondered how many kids we could cram inside Chateau Falco. Hell, I could donate so many toys that the kids would be ruined for Christmas forever. I could quite literally change some lives with a Yulemas party like this. Dean was really onto something magical here.

Why hadn't I ever thought of it? Probably because I spent too much time focusing on fighting.

I also decided that I would treat Huginn and Muninn a lot better for the rest of the year. As long as they didn't provoke me—which they often did on purpose.

Talon, I knew for a fact, was getting absolutely nothing from the Yule Father—if the Ravens had any say in the matter.

I'd get him some extra boxes of Fae catnip to make up for it.

Tory piped up, her voice full of raw emotion. "The kids at Shift..." she said, her voice growing throatier with each word. "I can almost guarantee that most have never had a Christmas in their lives, let alone a family to celebrate with. Coming to a party, invited in as family..." she began sobbing, and Alvara reached out to tuck her into her shoulder.

Alvara's eyes were red with happy tears of her own, overcome with Dean's idea. Alice was vibrating with so much excitement that it looked like she might be about to take off into space.

Gunnar and Ashley sat entirely still, murmuring softly to one another as they no doubt grew concerned, considering they had several hundred pack members to worry about. Dean noticed and smiled. "I think it's fairly apparent that wolves are a favorite of Odin. Don't think you'll be restricted to a limited number. In fact, you'll be celebrated for bringing the largest addition to the family. And you two are quite literally part of the family already," he said, indicating the runes branded into their wrists—the runes that marked them as family. I had given Ashley hers, but Gunnar had received his from my parents long ago to help control his shifting.

The pair smiled, dipping their heads gratefully.

"Who will dress up as the Yule Father?" Alice asked excitedly. It kind of caught me off guard, since she was pretty much the only one present who might have believed we really invited the Yule Father in, but her comment made me reconsider her age. She might look like a young-year-old, but she very likely could have been an old-year-old. Fae were strange like that.

Gunnar lowered his eye. "I don't know if anyone could do better than Nate's dad, Calvin."

"Enough of that," Dean chastised. "Every son must one day step into the role of his father, and none of them believe they are up to the task. But they all do just fine. To you, Calvin was the best. In his own eyes, he probably thought his father did it better."

Gunnar nodded in embarrassment. "I'm sorry, Dean," he said, sounding entirely too affected by the mild reprimand. What was up with Gunnar? He was acting so strangely lately. What was going on with his pack to cause him this much stress?

"Master Temple will make his father proud," Dean said, smiling reassuringly at me. Chateau Falco purred her approval around us, and the Ravens hopped about for a moment, ruffling their feathers with displeasure.

"That's one vote," Tory said, laughing despite her still-wet face.

Alice looked up wondrously at the ceiling, searching for the source of the rumble. "She's beautiful..." she whispered. "And she sounds so happy."

I blinked incredulously. "You can see her?"

Alice didn't even look over at me, still grinning up at the ceiling. "Of course." She turned to her mother, beaming. "This will be the greatest celebration ever!" she giggled, tucking her head into her mother's bosom. Alvara gasped in a breath at the sudden hug but instantly clutched her daughter right back and petted her hair. She smiled as she no doubt envisioned the future party.

How long had it been since she'd had a family to celebrate with? Ever? They'd been banished from their homes—from Fae. But how long ago?

Already, it looked like Yulemas was about to change some lives. Dean ordered us to eat before our food grew cold and, for the first time in a very long time, I smiled as I saw him sit down with us. He usually hovered around the table, serving us, choosing to eat only after all the guests were finished and loaded with after-dinner refreshments. Or, more often than not, after everyone had left or gone to bed for the night.

He looked incredibly awkward eating with others all around him, and even took a deep breath before carefully picking up a knife and fork. He looked up at me and I lifted my glass subtly, no one else even noticing.

He smiled slightly, dipped his chin, and methodically began cutting into his ham.

"To Dean," I said loudly, hoisting my glass.

The table belted out their agreement, and I could have sworn I saw Dean's eyes mist up before he regained his composure.

When he wasn't reprimanding me, Dean was one rock-solid guy.

I would forgive him for not waxing poetic about my awesomeness.

This time.

8

The table chattered on through the meal, ideas thrown out left and right as we stuffed ourselves to the brim for about an hour. Talon wandered in at one point, and Alice instantly commanded him to sit beside her where she could keep an eye on him.

Everyone laughed at that, but since it was on the opposite side of the table from the Ravens, he hadn't bothered arguing.

I watched everyone, pleased to see how much a simple idea had invigorated them all. Tory oh-so-innocently nominated Dean for Yule Father, saying I already had a hammer, and that it would be confusing, but she grinned at me near the end.

I had been preparing to flick a cranberry at her until Dean cleared his throat pointedly. I lowered my spoon catapult with a sigh. He couldn't watch me all the time. Tory would pay.

Tory smiled suddenly, turning to look at me. "I can take the Shift students caroling to get them in the spirit. It would also serve to scout the city and discreetly hand out invitations."

Yahn piped up. "We can hire a delivery truck, fill it with toys and gifts, and deliver them around town."

"We can be Odin's little helpers," Sonya said suggestively.

Alvara arched a brow at the dragon's smoky tone but, as usual, Sonya had no idea how her words had come across. Aria just rolled her eyes at her sister. "It would also be good for the Round Table Initiative. Nate Temple and Grimm Tech delivering Christmas gifts around town might give them something else to focus on."

Alex nodded. "It would help rebrand him from that stupid viral video with Mordred. Change the narrative. And it would serve two other purposes: the Freaks would see Nate honoring his people, being benevolent, making them more likely to side with him when Mordred returns, and the Regulars would see a good piece of news to focus on. Santa Temple. Or Temple Claus. Maybe Othello could help build some buzz with her internet magic?"

I nodded thoughtfully. "Othello is busy right now, but those are really good points." It wasn't common knowledge that Othello was on the beach with the boys, keeping the Biblical Horsemen as far from St. Louis as possible. Or that my ancestor, Matthias was with them. Thinking of Matthias, I wondered if he had ever played Yule Father. Because with him still kicking around, maybe I could weasel out of it. I sipped on my wine, considering how dangerous it was to ask a man who had once believed he was the Mad Hatter to pretend to be Odin, the Yule Father.

Probably not my greatest idea. I drank my wine and felt sorry for myself. I would have to dress up, damn it.

Dean stood and swept the table with his eyes, judging that we were ready for dessert. He returned a few moments later with a freaking sword and a large baked pie.

"What in the world?" I belted out, choking on my wine.

Dean handed the sword to Gunnar, who took it with shaking hands, his lips set in a determined line. The table went silent, everyone frowning in confusion. Especially at the grim look on Gunnar's face. My skin began to itch, not liking this one bit.

Dean walked over and carefully set the pie in front of me before silently backing away.

Ashley smiled brightly as she placed a reassuring hand on Gunnar's lower back, urging him forward. Gunnar finally took a deep breath and walked over to me, holding the sword hilt-out.

"Can you please cut into the pie, Nate?" he asked in a low growl.

I blinked, accepting the hilt of the sword more out of awkwardness than any commitment.

"Um...we have cake knives—"

He leaned in closer, his lone eye practically on fire as he murmured a phrase. "*Defiance.*"

Defiance, as in Chateau Defiance? Our old treehouse? That had been code for us to simply not ask questions, be entirely honest, and do the damned thing.

And I followed our code, come hell or high water.

"Of course, Gunnar." If he wanted me to cut a damned pie with a damned sword, I would cut the damned pie with a damned sword.

I stood, dramatically touched the blade to my head and closed my eyes, and then I carefully lowered it to cut into the pie, not wanting to destroy whatever was inside. Maybe they had gotten me a puppy or something.

The sword cut a straight line from the center to the edge, but nothing jumped out at me. Gunnar scowled, practically shaking as he motioned for me to cut out a *piece* of the pie, not just a line. I did and scooped up the slice with my sword.

A cascade of blue and pink M&M's poured out of the pastry, spilling down and off the table, revealing that all I held on my sword was a hollow, dry crust.

I frowned. That was odd. Who baked a pie with M&M's? And why hadn't they melted in the oven? There was a mystery here somewhere...

Someone gasped, and others began to squeal and laugh and clap as I frowned at the pie.

Gunnar, like a puppet with cut strings, abruptly collapsed as his legs gave out. He head-butted the table—the hard-as-iron wooden table—on the way down, crunching a few M&M's in the process, before sliding to the floor like a limp noodle, entirely unconscious.

I dropped the sword instinctively, and the heavy hilt struck him in the groin before toppling to the side.

He lurched back up with a reedy gasp at the groin blow and head-butted the table again with a *thump* that made me wince as it shook the table and spilled more M&M's from the curious pie. This time he was knocked out for good.

Everyone began shouting and yelling—at me.

But I had absolutely no idea what had just happened. Was the sword supposed to be symbolic of something? Me being King of St. Louis? And why the hell had Gunnar collapsed? He hadn't done anything worthy of that response. This was *my* mystery, *my* moment. Some obscure gift to Master Temple, King of St. Louis.

I nudged Gunnar with my boot, watching as more M&M's fell from the table onto his chest and burrowed into his beard, but he didn't stir. I turned to Ashley. "I think your husband just died, and I don't entirely understand why." I mumbled before kneeling down beside him. "And he's probably going to need the coldest ice-pack we can find. That sword was pretty heavy."

9

I patted Gunnar's cheeks a few times, but he still didn't wake. So I slapped him—this time with as much force as I could muster. Gunnar jolted awake with a gasp, gripping my arm and staring at me with one crazy eyeball.

Ashley was suddenly kneeling beside him, her face a mess of running mascara as she laughed and cried and squeezed his bearded face, kissing him about a gazillion times.

Tory grabbed me by the scruff of the shirt with one hand and yanked me to my feet, so Ashley could apparently molest my best friend. Tory then pointed down at the pile of M&M's on the table. She was also crying happily. I shot a look towards Talon, but he simply shrugged and went back to eating his meal, not even having bothered to get up since I wasn't in any danger.

"*Twins*, you fucking imbecile," Tory hissed into my ear. "Pink and blue. They're having a baby boy and baby girl!"

I heard a fizzing and popping sound in my ears, followed by crackling static.

Then I, too, was suddenly lying on the ground, staring up at the ceiling, bewildered.

Talon and Tory were staring down at me from inches away, looking concerned. Well, Talon looked concerned. Tory looked satisfied at my current situation. "Men," she huffed, climbing back to her feet and storming away.

"Wylde, are you okay?" Talon whispered carefully.

I nodded. "Yeah, yeah. Nothing to do with that. Just...I'm suddenly really stressed out," I mumbled, abruptly remembering what had caused me to fall down. Twins...

Talon frowned. "Why?" Then his eyes widened, and he shielded me from view, leaning closer. "Please tell me those are not your children."

"*What?*" I shouted. "No! Jesus, Talon!" I hissed, hoping no one had heard him.

He frowned, leaning back. "Then I don't understand. Why would you be stressed out?"

A big meaty hand suddenly shoved Talon to the side and yanked me to my feet without any noticeable effort. Gunnar stared at me from inches away, looking both excited and sick to his stomach. He had two massive red welts on his forehead. "What do I do?" he whispered.

Seeing my best friend more stressed than I felt, somehow helped to calm me down. "Hell, man. Why are you asking me? I almost had a panic attack even hearing it."

Gunnar smiled crookedly, but I saw the terrified gleam in his lone eye. "I've never felt like this. I feel violent enough to go destroy something—to protect Ashley from even a hint of a threat! But I don't think I've ever felt so happy before either. Or so terrified. How is that even possible?" He grabbed my shirt and yanked me close again. "What do I do with my *face*?" he hissed, pointing at the bizarre expression he was making, which really did look like a Frankenstein mix of emotion.

"Try to make it look happier," I suggested, shrugging.

Alex and Yahn sauntered over, congratulating Gunnar, but immediately blanched at the bizarre look on the soon-to-be-dad's face. "Are you concussed, and stuff?" Yahn asked. "You hit that table pretty hard, yah?"

"I've never felt better," Gunnar growled angrily.

"Maybe you should inform your face of that," Yahn suggested, chuckling.

I quickly shoved him out of harm's way and into Alex right before

Gunnar swiped at him with a werewolf claw. Gunnar froze, staring down at his claw in horror. "I...I'm sorry, Yahn," he stammered.

Yahn's eyes were wide—not with fear, but with utter bewilderment. "Toe-tah-lee fine," he finally grumbled in a much less jovial tone.

"Let's go take a walk, Yahn. Let them talk for a minute," Alex suggested, guiding Yahn away.

The women were all bubbling with overflowing joy as they laughed with Ashley, taking turns touching her belly and playing with her hair. The sound was deafening to my ears, all high-pitched coos and exclamations of some strange language while Gunnar and I were over here freaking the hell out.

I shot Gunnar a weak grin. "You'll do great—"

"Oh, the hell with that," he snarled over the loud sounds of the shrieking women. Then he picked up a wine glass and slammed it on the table, loud enough to cut all conversation like he had pulled a fire alarm. Dean was openly smiling, which absolutely caught me off guard. He would have skinned me alive for purposely breaking a glass. And he *never* smiled like that.

"I want to make an announcement!" Gunnar bellowed, even though the conversation had instantly ceased. "I'm sorry I made a mess of this. I don't quite know how to explain it, but I can say from the bottom of my heart that I have never been so happy..." he said, lowering his head apologetically. He was crying, now. "I'm so happy that I'm terrified I won't do a good job," he admitted. Someone on Team Female began to sob, and like a flicked domino, they were soon all snuffling and crying, but I couldn't see Ashley through their defensive ring.

Gunnar turned to me in an almost aggressive manner. "Which is why I want to personally thank Nate for offering to become the Godfather to my children." My face went entirely slack. I'd done *what*? That bit must have happened when I was unconscious. Gunnar continued, and I fought to keep my face calm against the internal horror at such a responsibility. "Figuratively speaking, of course. I would expect nothing less from my best friend, but I'm honored by his choice." Then Gunnar bowed and smiled at everyone. "I think I need some fresh air. Or a drink."

Ashley emerged from within her defensive ring to grab him on the way by and give him a very passionate kiss. "You'll be exceptional,

Wulfric. Your only competition is yourself, and because you're such a great man, you're terrified to look in the mirror at your opponent. Because *that* is the only time you get to see what everyone else *already* sees. And it scares you to go up against such a formidable man on a daily basis. This is the height of greatness," she whispered, loud enough so that only we heard it.

Gunnar closed his eye and set his forehead against his wife's, kissing her on the nose and holding the back of her head like it was a lifeline in a turbulent sea. Amazingly enough, I watched his entire body slowly relax. He opened his eye and smiled at her. "You're wrong, woman. I see greatness every time I roll over in the morning," he whispered back.

And her face split into such a wide grin that I feared they were about to try making triplets on the dining table.

Ashley, sensing my discomfort, nipped back at Gunnar's nose, shoved him towards me, and then slapped him on the ass. "Go, my Kings. You two could use a drink."

She didn't have to tell us twice. We headed for the nearest booze-station a few rooms down from the kitchen in one of the sitting parlors. I knew we had some of the nice Macallan stashed there.

I poured us each a liberal splash and we sat down in separate chairs with matching sighs of relief. We clinked glasses and downed them, saying nothing for a few minutes, regaining composure. I chose not to tell Gunnar that he still had a couple M&M's stuck in his beard—one pink and one blue, coincidentally. I spotted Talon just outside in the hall, but he chose to give us privacy, likely keeping an eye out for any intruders so we could talk in peace.

"I would have offered if I would have known you wanted me to," I finally told him.

"I know. That's why I announced it. Also...I want you to hold me accountable for being a good dad. You're the one who actually had a decent father. Despite his faults, Calvin was a great man."

I narrowed my eyes. "Except for all the lying."

Gunnar slowly turned to look at me, his stone eyepatch glinting in the fire's glow. "He gave me a *home*, Nate...a *family*."

My anger flickered out and died at the intensity of his glare. "I know. It's just...he lied to me about a lot of things. And not little things. He literally chose to lie about half of my entire life, and that lie is messing with my head right now, threatening to actually make me go crazy."

Gunnar nodded, refilling our drinks. "And his first order of business, after making what had to be the toughest decision of his life, was to make sure you had another ally like Talon. Someone to help keep you grounded, and subconsciously remind you of Fae. In effect, that act of compassion gave me a home. You might say he harmed you, but if he hadn't harmed you, I wouldn't fucking be here, and you wouldn't have me as an ally. I would never have met Ashley. Never have become a father..."

I downed my drink guiltily. "I'm sorry, Gunnar. I'm...not myself right now."

He snorted loudly. "Did you not *see* me in there? I still can't make my face work!"

I smiled. "Dude...you hit your head *so* hard. Twice!" I shook my head in amazement. "It was unbelievable. I felt it in my stomach." I found my smile stretching wider as I thought about him hitting his head once for each of his two future pups. But I didn't voice that.

Gunnar burst out laughing, spilling his drink. He shifted in his seat almost uncomfortably. Finally, he set the glass down and leaned his elbows on his knees, shaking his head. "Wait. Twice?" he asked, frowning in confusion.

I told him about the sword hilt and his jaws dropped open.

"*That's* why my balls hurt! That thing weighed at least ten *pounds!*"

We bantered back and forth after that, and I told him about thinking the pie had been for me. Some royal gesture. He could hardly breathe through his laughter.

I found myself idly playing with my new title. Godfather...

I'd have to find a book or something, because the only reference I had on that was a trilogy of movies, and they were likely not what Gunnar had in mind. Then again...I'd kind of done a lot of Godfather-like things in recent years. Becoming the King—Don—of St. Louis and taking down my foes with extreme prejudice.

I had a while to think on that future migraine. And tonight wasn't the night for it. Because I suddenly remembered that I had invited Gunnar to go with me to Fae tomorrow.

Well, shit.

10

We had joked around for thirty minutes or so and drank enough to marginally calm our nerves. Gunnar had made me promise to take him to Fae about a dozen times, arguing that he really needed some violence, or he was liable to do something stupid here in town. He needed an outlet for the storm of emotions within his heart.

The big bad wolf of St. Louis was going to be a daddy.

I had finally agreed to stick with the plan. He was the most loyal person I knew besides Talon, and in a way, it felt poetic to include my two oldest friends on this enlightenment journey I was about to take. Because I had spent a childhood with each of them—and they were both bitter about that, possessive on who had been the better friend. Maybe this would bring them closer together. Let them realize that they weren't all that different from each other.

Or they would try to kill each other. I had forced that unhelpful thought away, promising that at the first sign of danger, I would get them the fuck out of Fae, or get them away from each other if that was the case. Because I had two new reasons to keep Gunnar safe.

Twins. I shook my head at the thought. Poor, lucky bastard.

Having a plan, I felt much better as I walked through the halls of

Chateau Falco. Gunnar had gone off in search of Ashley to tell her we were headed out to the bar to celebrate and tell Achilles the big news.

I doubted he planned on mentioning Anubis, but that was my own problem to deal with, and really had nothing to do with Gunnar or anyone else.

Unfortunately, it was a requirement for me. If I skipped off to Fae without telling him, he was liable to revoke our agreement and drag me kicking and screaming down to Hell to become his permanent live-in guide. So, I needed to convince him that I had a plan.

It should be noted that I did not, in fact, have a plan. Not really. A crayon drawing would have been more professional than what I currently had: smuggle some banished Fae, meet new friends, kill or spy on Mordred.

I spotted Alvara leaning against a wall by herself, suspiciously peering around a corner, but I could hear laughter from the room she spied on. She heard me approaching and made no move to conceal her actions, but she did turn to face me. I glanced past her shoulder to see Talon showing Alice how to grip his spear properly for a fight. But he kept making it disappear on her, and then giving her a mock frown as he told her she must be doing something wrong.

Her indignant squawks denied the allegations. Rinse and repeat with increasing volume.

I smiled, proud to see Talon venturing out of his element and nailing it. He'd just become the default babysitter if we needed it in Fae, but I would wait to tell him about that promotion. I turned back to Alvara. "You two need anything?" I asked. "We're heading out for a little while to celebrate."

"Just assurances," she said, sighing.

I frowned. "About?"

"We're not welcome in Fae, and I'm scared to put her in danger," she whispered.

I'd already chased that ball of yarn in my own head and was pretty sure Alvara just needed to talk it out with someone. "She doesn't have to go. Dean could look after her here—"

"No," she said adamantly. "She's going. I don't want to leave her." She saw the puzzled look on my face and smiled in embarrassment. "Thank you for the offer, but if I walked in there right now and told her—the night before we are to leave—that she can't go..." she shuddered.

Which was the exact conclusion I had come to, but I pretended it was the first time I'd thought about it. Alvara was raising Alice all on her own, and I bet it could be a lonely, thankless job at times. "Yeah, I can imagine. But you two will be safe with us. You have me, Talon, Gunnar, and maybe even a few other friends once we get there. We'll be fine. We won't be looking for danger."

She nodded, but her eyes seemed far away. "Answers are the second most dangerous thing in the world."

"What's the first?"

She met my eyes seriously. "Questions."

I sighed, nodding my agreement. "I need this, Alvara. Most of what I've been told by others my entire life has either been a lie or barely a half-truth, so I'm seeking my own answers. And you promised to help me. I'm not kidnapping you. This was *your* idea."

"I know, I know. I'm not backing out, just voicing my concerns. It's just... I fear what you will do when you find the answers you seek. Maybe your parents lied for a very good reason."

I frowned at her. "I would never hurt you, Alvara. If you're afraid of that, I'll make it very easy for you. Tell me where your friend is, and I will visit her myself. You'll be safe here. Both of you. Remember that Baba Yaga and Callie Penrose said you could trust me," I reminded her.

She shook her head firmly. "I live by my word. We had an agreement. There is no option for me to back out." She pulled me by the hand to move further away from the room where Talon and Alice played—close enough to still see but not be overheard. "Answers are not always what we truly seek. The fruit of honesty often sours on the tongue. Sometimes, a lie, especially one of omission, is best."

"Well, I've had my fill of lies, and they definitely grow sour on the tongue," I told her.

"What if a lie keeps you safe? From others or from...yourself? Would you tell a child that their father was a serial killer, knowing the likelihood that it would forever taint their view of the world, making them feel inherently evil? Would you tell your child that Santa Claus is real for as many years as you could get away with it, or would you steal their joy and excitement with a truth? In a fatal accident, would you lean over to your child and promise them everything was going to be okay, or would you steal their hope in those last moments?"

I sighed in understanding. "I'm not saying lies are always bad. I'm saying that at a certain point, the truth becomes necessary. Lies are like Band-Aids. They help in the moment but must eventually be removed for a wound to fully heal. Replacing them with new Band-Aids—lies—only works in the short-term."

She sighed. "I hold little love for lies, Wylde. They have caused me great harm in the past as well." She sniffed, looking mildly angry. "Alice's father lied, too. Told us he would never leave...yet here we are..." she let out a weak sob as Alice giggled uproariously in the background. She finally met my eyes. "I am sorry to throw that at you. It was unfair. I see your mind is set, and I empathize with your position. Truly. I just needed to be certain."

She let out a sigh—both of anticipation and trepidation. Like a great weight had been lifted from her shoulders, but one that she was so used to carrying that she feared *not* carrying it any longer. She slowly walked back towards the sound of her daughter's giggling squeals.

"It is time to finally return home," she said almost under her breath, smiling over at Alice, who now seemed to be chasing Talon's tail as he hopped from couch to couch, egging her on. Alvara suddenly gripped my wrist tightly. "You will keep her safe over there, won't you? I need you to swear it. As much as we wish to return to Fae, we are not welcome back after our banishment. If they discover us, it would be the end. Promise you will do everything in your power to keep us safe."

I wanted to learn some more details on her banishment, since it seemed to involve Carl's parents, but her fingers dug into my wrist until I felt my bones creaking. "Yes. I'll do everything in my power to keep her safe."

She let out an anxious breath, and finally released my wrist. I shook it absently, surprised by her strength. "Good. Now, if you'll excuse me, I would like to braid my daughter's hair before bed. Big day and all that," she said, sniffling and dabbing at her eyes to conceal her tears.

Then she strolled into the room, speaking softly to Alice, telling her it was time for bed, and wouldn't she like a shower so they can braid her hair for their big day tomorrow?

I frowned at her back. Maybe it was a Fae thing. To have been banished for so long and then to realize you would be back home tomorrow... that had to be tough to wrap your head around.

I spotted Alex and Dean waiting for me down the hall, so I made my way over. Talon slipped out of the room behind me, following me on silent feet. Since the bar we were going to would have Regulars, he couldn't go with us. Thankfully, he'd said it would probably be best if he slept anyway so that one of us was clear-headed in the morning for our trip.

Even with that, he wasn't happy about leaving me unprotected and had made sure we each carried a pair of Tiny Balls—portable Gateways—on us in case we needed a quick escape, or got separated. Or in the event that I was unconscious from a flashback and would be unable to create my own escape, I was pretty certain.

"I need to talk to you in private before we leave," Alex told me, and then he took a few steps back to wait, even though that was entirely unnecessary.

I turned to Dean. "Can you find some chocolates and bring them to Alvara's room?"

Dean's mouth clicked shut and he blinked at me a few times. "Of course, Master Temple..." but I could sense the obvious question on his face.

"I think Alvara is anxious about tomorrow and wants a little mother-daughter time. She told me they're braiding hair, and that sounded suspiciously like code for *bring us chocolate or those with genetic outies are doomed.*"

Alex, despite giving us space, seemed to be mentally repeating the secret code for future use.

I wondered if he had any idea what I'd meant by genetic outies, hoped he didn't, and then prayed that he would try using the phrase with a woman where I could hear the reaction.

Dean nodded. "Your father often brought your mother chocolates when she seemed upset. I think I have just the thing." He paused to study me for a moment. "Might I say, it is very considerate of you to go out of your way for what most would consider a trivial matter. You could have just feigned ignorance, but you instead suggested a way to make them happier."

"It's not like I'm making the chocolate myself, Dean. I'm asking you to pilfer the pantry." Dean continued studying me in silence until I let out a breath. "Maybe I'm trying to get back on the Ravens' nice list," I said, smiling guiltily.

"Ah. That's more like you. Do try to stay out of trouble tonight. I have a bad feeling for some reason." And he truly did look troubled. Probably just envisioning the volatile Gunnar at a bar.

"Maybe you should have some chocolate, too." He narrowed his eyes at me, so I let out a sigh. "It's probably just knowing what we're doing tomorrow. Don't worry. It's only a few drinks."

That didn't seem to appease Dean's concern in the slightest, but I didn't let it get to me.

He left, heading back to the kitchens to scrounge up some lady-drugs.

AKA Chocolate.

Alex swept back in and spoke softly in case anyone was close enough to overhear. "Pandora wants to see you. She doesn't want to talk to you if you're drunk or hungover so she wants it to be before we leave. Won't take long at all."

I frowned at him suspiciously, but finally nodded. Pandora had only recently reopened the Armory, having locked it down while Mordred was in town. And I did have a few questions for her. "Deal."

Gunnar abruptly rounded the corner in a mad sprint and Talon darted clear, hissing instinctively. "Fly, you fools!" he snapped in a loud whisper. "I just got the green light and don't want her to change her mind!"

"We were just going to talk to—"

"I don't care where, just get me out of here!" he urged.

And he was suddenly shoving me after Alex, who was sprinting down the hall to avoid Gunnar's Heisman Trophy interpretation for Most Valuable Baseball Player.

"Heisman is baseball, right?" I asked.

Gunnar groaned, shoving me harder. "Just stop talking about sports. Forever."

I'd Google it later, but I was pretty sure I was close.

11

Pandora welcomed us to the Armory clad in fresh-off-the-bush mistletoe lingerie.

Or fresh-off-the-branch. Wherever mistletoe came from.

I'm not really sure how to describe her outfit, other than to say it got my attention up, and the placement of red berries had been given very careful consideration.

"Oh, I thought it was only you, Alex," she grinned. Then, accepting that she now had an audience, she gave us a little show. "How do I look?" she asked, twirling.

Gunnar froze midstride, one leg raised in the air so that he resembled a hunting dog going on point to indicate prey.

"Bird dog it!" I crowed at him, drinking down the fury from his glare, and using it to nourish and water the darkest parts of my soul so that it could grow even darker.

Alex grinned from ear-to-ear. "It's a long time until Yulemas, My Lady."

I frowned. My lady? They were well past *that* stage in their relationship. They were deep into the fuzzy handcuffs, Enya, and maple syrup stage.

"Can you put something else on, Pandora?" I asked. "I forgot my squirt bottle, and Gunnar is having a rough day," I said, pointing a thumb at him. He scowled back.

"Is that why he has candies in his beard?" she asked, cocking her head. Gunnar began raking his fingers through his beard, glaring at me.

In response to my request, Pandora snapped her fingers and the mistletoe was abruptly gone, leaving her entirely naked. Then she bent over at the hips to search inside a chest behind her, tossing out all sorts of strange garments, masks, sashes, and belts. "Let me just find something else."

I groaned, and Alex grinned. Gunnar slapped both hands over his face —even though he only had one eye to worry about. Old habits die hard, I guess.

"If that isn't a waste of resources, I don't know what is," I told him, laughing.

I turned back to Pandora to find her fully clothed in a pleasantly sheer toga. The show wasn't entirely over, but one would have to stare harder to get a good look.

I found her studying me, so I let out a sigh since she could read my thoughts. "Explain how you showed me Excalibur, but when I came back it was missing."

Because there had been a time or two when unwanted visitors had entered the Armory, and I was desperately hoping they hadn't nabbed Mordred's family sword for themselves.

"I've been waiting for you to remember that. I wonder why you forgot?" she asked with an amused smile.

I blinked at her a few times to show her my brain was cranking on and to give me a minute—like those spinning wheels on Apple computers, but at the blazing speed of 1995. I honestly had no idea if she was goading me or teasing me. "Is there a reason I forgot?" I finally asked.

"There often is, and your mind looks very dark and filled with holes at the moment." She studied me clinically for a second or two. "You have time to fix it. Not much, but enough. If you listen to the Wanderer."

"Who is the Wanderer?"

"You'll know soon enough. But the forgetting isn't important yet. It's the remembering that matters, is it not? That's what your whole plan is based on. To go wander Fae and remember all manner of childish things."

I turned to see if my friends had anything to offer, only to realize that they had wandered over to the balcony and were speaking in soft tones.

I turned back to Pandora. "I really just need you to help me, Pandora. I'm drowning here," I whispered—the first time I had admitted it to anyone. I hadn't been able to contact Callie and I hadn't wanted to talk to anyone else about it. Not because of any trust thing, but because I'd found that in my position as leader of this strange group of Freaks, I often couldn't afford to be too honest—even if I trusted them all with my life. Because at some point down the road, one of them would need to lean on me, and knowing that I had been on the brink of a meltdown only weeks before, and that I had relied upon them for advice or solace...

Then they might choose to not lean on me when they needed help, not wanting to burden me with their problems, and putting themselves at risk for no reason. In a way, I was martyring myself so that I could always be available to help shoulder their pain, and that wasn't a problem for me. It wasn't a hard request to fulfill most times, because my friends only asked for aid when they truly needed it, and I typically wanted to assist them.

I understood the contradiction—that I was doing the exact thing I didn't want them to do, but...wasn't that the freaking point of a leader? To take the first punch so they didn't have to?

To be the guy at the top...I was learning it was a lot lonelier than portrayed in the stories.

"Calvin Temple taught you that..." Pandora said gently.

I froze, realizing she was right. "Yeah. I guess he did. My dad had some good points every now and then." And I also realized that maybe he had passed that personality trait on to me. I let the topic go. "Pandora, please, just speak plainly."

"As best as I am able, Wylde, but my desires aren't really a factor. Some things I simply cannot speak of yet," she said sadly. I nodded in understanding, knowing there were strange rules to this place, and her existence within was bound by them. "When I showed you Excalibur, I showed you only a fragment of it. A placeholder. There are a few items like that in the Armory. Items too powerful to be contained in their entirety."

I frowned in rapidly growing alarm. "Isn't that the entire point of this place? To hold dangerous items? How can something be too powerful for the Armory?"

"Maybe powerful isn't quite the right word. Impacting, perhaps. Items that were destined to not be locked up. Items that absolutely had to end up back out in the real world at some point in time."

My eyebrows might have crawled off my scalp. "That would imply fate being fact."

She smiled. "Is it fate to say it will rain next year?"

I scowled at her. "That's cheating."

"Isn't magic cheating?"

I scowled harder. "You're saying that some things are entirely too powerful to be left locked away, and that Excalibur is one of those items?"

"I'm saying that some items haven't yet fulfilled their original purpose, so cannot remain locked up until they have done so. And...Merlin *was* one of the last to regularly manipulate time."

A cold shiver went down my spine, but I couldn't quite think of what to ask next. None of this was important to me right now. Later, definitely, but right now I just needed to know it was safe from Mordred's hands.

"You saw a piece of it here. Its astral form." She saw the alarm on my face and waved a hand dismissively. "These things happen from time to time. But it's nothing to be alarmed about. Without all the pieces in the same place at the same time, it cannot function at its full potential. Missing pieces are important, as you well know."

She stared directly at me, and I flinched. "Yeah. I'm learning that." Because a huge chunk of my life was missing from my memory, and I was about to go try and find it. "Where is the piece I saw, then? Where did it go?"

"It's still here," she said, shrugging. "I locked it away where none may find it, not even you. Not until you put yourself back together again, Humpty Dumpty."

"Swear it, Pandora. I have to know it's safe, and that Mordred cannot get to it."

"You know that is an impossible promise, Wylde. I can say that right now it is perfectly safe, but tomorrow? The next day?" she shrugged. "I cannot say. But Mordred is no closer to finding it than he ever was. In fact, it's as safe as your Round Table. Does that make you feel better?"

"It's better than I expected. If I keep the Table safe, I'll keep the sword safe?" I asked. "And just to clarify, the sword isn't wedged inside the leg of the table or anything, right?"

She smiled. "The sword is not a part of the table and is not hidden within the table. It is here, as I've told you."

"And the other pieces? Where are they?"

"On their way here, I imagine. I can feel their echoes. Now, do you like bears?"

"What?"

"I know you like dragons, but how do you feel about bears?"

"What are you *talking* about, Pandora?"

"Find the bear and you will find the last piece of Excalibur. Or you can just wait a bit longer. It should show up eventually. They always do." She cocked her head at me, listening to the storm of questions flooding my mind. Then she sighed with mild annoyance. "Mordred is no closer to obtaining Excalibur than he was when he was released from Hell. In fact, he's further away, because it is *here*, in the Armory. Excalibur finds the person; the person does not find Excalibur. You could run up to him and tell him it is here. Even invite him inside to search for himself, and he would not find it. Four more pieces must be reunited, or it will not be complete. A powerful sword, yes, but not its true potential. The Name, the Power, the Soul, the Blood, and the Blade must be forged back together. Reunited."

"The blood..." I said absently. "Do you mean the ichor in the Round Table?"

She. Just. Smiled. And I felt like I had won Jeopardy on live television.

But I had to consider it from all angles. I stared at her, trying desperately to understand the meaning beneath her answers. Then it hit me. Why she was being cagey. She was following rules. Commands. And two people in particular had given her commands before I came along. "I'm going to take a quick trip. I need to kill two people. It won't take me long."

She gripped my arm. "Killing your parents will not change anything, won't accomplish anything since they are already dead, and will still not give you what you seek. But you have guessed correctly. They forbade me to speak of it. And they lived by that same oath for a very particular reason, even if you cannot recall it at the moment. Your mind is too fragmented to see what is right in front of you. Excalibur is just one cog in the machine. The Catalyst is both the fuel and the machine itself. You're asking all the wrong questions!"

I ground my teeth, struggling to keep my composure. "I'm the new Master. Tell me."

Pandora sighed sadly. "Alas, I cannot. And I wouldn't even if I could because, as painful as it is, I've come to believe that they were right. But your parents did put one of my gifts to good use," she said, eyeing me up and down.

I blinked at her a few times. I glanced over my shoulder, wondering if she was indicating an item. Nothing caught my attention, so I turned back to her. She was suddenly two inches from my nose and she nipped me playfully with her teeth.

"I hope you don't waste it. Now, you need to leave, and I need you to sign some paperwork." She plucked a stapled stack of papers full of legalese off of a table.

I frowned down at it, scanning the pertinent information. "This is a lease agreement. What am I leasing?"

Pandora waved one hand in the general direction of the Armory as she flipped the pages of the agreement with the other. "Here. Sign right here."

"Wait, we're leasing the space for the *Armory*?" I asked incredulously. "From the fuck who?" I snapped, leaning down to read the document. "Who the hell is Last Breath?" I demanded.

Pandora gave me a stern look. "If you don't sign, we get evicted. Your call, but they've been perfectly good landlords for over a decade. I'm sure we can find another interdimensional unit if necessary, but your parents trusted this one."

"What if they come in and rob us blind?" I demanded.

Pandora arched a brow at me. "Well, genius, looks like your parents overlooked that one. Brava." She flipped back a few pages and stabbed a finger down. "They cannot physically, nor magically, set foot in here for any reason whatsoever without a guide—me or you—or express written permission from one of said guides. Or if we don't pay as agreed and refuse to balance our accounts after a six-month period of no payments—in which case, we would empty the Armory of all property and run for our lives. But the funds are already set aside to be paid in full in advance for a twenty percent discount, so that's not an issue. It's iron-clad. Your parents were merciless with contracts."

She handed me a pen, and I stared down at it for a solid minute, flipping the pages. "No changes to their original agreement?" I finally asked, warily.

"None," she said waiting.

I stared down at the blank line, hesitant. Signing contracts—magical ones, especially—could be fatal. I realized there was one more page behind the signature page and flipped it.

I froze, staring down at it. My parents' signatures on the original signature page block. I let out a breath, turned back the page, and signed.

"I want to meet them. Soon."

Pandora nodded, folding up the paper in a deft trifold. "I'll let them know."

"Let's go get a drink, guys," I called out, motioning for Gunnar and Alex to join me. We were walking out the Door to the Armory when a thought hit me. "Hey, how are you planning on mailing that out?" I asked Pandora.

"I don't need to. They're in the neighboring unit."

And the doors slammed shut. "Neighboring unit?" I demanded incredulously.

Gunnar scratched at his beard. "It's beer-thirty, and I need another ice-pack, stat."

Alex piped up casually. "You have an important meeting at the bar, and he's probably waiting."

I let out an annoyed sigh. I would look into this Last Breath business later. I had more important things to worry about. Like Anubis.

"I need all the drinks. Let's go."

12

Gunnar had practically guzzled the first pitcher he got his paws on, not even bothering to ask what anyone else wanted before specifically ordering a pitcher for himself. And he finished it about the same time we finished our single beers.

I'd carried my satchel with me into Buddy Hatchet—ignoring the strange looks I received for carrying around what looked like a white lizard-skin laptop bag with medieval chains for a strap. The satchel was bottomless—my own little pocket dimension—so I used it to hold anything I deemed too important to leave lying around, and also too important to have locked away in the Armory where I couldn't quickly grab it on a whim. Essentially, things I might need at a moment's notice.

I'd shoved the three artifacts my parents had left to me as an inheritance inside, knowing how important they were for the future: my War Hammer that said *Birthright* on the stone mallet, the Hand of God that contained the essence of a Maker, and the Hourglass they had stolen from Fae that could control time between our worlds.

I'd already packed everything for my trip to Fae in there, just in case. Food, water, clothing, and medical supplies.

My Devourer, I had found, no longer needed to be carried. Much like Talon's spear, I could now call it to me at will. That little trick had come about after I had officially become the Horseman of Hope in my fight against Mordred. If I put on my Horseman's Mask, it was suddenly there hanging from my magical chain. Just like Death and his Scythe.

Watching Gunnar wave a hand at a bartender for another pitcher, I gave Alex and Achilles a frank look and jerked a chin at Gunnar. They nodded and urged the Alpha werewolf to join them at the hatchet throwing area for him to let out some aggression. Because Gunnar was still acting recklessly—even by my standards. Perhaps he really did need to get to Fae, to workout whatever was going through his head about becoming a father. Maybe a good old-fashioned killing spree in Fae was just what the doctor ordered.

He was acting almost like...a berserker Viking. At least compared to his usual self. I wondered how much of that had to do with him being an Alpha, or maybe just a werewolf. They were big on family, so maybe that instinct was fanning the flames, turning his excitement into fear and over-protectiveness. Dialing his paranoia and dominance streak up to eleven.

The bar was a cool concept, especially for East St. Louis—which had a stigma for friendly strip-clubs and all-night bars. The back wall was a line of targets and the patrons could rent a bucket of hatchets or other throwing implement—but come on, everyone was going to pick the hatchets—to hurl at a target. Each throwing booth was set up with a list of fun drinking games one could play. Bouncers were plentiful—what with all the tools of destruction flying around—but overall, the place had a calm vibe to it.

Even though a Valkyrie ran Buddy Hatchet, she catered to Regulars and Freaks alike, not that any of the Regulars knew that. Surprisingly, we seemed to be the only Freaks in attendance, as far as I could tell. Which was for the best since I was sitting across the booth from Anubis, the King of Hell. He had chosen a latte-colored flesh-suit of a handsome man with long black hair that grayed out at the temples. He wore jeans, alligator loafers with no socks, and he was obviously allergic to buttoning the top half of his dress shirt. Maybe it reminded him too much of a collar.

"Did you..." I leaned closer, inspecting his glistening, hairy chest, "oil your chest hair?"

He studied me in silence, ignoring my comment as he drummed his fingers atop the table and considered my retelling of events about the fight with Mordred. I had laid it all out for him, even though I was certain he'd already heard the highlights of the fight. I'd explained away my delay in speaking with him afterwards by telling him that I'd been trying to track down Mordred to finish the job, but had been unsuccessful so far, so I was planning on heading to Fae in the morning to find out what he was up to. And I hadn't wanted to leave before talking with him.

And none of that was a lie.

Because you really couldn't lie to Anubis without a whole lot of effort. And if I put in a whole lot of effort to lie to him, he would know I was putting in a whole lot of effort, which meant I was definitely lying about *something*.

So I played it straight. Close to the chest, maybe, but straight.

I heard Gunnar roaring triumphantly over the hum of the other nearby patrons, and saw he was attracting a small crowd. Probably just women swooning over his biceps more than his hatchet hurling abilities. Anubis took a sip of his mead, murmuring his approval. "Our agreement still holds," he finally said, almost begrudgingly. "To be honest, you did much better than I had anticipated. Especially with only one Devourer."

I tried not to let my relief show, but I did close my eyes and dip my chin in gratitude, because he was definitely doing me a favor. And that deserved recognition. "Thank you."

"Who gave you the idea to go to the Dueling Grounds? That was quite ingenious."

I took a long pull of my mead, licking my lips after. It was a strange drink, but I was getting used to it. "No one. Cheat like a bastard to win like a king," I told him. "I knew I didn't have the strength to stand toe-to-toe with him, or the time to find another Devourer, so I sought an alternative. My time and ability were limited, what with some handicaps I recently discovered. Handicaps you helped me discover by throwing me into your lava ocean." He didn't react, so I mimed rolling waves with my hands and then fanned my face. "You know, in Hell."

"Yes. I picked up on your meaning from your hand gestures," he said, rolling his eyes. "It was the easiest way to show you the severity of your affliction. Merely telling you wouldn't have been enough to persuade you. You needed something more...extreme."

I nodded bitterly, accepting the truth to his statement. "I know that you set me up so that no matter which way I pivoted, you had something to win. Some way to benefit. Because you're a schemer," I said, careful to keep the last word an observation rather than an accusation.

Anubis frowned at me. Then he squinted suspiciously. "Odin talked. That sneaky bastard."

I shrugged, making sure the satchel was secure at my feet. Part of it poked out from beneath the table, but it meant it was closer to me than Anubis, so I left it. "Odin didn't tell me anything I hadn't already heard you say, he just used less lava to make his points."

We both looked up suddenly as Gunnar roared even louder, demanding more beer. The crowd around him was noticeably larger, but they were all laughing good-naturedly. What the hell was up with him?

Anubis grunted, turning back to me. "Teaching was never my strong suit. Since you are such a clever boy and found an alternative way to take back the Nine Souls from Mordred, I don't think you need to worry about finding a second Devourer for your cat. It would definitely be a benefit—Devourers are worth their weight in ichor if you can find one—but it's no longer necessary. If Mordred consumed the last Soul for himself, it looks like you're aimed directly at a brawl. And...of all the *schemes* I set up, that definitely wasn't one I considered," he added unhappily, taking another sip of his mead. "Speaking of Devourers, where is your pussy—"

"Meeeeoowwww," a sultry voice purred from beside us. I jolted like a frightened rabbit and saw a stunning, fiery-haired, middle-aged woman in a skin-tight red dress flashing a suggestive smile at us from beside our table. Her skin was as pale as marble, reminding me of milk. "Did you two just order room service?" she asked with a dark grin. "Because I can do service like no other."

I burst out laughing at her brash pick-up line. "Wow. That's a bold—"

She cut me off by sitting down beside me and placing a very warm palm very high on my inner thigh. "Boy, fortune *favors* the bold."

Anubis had stopped breathing and stared at the woman gripping my inner thigh. The only motion from his side of the table was his hand shaking as he held his pint of mead.

"Down, boy. She's not a fire hydrant," a new voice teased Anubis. I looked up to see a tan man with sand-colored hair wearing a burgundy suit and bronze ascot. He was chuckling amicably at Anubis. The King of

Hell did not peel his eyes away from the woman gripping my thigh—more specifically, he did not peel his eyes away from her cleavage

The woman tittered like chiming glass, and I picked up the scent of cigars and leather.

"Come now, Dear," the man said, holding out his hand like a gentleman.

The woman sighed, working her naughty fingers across my thigh like she was playing the piano. "Oh, Darling. How many times do I have to tell you? It doesn't *work* like that. Foreplay is involved, of course."

I felt my ears burn at the double connotations.

Then the man looked me right in the eyes, and I gave him perhaps the most awkward smile I had ever attempted—since his lady seemed intent upon braiding my inner thigh hair with her wiggling fingers. Except...he didn't look the slightest bit territorial. He turned to appraise Anubis and finally gave a shrug. "What a coincidence. There are four of us. Shall we go play?"

Sweet Jesus. Was this really happening? Anubis now looked about to choke on his own tongue. "We were kind of in the middle of a meeting."

"It looks like there is enough meat to go around. I have quite an appetite."

I coughed, feeling my ears burning hotter, and that was *before* her fingers began inching towards my wild west like she was reenacting the Lewis and Clark expedition to establish trade partnerships with the natives —in my pants.

"I think we're all set," I told her frantically. "It's been a long night."

She pouted her lush lips at me, coyly. "What do you think I came here looking for, sailor?"

Good lord. I needed another beer. "Nice ascot, man."

"I know," he said, pruning it lightly with his fingertips.

"Would you like a White Rose?" the woman asked me.

"Um, sure," I said, hoping it would get her hand away from my Thunderdome.

She leaned in close, practically touching my ear as she squeezed my thigh. "Then you should go find it," she said in a breathy whisper.

13

Before I could reply, she was suddenly standing beside the man again. The two of them blew a kiss at us before sashaying towards the front door, on the hunt for...bolder prey.

Anubis let out a shuddering breath—the first sound I'd heard him make in quite some time. "You have got to be fucking kidding me."

"I know! Can you believe that?" I croaked, glancing over my shoulder to watch them exit through the front door. My leg still felt hot from her pleasant palm and friendly fingers.

"I thought they were locked down to Kansas City!" Anubis hissed.

I turned to look back at him, my smile faltering. "Wait. You *knew* them? Why didn't you say anything, you weirdo? I've never felt so outclassed in flirting banter..." I said, shaking my head.

"There is no such thing as friendly banter when it comes to Darling and Dear," Anubis snarled, his eyes a million miles away. "How did I miss this?"

I stared at him, my mouth falling open. Darling and Dear? As in, the ones who had made my satchel and sent me that random bondage gear? I had been dying to meet them. Why hadn't they simply introduced themselves?

I swore, pounding my fist into the table. "Goddamn—"

"Touch my hatchet again, and I'll rip your arm off!" Gunnar roared, loud enough to drown out every other sound in the bar. I jumped to my feet, sensing that the crowd around the closet-werewolf had grown noticeably larger—and no longer seemed as friendly.

Anubis cursed. "He's about to shift, which means I'm leaving. This city is fucking ridiculous." I glanced back at him to realize he'd already made good on his word, leaving his half-empty glass of mead behind. Fuck.

Achilles and Alex were already dragging Gunnar towards me as I scooped up my satchel and flung it over my shoulder. I waved at the crowd behind him. "Sorry, guys. He didn't mean it. He's going through a rough patch."

"Then maybe taking him to a bar wasn't the best idea," someone shouted out angrily.

I nodded, rather than making an example of the prick. Because...he had a good point. And I couldn't just swat him upside the head with a current of magic. That would be as bad as Gunnar shifting.

"Hey! That's Nate Temple!" someone shouted excitedly.

"When are you meeting Mr. Dredd again?"

"How is the Round Table Initiative going?"

I pursed my lips, waving a hand as if I hadn't heard, and turned my back on them to look like I was too busy taking care of my too-drunk friend. This was bad. So bad. Because Gunnar was panting, swearing, and struggling against Achilles and Alex, demanding to be released so he could go teach them a lesson.

Achilles was gritting his teeth as he glared at me over Gunnar's shoulder. "Get us the hell out of here!"

Alex nodded. "He obliterated the target. Literally. Then he snapped the haft of a hatchet over his knee." He jerked a chin at Gunnar's arm, which he was trying to hide from the crowd. It was covered in white fur, meaning Gunnar had already partially shifted.

Fuck, fuck, fuck.

"Gunnar," I hissed, getting right up in his face. "Defiance, man. Fucking Defiance. Calm down or this will go viral by midnight! Let's get out of here, and you can shift at Falco." His lone eye latched onto me, and he visibly shivered, blinking rapidly. I could smell the beer on his breath, but it looked like he had at least heard me, no longer threatening the crowd at the top of his lungs. "Good," I encouraged him. "Just breathe. We only need to get to the parking lot, and I can—"

A booming explosion erupted behind me, and the concussive force slammed my forehead into Gunnar's jaw, knocking him out cold, and sending Achilles tumbling to the floor buried under the Alpha werewolf's deadweight. Luckily, Alex had managed to let go in time and was staring over my shoulder incredulously.

"Where is Nate Temple?" a basso, thunderous voice demanded from the source of the explosion.

I ignored the stars in my vision from headbutting Gunnar and put my best Clint Eastwood face on. Then I slowly, casually, turned to look. A bear of a man with a wild, tangled, chest-length beard, and even gnarlier long, reddish hair, stared back at me from the now permanently-open doorway. His beard was bundled together at the tips with silver bands of some kind, making him look like he was chewing on the head of a dirty octopus. He wore primitive leathers and a fur cloak, and his boots also seemed to be made of leather and furs. His face was scarred, and his eyes crackled with flickers of light.

I sniffed with disdain before smirking over at Alex. "Looks like Hagrid went to Burning Man," I told him, pointing a finger at the newcomer.

The man snarled, stepping through the shattered doorway and into the bar, ignoring the falling wood and drywall as he elbowed the broken door from the lone remaining hinge. "You..." he growled.

"I," I growled right back, theatrically mimicking his exact tone and posture.

Someone in the back let out a nervous laugh, but the rest of the room was eerily silent.

I needed to try to keep him off balance long enough to gather my wits from smacking skulls with Gunnar. I had no idea how the blow had knocked him out. It must have been the perfect storm, because I'd seen him take harder hits than that dozens of times throughout our life.

I was pretty sure I knew exactly who this asshole was—and I wasn't very excited about the next few minutes. But what happened next wasn't really up to me. He'd already made a big entrance so obviously had a point in doing so, and I wasn't sure I had the stones to tell him to cut it out. I didn't see anyone else stepping up, though...

My only hope was that the Valkyrie owner would step in. Quickly. I needed to stall.

The intruder had no interest in that option, and simply began stomping towards me, his hands outstretched to show me he planned to choke me to death. "You have something of mine, and you're about to give it back to me. I'll hurt you less if you make it easy."

"I'm not an easy kind of girl."

A metal door slammed down over the entrance to the bar, looking like solid steel. "Enough!" a somewhat feminine voice boomed from behind the counter. The intruder smirked at my response, but he didn't stop advancing, so I didn't risk taking a look to see who had spoken. I was really hoping it was Achilles' Valkyrie.

But no woman in shining armor swooped in to save the dudes in distress.

And I couldn't just throw around my magic in front of so many Regulars. Well, I didn't *want* to—because it would give everyone proof that magic was real, and if humanity was consistently reliable about one thing, it was that some asshole was probably already recording this on his phone. But I also wasn't about to go down without a fight. Alex was suddenly moving, reaching my side right as the intruder did.

"Let's take this outside," I told the man, hoping he would agree. "You don't want to piss off one of them," I urged, jerking my chin towards the suspected Valkyrie without breaking eye contact.

"Deal," he said, right as he came close enough to grab me.

"NO!" the woman shrieked.

The intruder must have been dragging his Ugg boots across the floor, because the static shock was enough to almost make my eyes pop and my fingernails crack and split down the center. I felt Alex grab me at the same time, and a rainbow-colored blast of light filled my vision.

I might have even peed a little from the static thing.

But I had sneakily reached into my satchel to wrap my hands around something long, hard, and always in the mood for a good pounding.

It was hammer time. *Can't touch this,* I thought to myself.

14

I was already swinging the War Hammer—laced with a healthy topping of magical oomph—as the rainbow light winked out and I found we were now outside the bar. The War Hammer seemed to siphon additional magic right out of me like a leech, building the power stronger than I had intended. I struck the intruder in the gut so hard that he flew twenty feet into a dumpster, bending it entirely in half so that it wrapped around him like a cocoon.

Then I fell to my knees, panting at the use of so much power in one go. Too much in one go. I had sprinted right out of the gate, and if it didn't pan out, I wasn't sure I'd have enough stamina to keep going. But I hadn't intended to use quite *that* much.

At least it looked like it had been worth it. I took a moment to verify that I still maintained my dignity and hadn't actually wet myself, so I now had two things to be proud about. Alex gasped, shaking out his hand frantically, startled by the static zap. "What the hell did he just do?" he demanded, scanning the area quickly. "And where are we?"

I surveyed the row of cars before us and pondered the back of a commercial building. "I'm pretty sure we're in the parking lot behind the bar, and I'm also pretty sure we just got Bi-fisted."

Alex stared at me, arching one eyebrow to let me know he had no idea what I was talking about. I hung my head, realizing it only meant that I had failed as a father and role model.

"Bifrösted," I explained as I climbed back to my feet. "The rainbow bridge that connects Asgard to Midgard—Earth. Maybe some of the other Nine Realms, too. We just lost our Bifröst virginity—"

An angry bleating sound interrupted my educational lecture on Aesir —the Norse Gods—mythology. "*Meh-eh-eh-eh!*"

I spun, glaring on reflex. "Put up your dukes, and say that to my face," I snarled.

A couple of stumbling drunk girls had been trying to take a selfie with two matted, shaggy goats about the size of mastiffs, but the goats were now glaring at us, having knocked the drunks down at our sudden interruption of their selfie. Their tall, curled horns looked chipped and aged, but were wickedly sharp at the tips. And in those eyes, I saw the fire that had inspired Inigo Montoya's quest for vengeance.

"They don't got no fucking *dukes*," one of the drunk girls stammered. "They're adorable goats, and they have pretty hooves." She followed that up with a hiccup.

I wondered if she realized she had just quoted the Adam Sandler skit, or if it truly was coincidental. Either way, it was a beautiful, beautiful moment. Despite the fact that the goats looked on the verge of charging. The worst part about it all was that I recognized them.

Seeing the fabled Tanngrisnir and Tanngnjóstr—teeth-barer and teeth grinder—live and in person confirmed my hypothesis.

The UGG wearing intruder was Thor—and we'd gotten off on the wrong foot, gosh darn it.

"Why are the goats harnessed to a chariot?" Alex asked, interrupting my moment. "Did someone really ride that thing here?" That *thing* was a very basic, primitive-looking wooden chariot with runes carved into the sides. Thor's goats carried him across the skies on it, according to myth. The two drunk girls flipped us off, blaming us for the goats' sudden lack of interest in photography. Then they left.

"Alex, this is about to escalate *very* fast. You need to get out of here. Grab your Tiny Balls—"

Right on cue, the metal dumpster exploded into a wave of hot shards and I managed to fling up a weak shield at the last moment, catching the blast. The UGG endorser stepped out, stroking his beard and rubbing his tummy where I had hit him. Alex looked dubiously at my weak shield— undeniable proof that I was running low on magical gas. Hell, I was concerned, too. Especially since I had caused Thor no lasting harm. Just pissed him and his goats off.

"Bro..." I began, hoping to calm the Norse God of Thunder down. I mean, I was cool with his dad—kind of. I didn't want to fight him, yet here we were. I had gone from a foursome invitation to standing in a dirty alley with a couple of angry goats, an even angrier god, very little magic, and Alex.

"We are not brothers," Thor snarled, spraying spittle into the air, his fist wielding a—

I frowned, feeling a very unpleasant wriggling sensation in my belly. "That's not a hammer," I said, pointing at the crude dagger in his fist. Which meant...

He nodded slowly, eyes riveting on the War Hammer in my fist. "*That* is my hammer."

Well, at least I now had official confirmation that I wasn't Thor— straight from the goat's mouth, so to speak. Because Odin had always been very sketchy about that whole line of questioning. And judging by Thor's interest in my Hammer, I was pretty sure I knew why.

Except...I noticed that Thor had frozen in place, staring at my War Hammer. His face contorted into a puddle of Shar-Pei puppyness, but I think he was aiming for outrage. He just had too many scars for it to look like anything other than a stack of soggy pancakes. "Where. Is. My. Mjolnir?" he demanded in a tone that definitely made up for the IHOP face.

Even though he was suddenly livid, I felt an immediate wave of relief at his question. My Hammer was *not* his precious Mjolnir. Praise Odin!

Unfortunately, it looked like he considered me guilty by association for leading him on.

"I have no idea where Mjolnir is, but you look dangerous enough with that dagger," I told him. "Why don't you put it down and we can talk about it like adults." He had other weapons he sometimes used, and I found myself absently wondering why he wasn't holding one of them.

"I was so certain..." Thor growled. "My Mjolnir needs me. I need my Mjolnir. We have been apart for far too long. Without it..."

Was their relationship like that Austin Powers flick? Had Thor...lost his mojo?

Or, perhaps his Mjol-jo.

Knowing my best shot had done very little to dissuade him—even with my War Hammer—I wisely didn't offer my thought up for discussion. Also, his hand was still quivering. After his teleportation magic inside the bar, I wasn't sure Shadow Walking us out of here was a great idea. He seemed to have a similar ability.

And now that he had my scent, so to speak, I doubted running was an option for me.

"Are we cool?" I asked. "Because I really want to take a picture with your goats—"

"No..." he interrupted, slowly turning to look at me. "We are not *cool*. No one hits me with a hammer..." His brows lowered as he lifted one fuzzy UGG boot of death, and then another, storming my way with nefarious intent. "If I can't have my Hammer, no one will have a hammer," he snarled, eyes locking onto the War Hammer I still gripped in my fist.

I panicked. This wasn't just any hammer. My parents had given it to me. It was important, somehow. I couldn't simply let him have it. It was mine!

I did the only thing I could think of. I shoved it where he would never get his dirty meat-hooks on it. In my satchel. Even if I died, he would never get it. He snorted at my futile act, assuming he could just retrieve it once I was dead.

"First of all, I don't think I like your attitude. Secondly, I can recommend a good spa and barber for...whatever you call that," I said, gesturing at his face.

"Pretty men die quickly in Asgard," he growled, not slowing down. "I'll show you."

"Explains a lot," I muttered. "Let's slow down a second, man."

"I'd rather not."

"Fine," I growled, taking a deep breath. I flung out my hand, drawing deep on my reserves. Unfortunately, like a car going uphill on low gas, I felt my knees shudder and my magic stall out. I gasped, stars twinkling into my vision alarmingly fast.

Before I could think of an alternative attack—or consider bravely fleeing—I heard a frantic bleat from off to the side. I glanced over to see one of the fucking goats hurtling our way. Thor bellowed in anger right before the goat struck him in the face with a hoof, getting tangled up in his beard-locks as they went down. I stared at Alex incredulously, since he had already hoisted the other goat over his shoulder and was spinning in a circle like he was winding up for a shotput personal record in track and field.

He flung the goat right as Thor disentangled himself, knocking him back down—but his dagger had been held outstretched and he ended up stabbing his goat—whichever one it had been. The resulting agonized bleating sound made me wince, but the roar of fury from Thor was enough to make every single one of my orifices pucker.

"Alex, we need to run. Now—"

But he had already covered half the distance to the fallen God and was singing as he ran. "Bah, bah, black sheep, have you anymore..." He leapt into the air, feet stretched out, right as Thor was climbing back to his feet. "Yes, sir, yes, sir, boots for Thor!" Alex belted out the last line just as his heels connected with the side of Thor's head, sending him cartwheeling into the pile of mother-bleating goats.

One of his UGG boots went flying off into a dirty puddle.

"Fuck, fuck, fuck..." I was cursing to myself, trying to think of a way out of this. If we survived, we would have to find Odin as soon as possible and convince him to get Thor off our backs. I could always hold the Ravens as hostage in a worst-case scenario.

Alex was laughing as he climbed back to his feet, brushing off his pants. "Come on, Godlet. Let's kiss knuckles," he taunted, lifting his fists. "Man to God."

15

T hor's wrinkled face purpled, and he jumped to his feet. With one missing boot, and one of his goats still bleating from the knife wound, the scene looked positively ridiculous.

"You're on a precipice, boy," Thor warned, his face livid as he squared his shoulders against the human aggressor. What the hell was Alex thinking? He was an incredible fighter, but against Thor? Was he nucking futs?

Alex, instead of advancing, turned his back on Thor and crouched down low, one fist behind him. He smiled from over his shoulder at the enraged Thor. "Bah, bah, black sheep, bootless Thor..." he began singing again, grinning like a loon.

Thor roared at the top of his lungs, the heavens crackling with a sudden storm that threatened to destroy St. Louis. And then it began to rain—great, forceful sheets of water splashing down upon us. It was as if he was casting his magic up into the sky so as not to accidentally use it in his fistfight. Or he was just setting the tone.

Thor charged him like a bull, his uneven gait looking awkward, but I could see the force behind the blow he had ready to slam down upon the back of Alex's head.

Five feet from contact, a small glass marble shattered between them, and two Gateways screamed to life, sandwiching Alex between them—one in front of stampeding Thor and the other on the opposite side of Alex. Where the hell had he gotten custom Tiny Balls of his own? Those definitely weren't the ones Talon had given him to send us back to Chateau Falco. Had Othello given him some kind of prototype that could be modified on the fly?

Thor barreled through one and appeared on the opposite side of Alex, looking startled to suddenly be facing his opponent head on.

Alex was already swinging in the uppercut of all uppercuts and struck Thor's jaw before he even had time to process it all.

Alex, I was beginning to realize, didn't like it from the back.

Thor cried out, suddenly airborne as the blow knocked him clean off his feet, but he still tried to reach out to grab hold of Alex.

But Alex had already darted out of reach, and succinctly grabbed Thor by the belt. Then he yanked downward as he lifted his knee, showing Thor the backbreaker move.

Thor gasped, tumbling to the asphalt and splashing beard-first into a puddle.

Alex smartly shuffled back, ready for round two. He didn't glance over at me as he spoke. "You have any magic yet?" he asked in a calm tone.

"Dude..." I said, shaking my head in awe.

"Magic," he repeated, watching as Thor specifically and colorfully cursed each of the Nine Realms while scrambling to his feet with a limp.

I tried and groaned. "No," I rasped. "I'm spent."

"Give me the Hammer. I've got this."

I shook my head immediately. "I can't, man. It's important. We can't risk using it for this."

Alex nodded absently. "Well, I'll buy you some time. Use your Tiny Balls to get the hell out of here."

"No!" I snapped, not liking him telling me what to do. "We'll *both* go!"

"The only place either of you is going is Asgard!" Thor roared, lifting a fist to the skies. Rainbow-colored light began to crackle around his fist and, unlike a Gay Pride parade, there was nothing lighthearted or carefree about these colors. The colors burned with fire, for one thing.

Thor hadn't done anything like this when teleporting us outside the bar, so maybe we were still Bifröst virgins. If he was actually calling the Bifröst this time, he was being entirely literal about taking us to Asgard.

"I wouldn't do that," I begged, waving my hands at a sudden nightmarish thought.

I was too late. A bolt of multicolored lightning clawed out from the skies to kiss his fist, rapidly growing into a fat column of pulsing, vibrant color. The Bifröst. The Rainbow Bridge between the Nine Realms.

Except...

Grimm, my unicorn, suddenly rode into Thor's happy moment on a Gothic lightning bolt of hate, swooping down from the skies to headbutt the Bifröst with his horn. A shockwave exploded out in a perfect circle across the skies, zipping ever-outward in an impossible display of flashing, fiery color that St. Louis could not have missed if they had been blind. About a hundred car alarms instantly went off in the nearby parking lots, and glass shattered from the windows of the nearby buildings.

It knocked Alex and me onto our asses, and we both stared up incredulously at Grimm neighing in the skies, entirely unaffected by the explosion. In fact, he was prancing about like a dog after he had dropped a load off in the yard, perfectly illuminated by the storming kaleidoscope of light above.

The Rainbow Killer had struck again.

The sky sparkled and glittered as the Bifröst fractured from the impact point outward, calving and collapsing like a glacier in the Arctic—a continuous, roaring rumble that grew in intensity and volume with each passing second.

Solid spires of Bifröst—as well as rainbow rain—slammed down into the parking lot, threatening to kill us all in the most undignified of ways.

Most of it rained down upon Thor, since he had been the one directly beneath the Bifröst and was currently staring up at the skies in utter disbelief. The pillar of rainbow chunks slammed into his mouth, making him gag and spit as it buried him alive.

But the Bifröst had been huge and, like a falling tree, the rest of the Rainbow Bridge solidified and fractured, falling down all around us. Grimm landed beside me and I risked burning out my wizard's magic to throw up a weak shield rather than dying by rainbow impalement.

The chunks of rainbow hammered into my shield, and my arms shook as my vision began to tunnel to a small circle—seeming to last for an eternity as it pressed me closer and closer to the asphalt.

It finally winked out, and I hoped I had held it up long enough to keep us safe. I realized I was lying flat on the ground, my cheek resting in a puddle of colors that swirled and rippled like a melted box of crayons. And it was pleasantly warm, almost hot.

I panted, trying to get enough breath to command Grimm to get us the hell out of here. Because I was pretty sure he had just broken Asgard's Bifröst.

And as smaller chunks of burning rainbow continued to fall all around me, it was oddly symbolic of what I was pretty sure had just happened to my budding friendship with Odin.

I finally caught my breath and climbed to all fours, noticing Thor struggling to emerge from the mound of rainbow guts that had buried him. I desperately spun towards Grimm, knowing he had enough time to fly us out of here before Thor—

Grimm was lazily gobbling down his fill of a pile of rainbow guts, murmuring contentedly to himself.

"Grimm! Get us out of here!" I snapped, panicking.

"YOU BROKE THE BIFRÖST!" Thor screamed, loud enough to make the very ground rumble. "DO YOU HAVE ANY IDEA WHAT ASGARD WILL DO TO YOU FOR THAT?" Thor continued, finally climbing free of his entrapment. He stood atop the pile of rainbow guts, panting, his eyes dancing wildly—both in disbelief at what had just happened, and an all-encompassing fury.

That look made me feel like I had just admitted to sleeping with his mother.

Then he saw Grimm actually *eating* the Bifröst.

Grimm shook his mane and swallowed the last bit, his lips dripping rainbow blood. "Big dog's gotta eat, ya know? Woof. Woof." he said in a monotone, flicking his tail. He slowly repositioned himself to face Thor, legs tensing as if ready for the obvious attack.

Thor sputtered incredulously.

And then, nonchalantly, Grimm squatted ever so slightly and pissed on the remaining pile of Bifröst. "It's hard to focus with you staring at me," he muttered, averting his eyes.

The look on Thor's face made me feel like I hadn't just slept with his mother.

I had forgotten to call her back the next day.

"Damnit, Grimm..." I wheezed.

Grimm snorted at my reprimand. "Sorry, not sorry."

I hoped Thor hadn't seen Achilles and Gunnar with us at the bar, or he would hunt them down when he finished making examples of us. Thor looked like he would hunt down anyone I had once bought a pack of bubblegum from. If I was dead, at least I wouldn't have to go to Fae anymore. Small victories.

I spotted helicopters in the distant skies, all seemingly aimed our way to get footage of whatever the hell fuckery had just gone down over East St. Louis. Maybe God had smited all the strip clubs in one throbbing blow.

Thor slowly climbed down from his perch atop the rainbow pile, his chest heaving, and tears running down his cheeks. "I will show you the many colors of a god's vengeance..." he promised, literally drooling in anticipation. The fact that his face and beard were dripping with rainbow blood almost made it impossible to take him seriously. Almost.

"Then I will hand you over to the rest of Asgard to atone for your crime with the Bifröst." Lightning crackled across the skies, somehow matching his steps, and it began to rain harder.

Between one flash of light and the next, a massive, hooded figure suddenly loomed between us and Thor, his back to us. He held a large spear at his side, and it crackled with yellow light, almost vapor.

I heard the sound of a file slowly drawing across metal and saw Grimm noticeably stiffen.

I followed his look to see an eight-legged beast of a horse—complete with an impossible rack of horns and a wide, bloody nose—slowly dragging one of his eight hooves across the asphalt, actually plowing a furrow in the stone.

I'd called him Rudolph once. He'd tried to bite my face off. Good times.

I turned to Alex, smiling hopelessly. This was it. Game over.

"I don't think Santa's here for us to sit on his lap. We just hit the top of his naughty list."

16

Thor stopped in his tracks, looking as if he had seen a ghost. "Allfather," he breathed, his hands falling to his sides. "Where... have you been?"

I pretended I was a very small fly on the wall, hoping they would forget about us.

"Stand down, my son," Odin commanded in a very soft tone.

Thor blinked in confusion. Then they narrowed. "They *broke the Bifröst!*"

Odin was nonplussed. "Because you provoked him. You fool."

Thor's jaw dropped in disbelief this time. "You have *got* to be kidding me! I haven't seen you in *decades*, father! And the first words out of your mouth are to side with him over your own son?" he growled, fists clenching as they crackled with electricity.

Odin nodded wordlessly. Gungnir—his massive, slate-gray war-spear crackled in his fist, the bright yellow Devourer at the tip steamed with a bright fog—a warning.

Where had Odin been for Thor to have not seen him in decades?

"Where did you take my Mjolnir, father? And what are you going to do about the Bifröst?" Thor asked in a very cold tone.

Again, Odin remained silent.

Thor cocked his head, glancing back at me with a frown, and then back at Odin. "How...do you even know Temple, father? The only other time I've seen you scoop up a stray is when you adopted Loki into our home as my foster-brother—" Thor cut off abruptly, taking two rapid steps back, shaking his head in denial. "No, no, no. That's ridiculous."

Wait a minute. What the hell was going on here? Alex was staring at me incredulously.

"That is not Loki," Thor demanded, pointing directly at me, "or I would know this to be one of his illusions. So, how do you know Temple?" Thor asked, much louder and angrier this time. "Why would you protect him like a son?"

"Nate is—"

"*Nate?*" Thor bellowed. "First name basis?! Are you his cupbearer, then, Allfather?" Thor hooted, belting out a sarcastic laugh at the ridiculous question.

Odin, for his part, was entirely silent, a solid boulder against his son's storm of emotions, only his cloak rippling in the wind.

His silence was...an answer in and of itself, and I felt my hand shaking as possibilities clicked into place. No...that really was impossible. Cupbearer was another term for...*butler.*

Thor had also read into Odin's silence, and was shaking his head in horror. Without another word, he lifted his fist to the sky, calling down a bolt of lightning big enough to destroy the world. "I will not stand—"

"Then you shall fall, my son," Odin said softly, stabbing his spear up into the air to intercept the lightning bolt and keep it from connecting with Thor's fist. The steaming Devourer atop Gungnir simply swallowed the bolt of lightning with a slight hissing sound.

Then Odin flung out a hand towards Thor, and a Gateway leading into a world of frost and darkness swallowed him up whole before winking out of existence.

Odin grunted, and then thumped the butt of his spear to the ground, and a bubble of some hazy substance suddenly covered us all in a vast dome. The helicopters from earlier swept by overhead, but we could no longer see them, only hear them. We couldn't see anything outside of our dome.

I don't think I would have even cared if the helicopters landed right on top of me. I was shaking my head, gritting my teeth in denial. Tears were streaming down my face, even though I didn't feel like crying. Tears of anger. Just like Thor, but for different reasons.

Without turning to face us, Odin spoke in a very low tone, almost a whisper. "I've sent him to his rooms, as it were. A time-out. I doubt the airsoft gun would have worked on him as well as it did on you," he said tiredly. "I told you I had a bad feeling about this night. Had I known all this would transpire..." He shook his head. "Maybe it's for the best."

I stared, shaking my head in denial. "No, no, no..."

Odin...shimmered to reveal a sharply dressed older man, his shoulders slumped guiltily. He let out a sigh, turning to look back at me empathetically. Over his pressed suit, he wore an apron with the Temple Family Crest on it. Dean's apron.

I fell to my knees, hyperventilating.

My butler, Dean, was Odin.

"Someone had to watch over you," Dean—Odin—said. "To make sure you tasted just the right amount of pain. Experienced just enough chaos to destroy the order you grew so accustomed to in your life. What better father figure to help with that than Odin? Even more so after Calvin and Makayla died..."

"Oh, Dean," I rasped, shaking my head.

"O-*dinn*, not O-*dean*," he corrected. "My idiot son had to give it away before I could tell it to you properly—at the right time. Now that you know, my help is limited. As Dean, I could work behind the scenes—do things that even now, you are probably not even aware of. Subtly. No one ever suspects the butler. Now..." he trailed off, sounding frustrated.

"How did you know we were even here?" I asked, trying to find something I could process. Dean...the man who had been there my whole life, watching over me from the shadows. The fucking Allfather had been my...*butler*. How had he even found the humility to accept such a role?

Odin didn't respond, and my mind slowly began to kick into gear. "The bar—Buddy Hatchet—is run by a Valkyrie..." I murmured.

"You are quite popular among my Valkyries," Odin said, smiling in amusement. "Consider how many souls you have given them over the years...all the battles and wars fought at Chateau Falco. It's like a buffet table of offerings. You are a legend in their eyes, even though they did not know my involvement. None of my pantheon knew. I didn't just lie to *you*, Nate; I lied to everyone. It was necessary."

That's when it hit me. I looked up sharply, shaking my head. "Anubis," I breathed.

Because Anubis was a schemer, always angling for his own gain, using others like pawns. And he was pals with Odin. If Odin's Valkyries liked me for all the souls I had lined up...Anubis had received his fair share as well, being the King of Hell. And I was his Golden Boy—his Guide. He wouldn't have wanted Thor ruining his plans. Anubis must have known.

Odin nodded, confirming my suspicion. "We share a vested interest in our favorite supplier of power. But that's not why I came to your aid," he admitted, looking embarrassed.

I scowled at him. "One of my ancestors made you their bitch, didn't they? You were forced to become our butler. Otherwise, why would you—"

I suddenly felt what it was like to have Gungnir tickle my testicles. And I wouldn't have wished it upon my worst enemy.

I flew.

Quite a ways.

I landed on a pile of rainbow guts, wheezing and coughing.

"And that was just the tip," Odin muttered.

Alex, the ungrateful little bastard, laughed.

I climbed to my feet unsteadily. So, no one had made Odin their bitch. *Message received.*

"I'm afraid that Thor was correct on one count. You do need to fix the Bifröst, or we are all in very big trouble. It must be repaired, or the entire might of the Aesir Gods will rain fire down upon Midgard, assuming Ragnarok has begun. At the very least, Alex would have to die as retribution. But...if the Bifröst is repaired...I will let him avoid that fate."

Alex abruptly stopped laughing, squinting his eyes as he measured up Dean from head-to-toe. "Let?" he began. "Such a funny word—"

"Damn it all," I muttered, interrupting Alex before he could pick another fight with an Aesir God. "I'm a wizard, not a civil engineer! I wouldn't even know where to begin!"

Odin pointed at Grimm. "Send him off to murder rainbows around the world and have him bring their carcasses back to you in Fae."

Grimm adamantly shook his mane. "Unless you plan on taping a shovel to my horn, it's going to take me a while." Upon our blank expressions, he lifted a hoof and his nostrils flared with a fiery glow. "Hooves, motherfuckers. *Hooves.* Not hands. Octodeer knows what I'm talking about." And he flicked his head back towards Sleipnir. "Am I right?"

Sleipnir didn't find the nickname even remotely humorous. In fact, it looked like he believed a justifiable response was to murder Grimm right here, right now.

17

Dean lifted a hand, halting Sleipnir without even looking—a stark reminder that this was *not* the Dean I had grown up with. This was Odin, no matter who he looked like.

Alex piped up. "I could go with Grimm."

Odin nodded his approval. "That would work. Grimm and Alex can gather rainbow carcasses from around the world and stuff them inside Nate's satchel. That way they only have to make one trip. It would be best to gather rainbows from nine different countries. Symbolic of the Nine Realms," he explained, waving a hand.

Then he turned to me. "But *you* cannot afford to waste any more time, Nate. You must go to Fae. *Now*. Before you break entirely. Coincidentally, a trip to Fae will be necessary to repair the Bifröst, because you will need Wylde's help in this endeavor. It's fitting that the three of you must work together to repair the Bifröst. That will help me calm my fellow Aesir down and explain away any...misunderstandings. You three made a mistake, you three fixed your mistake. Odin has returned after a long absence."

I clenched my fists, not liking this one bit. It fit just a little too perfectly to be coincidence, as Dean...

As *Odin* had so casually stated.

Sending Alex off to...

"You say to gather rainbow carcasses as if it is a totally normal request. How, exactly, are they supposed to do that?"

"Grimm can fly around Midgard and hunt rainbows to his heart's content. Shove nine fistfuls of each rainbow's guts into your conveniently bottomless satchel."

"And if I'm balls deep in the bush of Fae wilderness, how are they supposed to bring me the...rainbow guts," I asked, shaking my head at the ridiculousness of the labor we'd earned.

"I can find you anywhere," Grimm said, not taking his eyes from Sleipnir.

Odin nodded. "You will need a vast line of sight to repair the Bifröst, so I suggest you take the rainbow guts to the top of a mountain—the tallest one you can find. Thinner air will also help you wield more power. Less friction. But you will understand all of that better than I can explain it—if you find what you need in Fae."

Realizing I could either be murdered now for not accepting the punishment, or later for failing, there wasn't really much left for me to say. And I was having a hard time even looking at Odin, my mind still in shock to learn that the man who had lived in Chateau Falco my entire life —had served me meals every single day—had been lying to me all this time.

Just like my parents, and so many others.

And the suggestion to celebrate Yulemas suddenly soured in my stomach as I realized it had really been Odin proposing to host a celebra-tion...of Odin. My family had celebrated it for as long as I could remember, and I now felt very conflicted about that.

In this exact moment, I didn't even care to ask if my parents had known about Dean's alter-ego. I just wanted to get as far away from him as possi-ble. To get to Fae and start killing as many things as physically possible.

Because if I didn't get this Fae business clear in my mind—recalling my childhood—I was liable to choke at the worst possible moment and get myself killed. Take Thor, for example. I had various tools in my figurative kit that could have helped me take him down.

My Horseman's Mask—but that was broken.

My Fae magic—which I couldn't access until I learned my past in Fae.

This Catalyst business, perhaps, even had powers tied to it. I knew already that it gave me the ability to sometimes adopt new powers for my use—but the answers to that were also in Fae.

Mordred was also in Fae. And if I didn't stop him, everyone I cared about would die, and I would be sucked down to Hell to work for Anubis.

So as sad, angry, heartbroken, furious, and whatever else I was at the moment to learn of this betrayal, none of it mattered if I didn't sort out this Fae stuff. I frowned, then shot Odin a suspicious look. "Why haven't I broken down over this revelation? Shock usually sends me over the edge..."

Odin dipped his head. "You are now on a quest for me, so until the Bifröst is repaired, I have some small say in keeping you safe. It will last until you enter Fae, at which time you will no longer need my protection."

I frowned at that, wondering what he meant. "Just like that..."

Odin nodded. "Just like that."

There was that loving compassion I knew so well from Dean. "This doesn't give me back my Fae Magic, it just helps with the flashbacks?" I asked, needing to clarify.

He nodded again.

"What am I supposed to do in Fae to actually fix my memories? Do you plan on letting me take a six-month vacation before I attempt to repair the Bifröst? Because if not, you may as well kill me now. I sure as hell don't have any idea how to fix them—just that I need to go spend time in Fae. But I imagine recalling over a dozen years of my forgotten life is not going to be a one-day event."

Dean considered me, and that once-familiar, sharp stare took on a whole new significance for me. How many times had I teased, annoyed, and generally caused problems for my butler—Odin, the Father of all the Aesir Gods? Something most people didn't dare to do, and definitely never more than once. I had...made a habit of poking Dean.

So that same look I was used to getting from him...well, it felt a whole lot different this time, knowing who truly lurked behind the eyes of this unassuming, proper, sophisticated butler.

Odin was known to be a master of magic and sorcery, so I was hoping that he may now be allowed to give me an idea or two on how best to proceed—from one wizard-type to another. Especially since he obviously wanted me to keep on living.

He had chosen me over Thor, after all.

And when he had mentioned someone paying for the crime of destroying the Bifröst, he hadn't mentioned me or Grimm—just Alex. But...my parents had been pretty adamant about Alex being very important to whatever it was they had spent so long setting up.

"You are familiar with Forcing, yes?" Then he shook his head with a faint smile. "It feels rather strange discussing magic with you so openly..."

I let his nostalgia roll off my shoulders, ignoring it. "Trying to draw as much magic as you can when you first learn how to tap into it on a consistent basis, and then maintaining that grip on it for as long as possible. Like holding your breath while going about your day." I met his eyes. "I've also heard it's a great way to burn yourself out." My parents had made me do it with my wizards' magic, only telling me afterwards about the risks.

Dean nodded. "Yes. Close enough. But in Fae, it will be unique. Fae Magic is best understood by experiencing the external—your senses, for lack of a better term."

I frowned. "Thinking too hard on Fae stuff has recently sent me into the fetal position, and that's just when I think about it. You want me to *hold* it?"

"In Fae, you will no longer have that problem. The reason for your affliction lies primarily in the contradiction of your life. You sit here, in Chateau Falco with televisions, mobile phones, tablet computers, radios, and fast food. And you're trying to force yourself to believe you lived in a world with none of that. You know for a fact you were born in this other place, but you have very little personal memory of it, so when you try to recall those memories, your...Earth mind...tells you you're crazy and responds appropriately—shutting you down before you begin to believe your delusion."

I almost fell over at such a concise, simple explanation. "You mean...all I have to do is go over there and live for a little while? And the flashbacks won't bother me?"

Odin scoffed. "Years, most likely. Hence, the Forcing. But yes, the flashbacks will not be a problem in Fae."

"That actually makes perfect sense." I thought about it some more. "And being over there won't cause any problems with my Earth memory, because I already have that in my mind. There is no reason to disbelieve it. I remember it all."

Odin nodded, looking reservedly proud. "In Fae, your senses will pick up on familiarities, helping you cope with the memories. Still, that will take significant time—which you do not have, for multiple reasons I do not need to explain," he said, letting me know he meant the Bifröst, Mordred, and any other number of things I had spoken about to him as either my butler or Odin.

"Now, using a...*significant* amount of Fae Magic can send you into shock. A shock that might even fill in the gaps in your soul with an over-abundance of Fae magic, making your mind more susceptible to accepting parts of your childhood as Wylde. Because over there, your instincts are on the edges of your soul—heightened. And shock is the moment when all your senses are overwhelmed and flooded with impulses from your body. Like striking a flint to kindling."

"In this example, am I the kindling or the flint?" I asked, not liking the sound of his plan.

He ignored my question. "Hypothetically, this could shock you back to *life*, as it were. And look, who just broke the Bifröst and needs to suddenly use a vast level of magic? But you must immerse yourself in your emotions and senses. One shock may not be enough. And you will need help to repair the Bifröst. You are not accustomed to holding such power. Perhaps your parents may have left you items that could assist you. Hypothetically."

I stared back at him, keeping my face blank. Could...that be true? The three artifacts from my parents were intended for this? But the level of foresight to make that possible...

"Forcing will get your body accustomed to the shock you will face when repairing the Bifröst. And between the Forcing and the Shock... perhaps your memories will no longer be a concern when you return."

"Hypothetically."

He nodded. "Of course."

"Did you set this all up?" I asked, thinking of my parents. How else could they have known that I would need these random artifacts? Maybe Odin had used them, not the other way around. "Maybe you set all this up years ago. Told them to get the Hourglass in Fae, where you knew they would conceive and birth me. Then carefully concocted a plan with Anubis, Pan, and whoever the hell else is behind all these lies, to get them to raise me there. Then, you told Thor where I was going to be tonight. That I had his hammer. The hammer you had to have stolen and hidden years ago when you last saw him. Right before you came to work for my parents. Then, here you are, saving the day to tell me what I need right when I'm begging anyone I can for advice."

I didn't voice another thought. Pandora had told me I would need to listen to the Wanderer, and I suddenly remembered why that had tickled my mind. Odin had many names.

And one of those was the Wanderer. It hadn't truly hit me until I saw him standing against Thor with his rippling robes and Gungnir.

Alex let out a long whistle, nodding his agreement. "Makes sense," he said calmly, not flinching under Dean's glare—which was a first, for him. He flinched from Dean, but not after learning Dean was really Odin? What kind of sociopath was Alex? Had he been a victim of this mad plan as well? Hell, maybe Odin had kidnapped and delivered him to Fae in the first place. Knowing I would rescue him, eventually.

Dean's lips grimaced with mild anger, and I recalled him talking about sensing trouble in the air tonight. Then saying the same thing when he arrived—about how he wished he had known the events that were to transpire. As if he might have locked me up in the house to prevent them from happening, to keep his identity a secret.

"I did not know," he finally said. "But...for the sake of argument, let's pretend that I *did* set all of this up. What could you really do about it? Seems like if I am the mastermind behind this crazy scheme, I just gave you the solution to your fairy drama. So...unless you like curling up into a fetal position whenever you have a flashback, does it really matter? At the least, you would need to keep playing my game in order to find a way to overcome your handicap and turn it all against me later, correct?" he said as if reading a scientific journal on the mating habits of dung beetles.

I grimaced. He was, unfortunately, spot on.

Odin studied me thoughtfully. "The only explanation I have is that you are beginning to learn things that were hidden from you—for very good reason—for decades. This awareness and knowledge—and the fact that you keep whining about it to everyone who will listen to how unfair your life is—has perhaps caught the attention of the very ones your parents intended to keep you safe from—for you to one day fight. And now they are retaliating, to find the reason why you are so special—how and why they involved so many entities and pantheons in keeping secrets from you —and from each other." He sighed, shaking his head. "Things have already changed from what I had anticipated—from what your parents told me to expect. You have painted a very large target on your head, and I think you have done it sooner than your parents hoped. You better...level up, boy. I no longer know what to expect, and even godlings can die."

Alex narrowed his eyes at Dean, not appreciating his tone. I was still trying to process the casual admission that my parents had essentially recruited Odin—and lied to him as well.

Dean snapped his fingers, and a portal made of water appeared behind him, opaque so I couldn't see where it led. "Now, I must go to Asgard to calm them down about the Bifröst and explain my absence." My eyes widened in alarm, and he smiled. "I will have to get creative. I am quite talented at weaving fictions, if you haven't noticed thus far," he said drily. "If Odin can pass as a butler to the most demanding little shit to ever walk the earth—somehow managing not to drown Master Temple to death in his bathwater when he couldn't follow simple, basic rules..." he grumbled, locking his eyes with mine. "If I—Odin—can maintain humility enough to not only act as butler, but to excel at it for decades without ever being discovered, by *anyone*...I'm sure I can come up with a convincing tale for my fellow Aesir."

"I've had enough Aesir meddling with my life."

He stared at me blankly for a moment, and I felt he was trying to impart something, but the look vanished before I could decipher it.

"Destroying the Bifröst truly is a Ragnarok-level event. I wouldn't waste time smelling the flowers in Fae. Forcing seems your best course of action. If not for the Bifröst, I imagine your foe, Mordred, requires expediency as well. And, take long enough and you might hear my favorite song."

"Oh?" I asked.

"The Aesir are coming, the Aesir are coming..." And his tone made it sound like a funeral dirge, or a war chant.

18

Alex cleared his throat, his hands clasped behind his back. "We should expect this fight to hit the news," he said, gesturing at the destroyed dumpster, broken windows, two unconscious goats, chariot, and the piles of rainbow guts lying here and there.

"Dean will take care of the goats and chariot. Other than that, we should be fine," I said.

Dean made a sweeping gesture with his hand, and the chariot and goats whipped past him into the portal of water. Sleipnir gave us one last glare for good measure before walking through the portal ahead of his Master. Then Dean nodded his head at me and stepped backwards into the portal. It closed behind him, and the dome above us dissipated into fog. Grimm let out a sigh of relief the moment Sleipnir was gone.

Helicopters hovered all around the parking lot, spotlights sweeping the area and buildings for any evidence of the cause of the explosion earlier—some smoking gun to point at.

Like us.

Alex suddenly gripped my arm. "What about that?" he asked, pointing at the ground near the pile of rainbow shards that had trapped Thor. A ten-foot tall message was scorched into the asphalt—actually carved into it in one-inch deep gouges. *"Nate Temple was here."* Thor's dagger—now broken—lay beside it, purpose served.

Or a smoking gun like that, damnit.

I growled, but a helicopter was suddenly angling right for us, and rather than let him get a sight of two dudes and a unicorn at a crime scene, I decided it was better to simply leave the message in the asphalt and get as far away as possible from the scene.

Alex cursed, walking backwards to keep an eye on the helicopter and stay out of the spotlight. "What about Gunnar and Achilles? Those people recognized you at the bar, and now this message. We can't risk Gunnar and Achilles saying something—"

Grimm neighed aggressively at the helicopters. "How do you think I found you? Achilles used his Tiny Balls to drag Gunnar—who was unconscious for some reason—back to Chateau Falco. Dean looked at me and sent me to—"

Grimm jolted as if only just now considering what he had said. Alex had an equally surprised look on his face. Dean—Odin—had sent Grimm here to help me? But...why had he chosen to make his own appearance, then? Because of the Bifröst breaking? He realized he had chosen the wrong horse for the job?

Without Grimm breaking the Bifröst, I might not have learned the truth about Dean being Odin. Then again, Odin had seemed genuinely frustrated to come clean about it all—not just to me, but the world—to his own son.

What would he have to gain by orchestrating headaches for himself?

Maybe he was being played, too. Because someone—possibly this alleged mysterious group of people my parents wanted me to fight—had sent Thor here tonight.

And there was always the chance that they would send Thor after us again, no matter how far away Odin had sent him. Or the rest of the Aesir.

Either way, we had a new deadline. Literally. I glanced down to see I was squeezing the War Hammer in my fist. I didn't remember even grabbing it from my satchel. But I didn't feel like letting it go either. Probably when I was thinking about Thor.

"We'll worry about that later." I threw down my Tiny Balls and jumped through the Gateway back to Chateau Falco. Grimm and Alex followed after me, and the Gateway winked out right as a spotlight locked onto the crude message carved into the asphalt. I heard police sirens converging on the site.

I turned to the two of them. "My timetable just jumped up a few hours, so hopefully Gunnar isn't still down for the count or I'm leaving him behind." I turned to Grimm. "I need you to cut loose, Grimm. Kill as many fucking rainbows as you can find, as fast as you can. This is your moment to become famous. Because I need you two in Fae as soon as possible since we don't know how bad the time-slippage will be between Earth and Fae. An hour here could be a week there. Or vice versa." I let that settle in.

Grimm licked his lips. "No problem, Hope. No fucking problem. Hop on, pooper-scooper. We've got some rainbow shit to bag up."

Alex grinned as he hopped up onto Grimm's back like he had done it for years. Then again, he had been friends with Pegasus for some time, now, and had gotten used to riding horses. He looked resolved to the task at hand, holding out a hand for my satchel.

I handed it over immediately and was already walking backwards towards Falco as my mind raced with conspiracy theories—who to trust, and who not to trust. "Hurry," I urged them, squeezing the War Hammer in my fist, "and keep an eye out for Thor or any other Aesir!"

"The shitty part about this plan," Grimm offered, "is that rainbows typically appear *after* thunderstorms. So, the timing could suck less if Thor does escape wherever Odin sent him."

He had a point. Pep-talk time.

"This is serious, guys. No fucking around. We already have enough to worry about. Just murder some godsdamned rainbows, collect their beautiful guts, and shove them in my magic sack. You know how to find me when it's full."

They both nodded, but Grimm locked eyes with me. "We'll be moving fast and won't remain long enough in one place to hear your call. We'll likely ride the Night Currents to avoid any potential meetings with lightning boy or his fellow Aesir."

I nodded, having no freaking idea what the Night Currents were, and having no time to really freaking care at the moment. I'd learned that ignorance suited me perfectly fine at times. I knew Grimm wouldn't risk taking

Alex anywhere that would inherently melt his face from his skull, and that was good enough for me.

I turned, sprinting towards my front door, thinking of anything else I might need to ask Dean to pack up for my trip—

My stomach suddenly roiled with acid. No. Dean wasn't here. And he wasn't my butler.

I could grab my own last-minute items. I'd already packed everything I needed. The essentials for survival, the Hand of God, the Hourglass my parents had stolen from the Fae, and the War Hammer currently gripped in my fist. A thunderous boom echoed through the night sky right as I reached out my free hand to tuck my satchel behind my back as I ran so that it didn't slap me on the ass—

I skidded to a halt, swatting my ass in confusion. No satchel. None of my parents' artifacts except for the War Hammer in my fist.

I sucked in a deep, calming breath, and shouted, "Motherfucker!" at the top of my lungs. The sound of Grimm's thunderous departure echoed through the skies in perfect harmony with my shout. I panted a few times, muttering under my breath and squeezing the hilt of the War Hammer as hard as I could. "What the hell are the Night Currents?"

19

I was as tight-lipped as possible as we wrapped up last minute preparations to leave for Fae, basically delegating any last-minute requests and reminders to Talon.

I was rummaging around in the pantry, stuffing items into my shirt—which I had fashioned into an impromptu bowl—when Ashley spoke directly behind me, making me jump.

"What are you doing in here?" She took one look at my stash and grinned conspiratorially. "You going to Heavyweights camp?" she teased, pointing at my items.

I scowled at her. "Just because you're pregnant, don't think I won't cut you over a bag of marshmallows," I warned, covering my stash by turning slightly away.

She rolled her eyes. "Good luck with that. I wanted to talk to you about Gunnar..."

I sighed, leaning back against the shelves of the pantry, motioning for her to go on.

"Keep him safe over there, Nate, and go easy on him. No teasing, unless he seems playful. But let him kill as much as he wants if he's angry. He needs the distraction, and murder always improves his mood when he gets like this. Although I've never seen him get quite *this*...this," she admitted, obviously having no idea what word to use to describe whatever was going on with Gunnar after his recent gender reveal surprise—both pink and blue!

Also, her suggestion was a little, oh, I don't know, insane? It made me nervous to even bring him along, as a matter of fact.

My eyes had widened a bit, but she rolled right over my silent surprise.

"Our children will know their father. *And* their godfather. If you let anything happen to you guys, I'll kill you. Oh, and don't forget to have fun."

"You cornered me in the pantry to threaten me?" I demanded, but she was already walking away. I was entirely sure that she was entirely unaware of the contradicting advice she had just given me, but I didn't have time to argue.

My first stop was the Sanctorum before anyone else got there. After my chat with Pandora—and now fearing that Dean might not necessarily be on Team Temple—I needed to protect the ichor in the Round Table. Just in case it was one of the pieces of Excalibur she had mentioned. Even if it wasn't, it was dangerously powerful—somehow helping fortify my Horseman's Mask—and I couldn't risk it falling into the wrong hands.

I couldn't leave it here, especially since I didn't know how long I would be gone. I reached the Sanctorum and walked each of the upper levels, checking for Huginn and Muninn. I sensed nothing, so pulled the War Hammer out of my old Fendi satchel—my replacement after stupidly giving Alex my Darling and Dear satchel before taking out the artifacts—and studied it, making my way towards the Round Table on the main level. At least I hadn't left the hammer behind, too.

I'd seen it absorb and amplify powers of several different flavors before, including Fae, Maker, wizard, some neat revenge action on an old dragon friend of mine, and even the ichor that had momentarily flowed in my own veins after I killed Athena. Now that I was certain that it wasn't Thor's hammer, I was betting it was actually some kind of container, like the other artifacts my parents had left me.

The Hand of God had also been a container—for a Maker's power. And the Hourglass was quite literally a container of flowing sand, able to control the time-slippage between Fae and Earth—if one wanted to risk a Fae army hunting them down the moment they activated it.

Where the other two artifacts seemed to have a singular purpose, the

War Hammer seemed to be a jack of all trades, basically waiting to gobble up anything you let it gobble up. It made sense for the War Hammer to also be a container. It would be the perfect vehicle to transport Merlin's ichor to safety—and no one would suspect it. Just in case I was wrong, I also pulled out a six-inch glass vial with a rubber stopper. I didn't want to put all my eggs in one basket, so would put some in the vial just in case. The vial would serve as a decoy if anyone caught us. They'd see the vial and think that was it, the vial of liquid gold was obviously Merlin's ichor.

And they wouldn't look too closely at the War Hammer.

As I approached the Round Table, I studied the shifting stream of liquid metal that circled the center of the table. What looked like Druidic Runes and alchemical symbols floated within the golden stream like a mystical alphabet soup.

I hesitated at the lip of the Table, remembering my talk with Odin in this exact spot one week ago, before I had fought Mordred. He had given me answers, in a cryptic way, leading me down a path that concluded with me realizing that the golden metal in the Table was Merlin's blood—that Merlin had found a way to turn his own blood into ichor—for whatever reason. Odin...had helped me. A week ago. Probably in the only way he had been able to.

Then there was Dean, also a week ago. I had returned home after my fight with Mordred to find him standing in the halls, and rather than giving me a sympathetic shoulder to lean on, he had punished me for breaking one of his sacred rules. No nudity in the main living areas of Chateau Falco. Or you get the million BB's of shame across your flesh.

Had that been Dean or Odin's personality in charge?

When Alex had broken the exact same rule minutes before me, Dean had given Alex a robe and hot cocoa rather than punishing him. Was there some hidden message in that, or was I simply overthinking it?

But that was the crux of the situation. I no longer knew what or who I could rely upon.

Both Dean and Odin had helped—and harmed—me in entirely different—and even contradictory—ways. Several times even on the *same* day. But they were the same person.

I let out a breath, telling myself I would have time to consider all these inconsistencies as I travelled in Fae. Maybe Talon and Gunnar could talk some sense into me. At least I no longer had to worry about freaking the hell out for no apparent reason. That was an unbelievable weight off my shoulders.

As I thought about the upcoming trip, I thought very hard on the Wild God, Pan. Because he, too, had lied to me about who he was. He had masqueraded as Mallory, a chauffeur and security guard for my father. Odin obviously knew about Pan—everyone did, now. But...did Pan know about Dean being Odin? My parents had recruited both of them in their bizarre spider's web of lies, and I wasn't sure if that meant they had been kept secret from each other or not.

Because Pan claimed to be done with secrets from me, implying he didn't know about Dean.

We were going to see him in Fae, so I was about to find out. He was watching over—and nursing back to health—the only Knight of the Round Table we had so far found. I had yet to see him because he'd been unconscious ever since, but I was about to wake the bastard up somehow. I hoped this Knight could shed some light on exactly what Merlin had done to his blood.

I felt a slight chill of excitement. I was going to meet a real Knight. A man so entrenched in his ideals that he radiated chivalry through every segment of his armor. I couldn't wait. I absently began murmuring names of the Knights, wondering which one Pan was looking after.

I cut off abruptly as symbols near the edge of the Round Table began to shimmer into existence at the sound of me murmuring the Knights' names. They were strange, crude symbols, and they glowed with blue light. They faded from view after a few seconds, so I went back through the list, trying to memorize the symbols to match to each name, wondering what it meant or if it would provide some answer to finding the other Knights later.

One section of the Table remained devoid of symbols the entire time. I took a deep, hopeful breath, and murmured, "Arthur Pendragon."

The empty space on the table flared to life with the same blue fire in a similarly strange rune. I studied it thoughtfully, making sure I had it down and shook my head as I stared at the Table in its entirety. That had never happened before, and I was sure I'd mentioned some of those names—at least in passing—while in proximity to the Table. Why react now?

I imagined what it would have been like to sit here with all of them, being all chivalrous and stuff: polishing their armor, bragging about damsels, and having arm-wrestling contests.

I grinned at a new thought. "Merlin," I murmured, knowing I had certainly said that name near the Table, and not even a week ago. I wondered if it was because I was entirely alone this time when I usually had someone else here with me. Maybe it had something to do with Odin getting rid of my Fae block, or something else had changed about me. Becoming a Horseman?

Or...maybe it was because I had adopted some of Merlin's blood into my Horseman's Mask, and the Table now saw me as part of the old crew.

But nothing happened when I said Merlin's name. I said it again, two more times to be sure.

At the third repetition, something happened alright. The circle of flowing metal in the center of the table suddenly pulsed and churned violently, glowing brighter and brighter until I feared it was going to splash all over the Table. Not knowing what else to do, and not wanting to risk spilling any of it...

I shoved the corner of the War Hammer into the liquid., and...

20

I was suddenly forced to hold on for dear life as the War Hammer began to quiver violently, seeming to want to come apart at the seams as it gobbled up the ichor. I gripped the hilt with two hands, trying to hold the Hammer steady as it devoured the ichor and finally stilled.

I let it go, panting hoarsely. I clenched and unclenched my fingers repeatedly, trying to get some feeling back into them. The War Hammer rested halfway inside the empty chasm where the ichor had flowed, and it throbbed steadily with golden light. The stone itself wasn't gold or anything, but it was almost like a dimmer switch turning off and on— glowing gold from within, and then dimming back down to the plain stone. *Birthright* was carved into the side, seeming to shine brighter than the rest, since it was carved into the surface, closer to the ichor now trapped within.

The strangest part was that I felt my coin necklace—my damaged Horseman's Mask—now throbbing in time with the Hammer, also glowing. The Hammer really *had* been a container, exactly like the Hand of God. I'd wondered if the Hammer would stop absorbing the ichor after a dainty sip, but it seemed to have a very healthy appetite. And it had only stopped because it ran out of ichor to drink. I wondered exactly how much it could hold...

And grew a little bit nervous at the thought.

I'd heard the three artifacts my parents left me described as Keys by Anubis, and was now even more curious what they might open. Why Anubis had wanted them in the first place.

I reached out and lifted the Hammer, surprised to feel that it now felt lighter than before, even though it had just consumed what had to be *pounds* of liquid metal. I leaned over the Table and noticed a thin sliver of liquid gold still inside the crevice, so I scraped it into the vial, popped on the rubber stopper, and shoved it in my old Fendi satchel—nowhere near as cool or light as my Darling and Dear satchel, but that's what I got for being a big, stupid idiot. I shoved the War Hammer into the thick metal ring I had attached to a sturdy leather belt designed for just such use and felt satisfied that it wasn't going to fall out. It might make running a little awkward, but I could live with that. I also had a Velcro strap I could wrap over it to make it more secure but judging by how it felt right now, I didn't see that becoming necessary. I placed my hands on my hips, feeling like a total badass.

Like the Knights who had once set out for the Holy Grail, I was now setting out to find the pieces of Excalibur. If Pandora's silence meant what I thought—which was in no way a guarantee—I now had the Blood. One of the parts was within the Armory—likely the beautiful sword I had seen long ago—the Blade, as she had called it. And she had said the other pieces were finding their way to the Armory, *as they usually did*. If I was on the right track, I still needed the Name, the Power, and the Soul.

Once I found those...well, I guessed I would hide it. I sure as hell wasn't going to FedEx it to Camelot for Mordred's Yulemas present. My only real goal was to keep it out of Mordred's hands, because he wanted to destroy it —or use it for himself.

I turned at the sound of footsteps to see Gunnar and Talon stroll in with Achilles on their heels. The Greek hero had returned to Chateau Falco after the bar fight, probably very interested in the protection the house had to offer one who may have been recognized by Thor at a rowdy brawl last night.

Talon and Gunnar dipped their heads at me and made their way over to the fountain, ready to leave. Gunnar was walking stiffly, making me assume he probably felt embarrassed about his lack of assistance during the fight with Thor. He was touchy about personal failures. And Talon was quiet because I had tasked him with keeping a close eye on Gunnar, since he was acting like a nut-job ever since finding out he was going to be a dad.

They were both quiet for another shared reason. I had very briefly told Talon about the night's events, and he had made Gunnar promise not to change our plan of going to Fae before passing on that information—because I had been confident Gunnar would instantly freak out and want to get Ashley out of danger, or spend a week fortifying his pack, or any other number of totally logical decisions, rather than leaving for Fae as planned. We couldn't—I couldn't—afford any speed bumps in my trip. The Allfather had made that very clear.

If we didn't hurry, Thor, or the rest of the Aesir Gods, would pay us a visit and, if history was accurate, I'd heard of very few locals who ended up appreciating a visit from Norsemen.

So, Gunnar and Talon were both up to speed, and were equally unhappy and nervous about it all. They were also brimming with questions for me, but I hadn't given them the time to corner me. We would have plenty of time to discuss that in Fae if necessary. And sitting around playing *what if* wasn't going to help me fix my Fae Magic. The only way to put a stop to this was to stick to the original plan of fixing my memories so I could repair the Bifröst.

But...I needed someone here at Falco to know about the potential shit-storm heading our way. My eyes latched onto Achilles, and I pursed my lips. He was a tough, hardened, capable warrior. He would be able to handle it. He was friends with several gods and didn't scare easily.

Achilles was also the only other one who had seen Thor in person, and probably wasn't too keen on leaving the protection of Chateau Falco.

I pulled him aside and caught him up to speed on events from the parking lot and, after hesitating for a moment, I told him the truth about Dean actually being Odin. Achilles, the legendary Greek hero, almost crapped his pants. He stiffened like a board, and almost fell over before I gripped his forearm. "Play it cool, man!" I hissed low enough for only him to hear, because Alice and Alvara had just sauntered into the room with Tory and Ashley.

"Are you fucking kidding me?" he whispered. "How the hell did you just happen to find Dean in the parking lot near the strip clubs of East St. Louis?"

Tory was speaking softly with Alvara and Alice, but Ashley had made a beeline for Gunnar, kissing him on the lips and hugging him close. I turned back to Achilles. "Well, Grimm kind of broke the Bifröst—"

"He did the fuck *what*?!" Achilles choked, his voice growing high pitched.

"Keep it down!" I whispered angrily. "This isn't a High School Musical tryout! Thor was upset about Grimm breaking his rainbow, and then Odin...Dean appeared. He stood up for us against Thor, banishing him somewhere cold and dark. I have no idea where, but Thor probably isn't going to be too happy about it when he gets out."

"I don't even know which part to start screaming about!" he hissed. "Let me come with you to Fae for crying out loud. I'd rather end up in an ogre's cookpot than let Thor find me!"

"No. I need you here, keeping an eye on the gang, on Huginn and Muninn, and if Dean shows up, keep an eye on him, too."

"No way! I'm not going to spy on Odin, you fucking lunatic!"

"He might be on our side."

"He might *not* be on your side!"

Gunnar cleared his throat behind us. "You ready, Nate? I was woken up early believing it meant we needed to *leave* early..." he said in a low growl. He had worn sweats and a plain tee, knowing that he would likely shift into his gargantuan werewolf form once we crossed over—but he didn't necessarily have to change if he didn't want to. After you came to grips with your Wild Side, you could kind of turn it off and on at will. I'd told everyone else to dress Fae-Casual—something you could easily run in and didn't mind getting blood on. And to bring backup clothes just in case.

I knew it wasn't the lack of sleep annoying Gunnar, but the fact that he had lost his marbles at the bar, and then been useless to keep us safe from Thor after. Or some of his crazy other baggage.

I nodded. "Just giving Achilles a quick update. We're almost finished." Gunnar grunted and made his way back over to the waterfall, waiting silently. Talon was studying me out of the corner of his eyes, his tail swishing back and forth behind him.

"No, we are *not* almost finished," Achilles squealed in a whispered hiss.

"You've got this, Achilles. Just put two pairs of socks on, and you're invincible," I teased, kicking his heel with the toe of my boot.

He glared at me. "Not against Odin, you half-wit!"

I waved a hand and told him about Alex and Grimm hunting rainbows to restore the Bifröst, but that they were traveling the Night Currents.

Achilles promptly passed out, crumpling to the floor in a sad heap. I stared down at him, blinking a few times. Well, that had been entirely unexpected. Maybe he hadn't been as equipped to handle the news as I'd thought. Tory glanced over and froze upon seeing Achilles unconscious, or that I was nudging him with my boot and whispering his name not-so-discreetly.

Tory rushed over, scooping up Achilles like he was a toddler who had fallen asleep in the car on the way home, and then she carried him over to a couch near the fire in the center of the massive space. I watched her warily, thinking, and finally made a decision. Rather than risk the same result as Achilles, I leaned in close to give her a hug goodbye.

"Don't react," I whispered into her ear. "When he wakes up, tell him that you know about Dean, the Bifröst, and that I give him permission to tell you and Ashley everything. He passed out before we got to that part. But no one else can know, okay?"

She squeezed back in acknowledgment, but it felt stiff and awkward as she no doubt reeled from my cryptic goodbye. She pulled back and gave me a fake smile, but her eyes were full of questions.

"Thanks, Tory. Keep everyone safe while I'm gone. I hope it won't be long, but you never know in Fae."

She nodded woodenly, her eyes drifting to Achilles with a pensive frown. She looked a hell of a lot more motivated to wake her patient than a few moments ago. I made my way over to the waterfall to find Ashley happy crying, and Gunnar holding a beefy palm over her belly. Alvara looked on the verge of her own tears, and Alice looked as excited as ever.

I stared at Ashley's belly and made a silent promise. *I'll keep your dad safe, guys. Or I'll break the world getting him back to you. I may not be much of a father figure, but I've got the wrath of a god burning inside me, and that will keep you plenty safe, no matter what.*

I looked up to find Ashley and Gunnar both staring at me curiously. I blushed. "Thought I saw a stain on her shirt," I said hurriedly. They narrowed their eyes in unison, but it looked more heartfelt and amused than anything.

"Can we go, now?" Alice begged, hopping up and down on her feet, her blonde, braided ponytail rising up and down along with her. She gripped the straps of her small backpack eagerly, Ready for her adventure in a wondrously terrifying new land.

I nodded and stepped up to the waterfall, holding out my hands to form a chain with them. "Go, go, gadget-Fae."

21

W e stepped into Fae about thirty minutes away from the cave I had been born and raised in. I hadn't wanted to go directly there so as not to terrify Pan with my small army. Also, I wanted to get a feel for the place, get everyone acclimated to the strange nature of Fae—especially since I had no idea what it would do to Alvara and Alice.

I hesitantly turned to the two, fearing what I might find and...

They hadn't changed.

I let out a breath of relief. I had been concerned they might become trolls or some other strange creature that would give Pan pause when we finally ran into him. Alvara had tears in her eyes as she spun in a slow circle, staring up at the sky in awe. I knew what it was like to return home after a long journey, but I had never come back home after being *banished*. Maybe it was like stepping out of prison after serving what had originally been a life sentence, only to be released a decade later when the true criminal was found, and they let you go with a bureaucratic *whoopsies*.

Alice let out a squeal of excitement, running her tiny fingers through the tall glass grass, grinning as it chimed back at her. I couldn't help smiling as I watched her—admiring that look of wonder on her cheeks and wondering myself if I would ever get back that childhood sense of joy for the world. Because I'd learned the hard way that life wasn't always that carefree and joyful.

I sensed Alvara watching me watch her daughter, and I smiled back at her. She mouthed *thank you*, and I shrugged it off humbly, waving a hand.

Gunnar and Talon both took deep, calming breaths, smiles slowly creeping across their faces.

Gunnar hadn't changed into his Wild Side—something that often happened to those who came to Fae who did not naturally belong. Fae brought out your inner...primitive side, was perhaps an accurate way to describe it. Or it brought out an inner part of you that typically lay just beneath the surface. An amplification of your powers given form. If things got hairy, Gunnar would get hairy, so I wasn't concerned.

Talon, of course, was always in his Wild Side, the bipedal feline warrior with long whiskers and shaggy fur, even sporting a beard of sorts. He wore velvet slippers that made no sound as he moved. His spear wasn't currently in his hand, but he could call it at will when necessary.

Alice had her hands on her hips, glaring up at Gunnar.

"Stop being shy, Princess Padfoot. You can't hide from me. I *see* you already."

Gunnar arched a brow incredulously before turning to Alvara with a questioning look. Alvara was studying her daughter thoughtfully, looking surprised.

"You see him, Alice?"

"Yes, and I want to ride the big bad wolf's shoulders," she huffed. "His fur looks fluffy, and I'll be able to see farther from up high."

"I...don't frighten you?" Gunnar asked in a very soft tone.

She shook her head. "You're beautiful," she said, grinning.

Gunnar looked totally out of place, and I realized what was going on. He'd purposely held himself back for fear of frightening the child. I wondered if this was some manifestation of his concern about being a father—that he believed he was a terrifying monster and didn't know if a child could love him or if they would run away screaming.

Talon smirked, shoving Gunnar lightly. "I would do as the Lady demands. And if she can already see you, there's no use holding it down."

Gunnar let out a shuddering breath, and I realized his shoulders had been rigid with tension as he struggled to hold himself in control. Between one moment and the next, he shook, and a seven-foot tall mountain of muscle and thick, wiry, matted white fur exploded before us, practically trebling his size. Bones were woven into his hair in places like a light armor, and his long fangs extended out from his closed jaws. His claws extended longer than usual and were made of the same stone as his eye-patch—which featured a wolf-head engraved in the center—and a tarnished bronze crown adorned his head, held in place by his braided fur.

Alice beamed. "There. That's better, isn't it? You look much calmer. Now, kneel."

Gunnar did so, staring at the child in disbelief to see her so unaffected by his appearance—as if it simply made no sense to him.

This trip was going to be very interesting indeed. Maybe it would even have a healing effect, of sorts, judging by how Gunnar was looking upon Alice right now—like he had just met blonde, lady Jesus.

Gunnar held out a massive paw, his long claws large and sharp enough to slice the small child in half. Alice stepped up into his palm, giggling as he lifted her atop his shoulders. She scrambled around his neck like a spider monkey and clapped delightedly. Gunnar stared straight at me, looking like he'd been bumped on the head and was terrified to step wrong for fear of hurting her—like he was walking on eggshells.

Alice let out a long sigh, and then wrapped both of her tiny arms around Gunnar's massive neck and squeezed him into a tight hug, closing her eyes as she nuzzled her face into his thick fur. "You will be the best dad ever," she whispered with a cracked voice—the first sign of a lack of composure I had seen from her.

And I abruptly remembered that Alice had lost her father. Stab. Twist.

Gunnar let out a low, hesitant growl, blinking rapidly Then, as slow as a shifting glacier, he lifted one paw to reach up and compassionately rub her tiny, toothpick legs. She squeezed him tighter into a hug and I watched as that tiny force of nature squeezed a fat tear out of Wulfric's single eye. He caught me looking and didn't bother hiding the slow smile that creeped over his muzzle, revealing his array of fangs.

Even though the smile looked terrifying, I gave him a thumbs up and a grin.

Alvara had turned her back on the pair, and I saw that her shoulders were shaking. The dad comment had hit her hard as well.

I took a deep breath of my own, wondering what Alice had seen when she looked at me—if she had some kind of gift for seeing the monster beneath the man. She hadn't said anything, and I hadn't yet felt Wylde poke his head out. But...I did feel something beneath the surface. The stirrings of someone on the verge of waking. Like smelling bacon when you're asleep in bed. You're still dreaming, but something is tugging at you to open up them peepers.

Forcing, Odin had said. I needed to Force my Fae magic to the surface. But I had to wait for the lazy bastard to get out of bed, first, I guessed.

"Let's get moving," I said. "Talon, why don't you and Alvara scout ahead of us in stealth. I'm not in the mood for surprises, and there's always the chance this area is now being watched by Oberon or some other suicidal idiot with a crown. And Alvara would probably get a laugh out of hearing about my new friend from last night," I added meaningfully. Because she needed to be informed of the danger now, before any of the Reading Rainbow thugs—the Aesir—showed up.

Talon and Alvara slipped away in silence, moving through the waist-high glass stalks without a sound. Impressive. Maybe it was a Fae thing. It definitely hadn't rubbed off on me, unfortunately. Despite being raised here.

Gunnar and I sounded like we were swinging hammers in a china shop as we began walking through the glass grass. It was also why I wanted Gunnar to lead—to make a freaking path for me. I studied the scene as we moved, marveling at the colors of the trees, the smells in the air, the whisper of magic on the horizon. I couldn't quite grasp ahold of it as I had before, but I could sense it floating all around me like colored fog. I think.

Unfortunately, like tantalizing tendrils of brewing coffee in the air, I couldn't grasp them. I briefly imagined Pepé Le Pew chasing his lover's perfume through the air and sighed. Not yet.

I'd once woven moonbeams and starlight, brought vegetation to life, caught and manipulated shadows, and other sorts of bizarre things.

And that—right there, I realized—was the problem. I subconsciously thought of those things as bizarre and impossible, which wasn't helping with my block.

I needed to remove all preconceptions and become open-minded. Leave the baggage at the door, so to speak.

I took a deep breath and, as well as I could, I did just that.

It was strange because as a wizard, I was used to doing all sorts of things people thought impossible. And here I was, having to start all over again. Having to abandon what I thought I knew and believe in the unseen. The word *can't* didn't exist. I needed to experiment, feel, learn, without any preconceived notions.

I tried focusing on my senses like Odin had suggested, hoping that it would give me an opportunity to grip the magic and hold on for dear life. The scents were dizzying, and entirely different from the human realm. Here, a fruit could smell like sizzling meat, and a rock might smell like a fresh pastry. The grass beneath my boots was obviously not typical of Earth, being made of glass, and let off a pleasant chiming sound when crunched underfoot. And, as I focused on my senses, I realized I couldn't sense any life nearby—not even mundane creatures going about their day to munch on some seeds or leaves. No birds flying by, no pixies zipping to and fro.

It didn't feel dead or abandoned, it was just uncommonly uninhabited —or they were all hiding from our party, which wasn't out of the realm of possibility.

As a wizard in the human realm, holding your magic in on a constant basis—which wasn't advisable—would let your senses explode with feedback. The smells, tastes, colors, tactile sensation was significantly heightened, akin to taking ecstasy. Allegedly.

But compared to Fae?

It was a weak gateway drug.

My parents had quite often made me hold my magic to the maximum, not letting me do anything with it, but simply telling me to hold it as long as possible.

They had...Forced me.

I hadn't really thought about it until Odin brought it up, because I had only been a child just coming into my powers, so it had been a fun game. And I hadn't known how to really do anything with my magic, so it hadn't seemed dangerous. But...maybe they had been conditioning me. Testing me.

Preparing me.

For this. When Forcing my *Fae magic* could literally be the difference between life and death. My only chance at repairing the Bifröst before the Aesir rained death down upon Midgard.

As we made our way onward, I pondered the loss of my Darling and Dear satchel, hoping Alex wouldn't lose it and that he would finish his rainbow hunt soon, so I could get it back. I'd been so wrapped up in the Odin thing I hadn't considered the items I had stowed away inside the satchel when I handed it over to him. And remembering that Odin had said I might need them to help with either my recovery or the Bifröst...

What if I needed them suddenly and he still hadn't returned, lost on these mysterious Night Currents forever? Achilles hadn't seemed like he would ever volunteer to ride them, and he was a brave son-of-a-bitch. What if not having the Keys got one of us killed?

I also didn't know what to make of running into the entirely strange Darling and Dear in the bar. Anubis had looked shell-shocked, assuming they were locked down in Kansas City—whatever that meant—and hadn't been pleased to see them coincidentally hanging out in the same city, in the same bar, and on the same night as us. The only significant thing they had said was that if I wanted a White Rose, I needed to go find it—but their riddle was lost on me. Even now. They sure liked to try new things, though...

I sighed, readjusting the War Hammer on my hip. It was no longer pulsing with light, but I could feel a pleasant thrumming sound when I gripped the haft. Almost a purr. Because it was fat and happy with all that ichor. Thinking on my parents' Keys, I wondered just how much power my parents thought I would one day need. Because giving me three magical containers seemed like overkill.

Unless my future opponent was unlike anything I had ever imagined. If Odin hadn't been lying about that as well.

I thought about how an already difficult—nigh impossible—task of retrieving my memory, or legend as Alvara had called it, had spiraled even further down the sewage system of my life. Now I had to repair the Bifröst.

Hopefully, Alvara's friend could shed some light on that.

But first, I wanted to meet the Knight of the Round Table who Pan had tucked away inside my cave, nursing him back to health. I hoped he would have some answers regarding what to do about Mordred or finding a piece of Excalibur. Or both. Even though Pandora had made it sound like the pieces were all on the way to the Armory, I hadn't liked the way that sounded. I wasn't trusting of delivery guys, in general.

Tuck a hat on your head with a logo, and they were supposed to be instantly trustworthy.

But what about the man or woman beneath the hat? What if they were cruel or wanted to steal the pieces of Excalibur for themselves. Hats didn't change a person. I flinched at a new thought. Could...a *Mask* change a person?

I shuddered, suddenly realizing my Masks were inside my Darling and Dear satchel that was currently joyriding across these Night Currents. My mother-freaking Horsemen Masks that I was supposed to give out. I had been so engrossed in everything else that I'd forgotten about them. What if something happened to them and the Masks were lost forever? Would that mean the Biblical Horsemen would die? Or would the Masks find their own way out of my satchel, find their own Riders—ones less squeamish about the silly concept of *right* and *wrong*.

I already had a list of potentials I wanted to speak with about becoming a fellow Horseman, but...I was hesitant. Was I asking them to accept a curse? Would it make things awkward where they would feel obligated to say yes but actually resent me? I needed those who *wanted* to become Horsemen—whatever being part of my new merry band of Horsemen really meant.

Were we opposed to the Biblical Riders?

As I considered that, a funny thought hit me. Maybe that answer was mine to give since I was leading them. I had named them, after all. It would make sense that I decided our purpose.

Still, I hoped Matthias learned something useful from them in Bali, because we quite literally had nowhere else to look as far as I knew.

It was a surprise to realize we were now climbing the hill towards my old cave—the place of my birth—but Alice's sudden giggle snapped me out of my thoughts as she leapt off Gunnar's shoulders to roll through the purple fields leading up to the cave. Talon and Alvara were waiting up ahead a safe distance from the entrance, waving at us. I was surprised to see Mallory, not the goat-legged Wild God. He had donned his human form in favor of looking like Pan, which must mean he recognized us. Indeed, he was staring out at us, smiling and waving.

I took a deep breath, wondering how this was going to play out. It could go fine, or get very, very ugly.

22

Gunnar stepped up beside me, and I pretended not to notice the golden ribbons woven into the back of his head. Maybe he was unaware, which would make me appreciate Alice even more. "Things got nasty last night. I knocked you out, end of story. Drop it," I told him, not wanting to deal with his pity party. I was dancing in one of my own.

He was silent for a time. "It's not that," he finally said. "Hanging out with Alice on the walk here...well, I think I really needed it. She kept messing with my fur and peppering me with questions. She's a never-ending stream of commentary, pointing out trees she thought were pretty, a shiny rock, she stubbed her toe on this morning—"

He caught my frown and laughed. "Exactly. Everything is a wondrous event to her because it's all new. And she wanted to share every single second of it with someone. She has no filter and...it was refreshing. I don't think I thought about Mordred or anything stressful even once on the way over here." How great for him. "Only after she hopped off my back, I saw a storm cloud," he said, shooting me a significant look. I grunted. He sighed with a shrug. "It's like the world got heavier after she climbed off my shoulders, which makes no sense, physically speaking. I just wanted to let you know that I feel better already, and we only just got here. I want to go home and tell Ashley all about that piggyback ride..." he trailed off, grinning like an idiot. "You should try it."

I narrowed my eyes at him. "If you don't want to give her another piggyback ride, just admit it. You don't need to oversell it to the next sucker." Then I smiled to let him know I was teasing.

He scoffed, shaking his head. "You're hopeless," he muttered, smiling over at Alice thoughtfully.

For the record, you would only know a werewolf was smiling if you spent a considerable amount of time around werewolves. To newbies, it probably looked like a death sentence.

"I'm glad she helped calm you down. Maybe being a dad won't be so bad. Your kids will love you, man. You're like a superhero. You even have those Underdog undies, remember?"

He smiled crookedly. Then he let out a long breath. "I know. I'm just used to being in control, and kids are the opposite of control and order. They're chaos. I want to make sure I bring them up safely. It's pretty much a dad's biggest job. Give them what they need to succeed."

I nodded, biting my tongue. Yeah. That.

"So...Bifröst," Gunnar muttered, shaking his head. "That...could have gone better."

I grunted my agreement. "The strangest part is that Odin—Dean—sent Grimm to protect us from Thor. Dean knows how Grimm feels about rainbows. Which means Dean either forgot, or he set it all up. I don't know which is scarier," I admitted.

"And Dean lied to you for decades already."

My eyes drifted to Mallory up ahead. My parents had roped him into their schemes as well, forcing him to lie to me—to omit his true identity as Pan, and that he had been here with me in Fae most of my life. "And Dean worked closely with Mallory for most of that time," I mused.

Gunnar missed a step, his lone eye suddenly latching onto Mallory. "Damn. I hadn't even considered that. But he already came clean about everything, right?"

"We're about to find out. If things get messy, get Alvara and Alice to safety," I said, walking towards the cave. It was entirely possible Mallory hadn't known—as Thor hadn't known about it—which meant Odin had lied to everyone. Whichever way the cookie crumbled, I needed to remember that these two had only lied at my parents' request. They were the puppet masters.

"What would make all this secrecy necessary?" Gunnar asked, jogging to catch up with me. "If they're all in cahoots, why keep you out of the cahoots—when you *are* the cahoots?"

"You should go back to your piggyback rides, Gunnar. This storm cloud is rumbling."

And I walked up to find that Mallory had started a fire—not because it was cold, but more for the symbolism of safety that a fire brought about. Fires made a place feel like home. Sitting around a fire and talking was therapeutic. I smiled, reaching into my satchel to pull out the bag of marshmallows Ashley had caught me stealing, and waved them at Alvara —who was busy listening to Alice blabber on about her walk and all the things she had seen. Just like Gunnar.

Alvara smiled at my marshmallows and pointed for Alice to see. I had never seen Alice move so fast. The bag was immediately torn from my grasp as she squealed delightedly, running off in search of a stick. Alvara let out an amused sigh and went off to help.

Talon was staring out at the Land of Fae as if surveying his kingdom, and I wondered if he remembered doing that as a child, because his memory had started coming back sooner than mine.

Mallory waved at me before walking over. Gunnar turned away to scan the surroundings, verifying no surprises lurked in the near distance.

Mallory was a big, beefy man, and wore khakis, a wrinkled dress shirt and no shoes. He looked like an old sailor turned model, his iron gray hair pulled back and his beard a little scraggly around the edges from Fae's lack of grooming products.

He still managed to look like a stud.

He was frowning curiously at Alvara who had returned to the fire with Alice. "Alvara and her daughter, Alice, are here to introduce me to a friend of theirs. Someone who may know some things that could help."

Alvara nodded politely. "She lives not too far from here, in fact," she said, studying the wilderness in the distance—towards a forest of yellow trees with blue leaves.

Mallory frowned, having tracked her gaze. "The Seer?"

I turned away from the trees to look at him, and then Alvara. She studied Mallory. "And how do you know the Seer?" she asked, frowning.

"I don't. I've just heard of her." Then his face grew somber. "She's...been gone for a long time. Or maybe she died. I don't know."

Alvara frowned at Mallory. "I highly doubt it. She's a resilient old woman. She's probably just hiding, but she will answer if I knock. We go way back."

I studied the two of them, not sure what to make of that conversation. If this Seer was dead, there went my only lead on the Catalyst thing, and I could return the women back home to focus on fixing the Bifröst without fear of bringing them into danger.

Mallory shrugged absently, but he didn't look too hopeful.

"Gunnar is pregnant," Alice chimed in, fiddling with about a dozen sticks for her marshmallows. I grinned. Was she planning on cooking all of them at once?

Mallory was frowning until Alvara clarified. "Ashley is pregnant. Gunnar is not."

Gunnar nodded, smiling. "Twins," he said.

Mallory promptly ran up to Gunnar and enveloped him in a bear hug. "Congratulations!"

Gunnar returned the gesture, but his eye was wary as he stared at me from over Mallory's shoulder—probably thinking of our talk moments ago. Talon remained distant, staring out protectively. Cats were anti-social by nature, and Talon was allergic to touching others' emotions.

Mallory finally detached himself from Gunnar. "Here's my advice. Simply being there is often the most important bit. The other things you're probably concerned about usually fall into place naturally."

Yeah. Not so much, in my opinion.

Mallory turned back to me. "Is that why you finally returned? To find the Seer? No offense to Alvara, but don't you have more pressing matters to worry about?"

"Like what, Mallory?" I asked with a cheerful smile. "I had nothing better to do, and according to my parents, unearthing secrets they kept from me is the most important thing in the world...and being the Catalyst is where X marks the spot, remember? You told me this."

He stilled, cocking his head at my tone. "I was referring to Mordred."

He looked me up and down critically but seemed to be looking beyond my physical appearance. "Or your Fae magic. You look like a fractured ray of light right now. Full of blockages and cracks."

The group grew silent. Except for Alice. "Oh, that's exactly it," she agreed.

We all turned to look at her, but she had resumed roasting her dozen marshmallows on the fire.

"Am I missing something? Why is everyone so tense?" Mallory asked warily. "Has something happened?"

"It's nothing. I just found out that Dean is Odin in disguise," I said conversationally.

Mallory's mouth dropped open, and there wasn't one bit of acting involved. "Impossible. You've been deceived."

I shook my head, watching him very closely. "Trust me. I have not. I saw him change."

"But...I would have known—" He stiffened in sudden understanding. "Ah. That's exactly what this is about. You think I knew and never said anything. Because of my past omissions." His shoulders slumped. "I understand, but you are wrong. So, so wrong."

23

I turned towards Talon and Gunnar. "Can you two show Alvara and Alice the cave? I want to take a walk with Mallory in private. We need to leave soon, so we won't be long," I told them, watching Mallory closely.

He watched the group, too, looking haggard and disturbed by the news of Odin.

I let out a sigh of regret. This next part was going to be hard.

"I truly didn't know—" he began.

"The Knight isn't here," I said, cutting him off.

Mallory froze, totally caught off-balance by my statement. It was why I had so casually mentioned the Odin thing in the first place. To shake him.

He didn't ask the obvious, but I explained anyway. "You didn't warn my friends to leave the Knight alone, or to be quiet, or not to go to a certain room, or any of the other number of things one who was housing an invalid would have requested." I met his eyes, walking backwards. "Where. Is. He?"

Mallory hung his head. "He escaped last night. I went searching for him but have found no trail."

I clenched my fists. "You should probably start with the part where he woke up for the first time," I growled, growing furious.

"I swear—"

"No more excuses and apologies. I want facts," I interrupted, my voice laced with scorn as I continued walking backwards. He followed me around the side of the cave, dragging his feet like a guilty child. "You know what? Scratch that. I don't care about the Knight. Maybe he'll go take care of my Mordred problem for me. I want to know about your buddy, Dean."

Mallory was blinking rapidly at my onslaught, as if putting pieces of a puzzle together in his mind, "Odin? Are you absolutely certain it wasn't some illusion?"

I nodded resolutely. I thought about explaining how I had seen Odin shift into Dean but realized that didn't address his illusion comment. And there was a certain god known for illusions—Loki. "Thor confirmed it," I finally said.

Mallory gasped. "Thor was there? What happened to him?"

"Thor thought I had Mjolnir," I told him, wondering why that mattered so much. It was all I could manage not to throttle him because my anger was just under the surface of my skin. "Thor has apparently been missing his hammer for *quite some time*. And his daddy has been working with my parents for *quite some time*. And you've been keeping this hammer safe for *quite some time*. So...let's imagine a Venn fucking diagram. Following the overlapping logic, here's my working theory. Decades ago, Odin fled from Asgard without leaving a goodbye note, stealing Mjolnir and hiding it in the chaos—I don't know where. Then he secretly gave my parents—and you—this replica hammer, leading his entire pantheon to one irrefutable understanding. That as soon as I picked up this fucking hammer, Thor would eventually hear about it, and we would throw down."

I was resting my palm atop the hammer, panting. It felt warm under my skin, but I didn't dare remove my hand because it needed to touch something. And I didn't want to grab the handle, or I might just lose control. I could almost taste my anger as I watched Mallory's eyes flicker back and forth, processing everything. Or pretending to. I couldn't tell.

"And when Thor does finally pay me a visit—last night—and learns my hammer is not his precious Mjolnir, he grows violent. Dean hears about my battle with Thor and sends Grimm to keep me safe. Grimm destroyed the Bifröst, by the way. Good times."

"*WHAT?*" Mallory roared in utter disbelief.

I went right on, not acknowledging the question. "Then the long-lost Odin appears to calm everyone down and chooses to side with *me* over his own son—who hasn't seen him in decades, remember. Thor pieces together that Odin is, in fact, my butler, and Odin uses his spear to blast Thor into another realm—not appreciating his clever little boy unveiling his clever little lie. And now, I have to repair the Bifröst before all of Asgard puts me on their naughty list and destroys Midgard. So, yeah...fuck the whole Knight thing."

"Thor...fell?" he whispered, sounding defeated.

"Yes!" I shouted, leaning closer. "But that's not the important part. How do you expect me to believe you didn't know any of this? You worked beside Dean for years, and you're both gods! How do you expect me to believe that one of the best liars I have ever met—rivaled only by my asshole of a father—didn't know who Dean really was? You guarded the fucking hammer, man! Gave me the target to put on my back for Thor!"

Mallory took a deep breath and then very calmly looked up at me, his eyes bloodshot and full of pain. "Be careful with your accusations, Wylde. Words have repercussions."

I laughed. "I will accuse whoever the fuck I please, Mallory. Because I am *right*! You *did* lie to me. You *all* did! You knew so much that could have helped me...but you bought into my parents' sadistic scheme. Let them infect you with their sociopathic treatment of a child—"

"Be very careful, boy. It is not wise to disrespect the dead. Or your own blood. Especially when their friends are near. And it is not wise to anger the God of *Panic*..." Mallory warned, suddenly flickering into his godly form. Pan, the Wild God.

He was a tall, gangly humanoid thing with the lower body of a goat. Great curling horns grew out from his head, and although slightly scrawny, his muscles were like cords of rope. A leather string around his neck held a set of pipes.

I scoffed, my rage bubbling up to the surface as I glared back at Pan. My chest was heaving, and I really felt like hitting him. Hard. "I can say whatever I please about my parents, Old One. They earned it."

"There he is," Pan snarled viciously. "The spoiled Temple boy. The one who got everything he ever wanted. His life perfectly ordered and perfectly safe. Tastes a little chaos and he wilts like a frozen flower rather than remembering where he was *really* born. I thought I had beaten that weakness out of you long ago, but it seems you can take the spoiled brat out of the mansion, but you can never take the mansion out of the spoiled brat. I liked you better as Wylde, and I'm not surprised he's ignoring you. He's ashamed of what you've become."

My eyes narrowed in outrage, my skin tingling at the rush of blood. "How dare you..."

"How dare *you?*" he roared right back. "You forgot your real fucking name!? But I'll remind you," he promised. "Even if I have to beat it out of you."

Pan punched me in the gut, sending me flying.

"Come on out, Wylde! Uncle Pan wants to play!" he bellowed, rocks crumbling from the top of the cave at the concussive shout. "No city-slickers allowed!"

My rage exploded at the challenge, and I felt Wylde roar up from within me like a shark from the depths of a black ocean. I climbed to my feet, clenching my knuckles until they cracked, my vision red with anger.

"Ahhh..." Pan sang in a loud shout. "So Wylde *can* hear me. He answers me, but not you, I get one boy for the price of two!" He was cackling like a lunatic.

Wylde roiled furiously within me.

"Why do you not bleed, Wylde? A god just punched you in the stomach, yet you do not bleed. Explain that, boy. Maybe it was all part of your parents' *plan*, you insolent, vapid child!"

My hammer was crackling at my hip, bloated with power and begging to be let loose. To take the power in for myself. To use it. To teach this liar his own lesson.

But this required a more personal touch. Flesh to flesh.

"I want to know if a god can cry," I snarled, licking my lips hungrily.

Pan laughed. "Your parents loved you more than any parent has *ever* loved their child. Trust me. I saw it in their eyes. Otherwise, I would have handed them and you over to Oberon and the Queens when I found you in the first place. But instead, I fell in love with a violent, dangerous, beautifully compassionate, and loyal boy. I even gave you Talon. I saw hope for the first time in centuries!"

"And you helped drown that hope in despair," I snarled.

He began running at me. "You've forgotten your name, Wylde. You traded it away for a mansion and a fancy car!"

"You helped me do that by hiding the truth!" I screamed, planting my feet.

"Boo-fucking-hoo! You think you're the only boy who is angry at the world? At his parents? Have you ever *read* about any of the gods, from *any* pantheon? It's par for the course! And to answer your question..."

He was pounding closer on his sharp hooves, and he was laughing so hard he was crying.

"Yes, Wylde. Gods cry..." Pan snarled, throwing a fist at me. "Every time they see their sons and witness disappointment."

24

My vision flared from red to white.

Wylde snarled savagely, grabbing ahold of the powers suddenly swirling all around us. I punched Pan's fist with my own, and a shockwave flattened the field of purple grass all around us, buffeting us both back. I slammed into the ground, furrowing a divot deep enough to sleep in and ten paces long. Pan had struck the cavern, sinking a few feet into it. He shook off the rock and debris and stepped out right as I climbed to my feet.

I felt no pain. Just rage.

We ran at each other and I leapt into the air, driving my knee up into his chin with a bone jarring *crack* as I dodged his swing. I landed as he hunched over, dazed, and I began punching the side of his head as hard as I could, Wylde snarling through my own lips. My fist was encased in wood as hard as iron, and I pounded the horn on the side of Pan's head, cracking it with each strike. My blood rushed to my brain with excitement, making my skin tingle. And I realized I was now laughing.

Although dazed and taking a beating, Pan laughed along with me before stomping on my foot with his hoof. I heard a cracking sound, but my foot was still functional, so I shoved him back, and kicked him with my damaged foot to get some space. Chunks of gravel slid off my leg like a broken cast, showing that Wylde had protected me from Pan's stomp.

"Wylde, Wylde, such a sweet boy, until you take away his toys!" Pan hooted, taunting me in a sing-song rhyme. He pointed at the War Hammer he had slipped from my belt. He threw it into the grass near the cave and rolled his shoulders in anticipation.

I roared, hurling a fist at him and striking with a blow of air that knocked him on his ass. Pan was cackling, still, despite the whooping.

"Likes his cars, likes his drinks, but in the woods, he forgets how to think!"

"SHUT UP!" I roared, hurling more blasts of air at him, knowing that it wasn't my wizard's magic, but my Fae side, even though I couldn't keep track of how Wylde was doing it.

It sounded like he was humming to himself while chopping wood.

"Cries for his mom, cries for his dad, but to anyone who listens, he hates them so bad!" Pan cried out gleefully, and a boulder was suddenly sailing right at me.

I held up a palm and the boulder dissolved to dust, but I hadn't considered choking to death on the cloud, so bent over double, coughing and wiping my eyes.

Pan had closed the distance and grabbed me by the belt to throw me into the side of the cave. I struck hard, sensing magic encasing me at the last moment to protect my head. The rock wall cracked, and a cascade of gravel and boulders rolled down all around me, sliding off the unseen shield I had thrown up. My head still spun, even though I had blocked the force of the initial blow.

"With all his baggage, and no Fae magic, this little Manling is oh, so tragic."

"ENOUGH!" I screamed, and I picked up the boulder beside me— easily twice my size—and hurled it at the taunting goat. It struck him like a tidal wave, sending him stumbling towards the edge of the cliff.

And Wylde's magic abruptly winked out, sending a wave of ice down my neck as I realized what I had just done. Like waking up from a night of drinking and suddenly seeing a video of yourself doing something you would never normally do.

I sprinted at Pan, screaming as I watched him trip, stumble, and fall back into open air.

I dove face-first and grabbed at anything I could find, managing to snag something hard and calloused. I dug the toes of my boots into the earth behind me and stared down to find Pan looking up at me through bloody teeth. His fingers gripped the edge of the cliff, and I was holding him by the horn I had pummeled and cracked during our fight. I felt my feet sliding so I latched onto the boulder I had thrown at Pan, digging my fingers into a crevice to help support Pan's weight.

I was panting frantically, and the sudden departure of Wylde was making me shiver.

What the hell had come over me? I had gone fucking postal.

And now...

"HELP!" I screamed, my throat raw from shouting at Pan. But I knew it wasn't loud enough for anyone to hear. My only hope was that Gunnar and Talon would come running to see what the hell had caused all the destruction outside the cave. We had basically obliterated one side of the mountain and torn up the field around it. They couldn't have missed it. They would come running, thinking I was under attack.

A cold chill rolled over my neck. Except I had told Gunnar to take the girls to safety if things got messy with Pan...

I didn't think I was going to be able to hold onto Pan for very long. I was too exhausted from the fight. Even though Wylde had done all the heavy lifting, my body was now feeling the repercussions. And Pan looked even worse, his fingertips were white where they clutched at the edge of the cliff.

I felt his horn creaking beneath my grip. I knew if I let go even for one second to switch to his forearm or other horn, his fingers would give out and that would be it. He was barely assisting me, and my shoulders and chest were beginning to burn from the strain. We were at a stale-mate. But this time not in a fight—to save him from dying.

"I'm so sorry, Pan. I don't know what came over me." I wheezed. "What the fuck is *wrong* with me?"

Pan coughed up blood, his face now entirely calm, no longer maddened with blood-frenzy. My eyes widened in chilling understanding. Pan nodded slowly.

"It wasn't your fault, Wylde. I made you *panic*. It's what I do. I used my power to push you over the edge. To Force you to rely upon Wylde. It was always going to be this way. What I promised your parents so long ago. I know this moment hurts—will continue to hurt long after I'm gone—but I've known about this day for years. It was my part to play. To know that I had to hurt you, to lie to you, to Force you...all so that we could *save* you. To help you save yourself, so that you could go on to one day help save *everyone*."

"What?" I whispered, ignoring the fiery pain across my chest as I strained to hold him, to pull him back up. But it was no use. It was all I could manage to hold him in place. *Come on, Gunnar. Talon. Anybody...*

"I really didn't know about Dean—about Odin—but as soon as you mentioned his name, I feared today was the day. All I knew was that the day I heard that Thor had fallen, I would have to teach you one final lesson before I too fell. To Force you to rely upon Wylde—to shock you into using your Fae Magic. Your parents said it was critical—and with my gift for inducing panic, I was the best god for the job. The most reliable. I swore not to admit it to you until now, in this moment—facing my certain death. Another lie to you," he whispered guiltily.

He coughed up more blood, spitting it out as he dangled over thousands of feet of empty space—and at the bottom of that fall was an ocean of roiling, liquid stone.

"There had to be a better way," I rasped, straining to use my feet to give me that little extra I needed to potentially lift him up. But my feet were barely secure as is. "My parents are not gods, Pan! They don't know everything!" I said, ignoring the tears pouring down my cheeks.

Pan shook his head. "They knew enough to see this moment, didn't they? And look at you, reuniting with Wylde again."

My fingers slipped in their own sweat, and I begged Wylde to come back for just a second—to help me at least lift him. I tried my wizard's magic, but I must have used that up in the fight, too. Or Wylde had used it to supercharge some of my attacks.

"I chose this, Wylde," Pan whispered. "And I would do it all over again. You made my existence worthwhile. Gave me hope." And then he began humming a song my mother had often sung to me to calm me down when I was frightened. *Star light, star bright, first star I see tonight...*

The song calmed me, reducing my hysteria. "No, Pan. I need you."

"You did, in the past. But this was the last gift I could give you."

I shuddered. "No, no, no..."

"We all played our parts, but you should know your parents played each of us just as much as you, the clever shits. But as their tapestry of deceit unfolds...I'm seeing a marvelous work of art." And he stared directly up at me, grinning through bloody teeth.

"We can heal you, Pan. Don't give up. I didn't hit you that fucking hard, you stupid goat!" I sobbed angrily, my tears splashing onto his bloody cheeks

He grunted, glancing down at his side, where a few shattered ribs poked out from his skin. I blanched, not having noticed until now. He was dying with or without holding onto the cliff.

"When the Knight woke, he spoke very little. Before he left, he was muttering about *time* as he drew something you should probably see. I couldn't make heads or tails of it, unfortunately. Maybe the Seer can find something in it, if you can find her."

Pan abruptly let go with one of his hands to snatch up a nearby rock from the boulder that I had thrown at him. "Know what this is, boy?"

"A rock!" I gasped, feeling his cracked horn straining at the suddenly increased weight since he had released the cliff with one of his hands. "Let go of it and grab back onto the ledge, Pan! If you fall, I'm jumping after you."

Pan frowned. "Feel it, Wylde. Feel the rock with your mind." Knowing he wasn't going to listen to me, I frantically obeyed, telling myself that doing so would somehow save Pan from falling. And...as I strained, I suddenly began to hear faint whispers. My ears popped, and I felt Wylde stirring within.

"Grab that feeling!" Pan hissed anxiously.

In my mind, I latched onto the sensation just as tightly as I gripped Pan's horn. Wylde struggled slightly, but I kept a fingernail grip on that conduit between us, feeling the wind and grass and earth beneath me suddenly humming to their own faint melody—almost too faint to hear.

I realized I was staring at Pan's fist—at the rock within. "It's a diamond," I whispered.

Pan grinned, squeezing his fist hard enough for the stone to crack. He opened his palm to show me a blood-coated diamond. "To remember me by," he whispered, dropping it to the grass between us. "To remember that you can do anything you want, Wylde Fae. You just have to take a deep breath and slow down."

His horn let out a loud crack.

"Help! Gunnar! Talon! Somebody! He's slipping!" I screamed, my voice raw.

Pan grabbed back onto the ledge, but I could tell he was already well past his endurance. My eyes locked onto the feather tattooed on the back of his wrist. The one he had gotten to immortalize the doodle I had drawn there as a child. As Wylde.

Pan noticed, smiling sadly. "It's time for me to float on, Wylde." One of his fingers slipped free, and the rest were already sliding as he lost more of his strength. "The Macallan," he hissed, gritting his teeth. "Check behind the white boulder in the cave. Raise a glass to me, will you? I meant well. We all did..."

Then his eyes glazed over.

And as his body went slack, the horn snapped, not strong enough to support his full weight.

He fell straight down.

"Noooooo!" I screamed, still clutching the end of his horn and punching at the earth with my other hand, blinking away my tears so that I wouldn't miss my last moments at seeing Pan in this world. He fell into the stone ocean with a faint splash and was gone forever.

I dropped my chin to the ground and cried. Hard.

I don't know for how long.

At one point, I realized I was staring at a strange root on the raw edge of the cliff below me, watching it swing back and forth in the breeze, ready to fall at any moment. My eyes widened, and I snatched at it a moment before it fell. Because I realized it wasn't a root. I lifted it up and stared.

Pan's necklace. The one with his pipes on the end. I rolled onto my back and clutched it to my chest, staring up at the sky as I tried to process the death of a close friend. That he had planned this death. I wasn't entirely sure I believed that or if he had just been trying to save me from myself—from my own guilt.

Because no matter how one cut the cake, I had killed Pan.

I felt the diamond under my fingers and shoved it into my pocket without looking at it, the sensation of Pan's blood on my fingers making me want to vomit.

I finally, unsteadily, climbed to my feet and turned away from the cliff. Gunnar and Talon were staring at me, tears falling down their cheeks, their eyes red as they stared at the broken horn and pipes in my hand.

"How…" I rasped, but it turned into a cough. "When did you get here?"

"Too late," Talon sobbed, his furry cheeks stained with a dark line from his tears. "We had to save Alvara and Alice…" he whispered.

Gunnar was nodding, glancing back at the cave. "It began to cave-in, and we didn't see you lying here. The wind changed slightly, and I finally caught your scent," he added. "I'm sorry, Nate."

Talon sniffled, wiping the back of his paws at his eyes. "I'm sorry, Wylde."

I hung my head. "Don't be sorry. He set it all up," I said numbly. "We weren't supposed to save him." I opened my mouth to say more, to blame my parents, but let out a breath of anger. I wasn't about to start trash-talking my parents. Pan had pretty much ruined that for me, and it wasn't the time.

Pan had believed in them.

Whether misguided or not, I wasn't about to cheapen his last words. Not here, only feet away from where he had martyred himself.

I still gripped the faintest of fingerholds on the conduit between me and my Fae senses, or Fae magic—I wasn't sure which. I clamped down on it like Pan holding the edge of the cliff. Wading out into those cold waters of lost hope, refusing to let go.

Like my parents had told him to do…years before.

All things considered, they were very lucky they were already dead. Or I may have made good on the old stereotype of most gods from most pantheons—the children killing their parents.

Pan had asked me to do something for him, so I took one unsteady step. Then another…

I picked up my War Hammer and set it in my belt hoop.

Then I continued on, and my two best friends followed me.

As did the screaming silence of grief.

25

I stared at the front of the cave—at the pile of rubble blocking half of the entrance. The damage from my fight with Pan had been extensive—both outside the cavern and within.

Alvara and Alice peered out at us from behind a fallen boulder just outside the cave—it had landed directly in the fire Pan had built, and it looked like the fire had spread before someone had doused it. I arched an eyebrow at Gunnar.

He nodded. "Wasn't worth mentioning," he said humbly.

Alice suddenly ran at me, tears running down her cheeks, and I felt like the worst kind of person for scaring her to death.

"I'm sorry, Alice—"

She leapt at me and wrapped her arms around my neck like tentacles, squeezing tightly as she sobbed into my neck. "You looked like you needed a hug, Manling," she whispered.

My eyes misted over, somehow not yet dry despite how many tears I had shed in the last half hour. I nodded stiffly. "I did," I rasped.

She squeezed tighter, petting my hair with one of her small hands. "It's okay, Wylde. We haven't found the happy ending, but the story isn't over yet. We haven't even seen a knight or a dragon. You can't have a happy ending without them. Every princess knows that."

I smirked at the bizarre comment. "Of course." I helped her down, but before I could turn away, she suddenly grasped my hand tightly, refusing to let go. Alvara smiled at us with a haunted expression—no doubt imagining her husband again. Or she was thinking about her daughter holding hands with the Manling who had just killed the god he'd called a friend.

I stifled that dark thought.

Alice began tugging me towards a small opening in the cave. "I already checked to make sure it was safe to go back inside."

We entered, and enough light shone through the opening to eventually point out an out-of-place white boulder, just like Pan had mentioned. But I didn't see the Knight's drawing anywhere. Probably buried under the rubble.

"What are you doing, Nate?" Gunnar asked gently.

I still held the conduit with Fae magic, but it was so weak that I didn't want to risk trying to use it. Just holding it would build up my strength, hopefully retrain my mental muscles.

So, I lifted the War Hammer from my belt, and struck the white rock as hard as I could. Everyone gasped and cursed behind me, but I stared only at my target. The white stone shattered like glass, exploding inwards to reveal a vast, echoing room. I scooped up one of the stone-lights from the floor since most had fallen down from the walls and used it like a flashlight. Others quickly did the same.

Alice—still gripping my hand—giggled devilishly.

I stopped in the center of a tall, maybe ten-by-twenty-foot room. Crates and crates of fifty-year Macallan lined the walls. All the good stuff Pan had hidden out of my reach for so many years. I had finally found Pan's mystical, secret stash. But my eyes were immediately drawn to something else.

I fell to my knees, my heart ripping in two. Alice squeezed my hand, gasping.

Others made similar sounds behind me, but I couldn't look away.

The entire wall was covered with papers. Children's drawings of horribly inaccurate stick figures, wizards, and even Talon. Awards, newspaper clippings, even an old sticky nametag that said Archangel—that I had worn to a convention soon after my parents died—was tacked onto the wall. I spotted a copy of the registered business license for Plato's Cave, pictures of me with my parents, me and Gunnar playing as children, and other pictures of me growing up that I had never before seen, from all ages of my life.

On a lonely looking desk sat a stack of leather journals. Alvara rushed over to them, scooping up a handful and scanning them. "Manling Tales..." she whispered. "They're numbered."

I held out my shaking hand and she gave me one. I flipped it open to find a page with a single sentence on it.

I'm sorry for what I said before the cliffs...

I shuddered, almost dropping the journal. But...this journal was old, not recent. I flipped the page to see it was an entry on the day I had first met the cat Pan had found.

...and that beautiful child Named his first Name! Talon the Devourer!

Talon was standing beside me, so I held it up to show him. He gasped after a few moments, and I pulled it back, slowly flipping through the rest of it. It was a private journal of sorts, documenting each day of his time in Fae with our family and Talon. I continued flipping pages to find dozens of entries, intermixed with ornate doodles that took up entire pages and made me feel slightly dizzy. I snapped it shut and looked at Alvara's stack.

Pan had been writing these for *years* to fill so many books. He really had known this day would come...

Talon tapped me on the shoulder with his soft paw and pointed at the opposite wall, his paw shaking. I hadn't even noticed the other walls were decorated.

In huge letters, Pan had painted a message.

Family isn't born in blood, it is forged in fire.

Star light, star bright, it's not your fault, I'll be alright.

Alice reached up and wiped a tear from my cheek, looking sad for me.

A small table sat below the mural. The table held three items. A piece of paper. A glass. And a bottle of fifty-year-old Macallan. I walked up to them, my legs shaking.

A small tag hung from the neck of the bottle. *Pour me.*

The glass had a similar tag tied to it. *Drink me.*

I obeyed, staring down at the paper as I uncorked the bottle and poured a healthy splash into the cup. The paper had a very short message, and old stains on it, proving that it was not freshly written.

Keep the journals safe. Someone will help you read them one day. This was my choice, boy, don't blame your parents for being right. Drinks on me.

I took a drink, marveling at the taste. It was my favorite. I scanned his letter again, thinking. Why would I need help reading the journals? He hadn't written them in any foreign language.

I turned at a sudden sound behind me. Gunnar was shaking his head at all the pictures, even letting out a slight laugh at one near the corner I couldn't see from here. Alvara was holding up the journal to one of the doodled pages, and Alice was taking tiny steps back and forth, squinting at it from about six feet away.

"Ah! There you are," she muttered to herself, finally standing still.

I frowned, but Alvara shot me a very dangerous look, warning me not to interrupt. Then she turned back to Alice, seeming on the verge of jumping with joy.

Gunnar glanced over, noticed my attention, and shrugged.

Alice stared unblinking at the picture for a full minute, her eyes darting back and forth as if reading something. She finally burst out laughing. "It's a story! About you," she squealed, turning to point at me. "An embarrassing one where you brought a baby Rarawk home, only to earn the ire of its angry mother! Your parents were not pleased."

Talon coughed suspiciously. "I remember that." I didn't, but that wasn't really the most important point.

I blinked at Alice incredulously. "You got all that...from a picture?"

She nodded. "Of course, silly Manling. Pictures are for kids!"

I hurriedly walked up to stand beside her, staring at the image, but it just made me dizzy.

"No, no, no," she chastised. "You're bigger. Tell me when to stop," she said, slowly tugging me back a few inches, then a few inches more.

"Stop!" I snapped, staring at the doodle intently. It abruptly sprang to life, almost like the words danced right out of the picture akin to a hologram. I scanned it quickly, realizing it was indeed about a baby Rarawk I had wanted to nurse back to health.

The mom had shown up—drawn by the baby's cries—and had not been pleased.

And just like that, I felt a very faint click in my mind. And my grip on

Wylde's magic, suddenly felt a hair easier to maintain. Nothing life-changing, but...better.

I shook my head at Alice. "That's...incredible," I whispered.

Alice let go of me and the words abruptly shimmered back to a doodle. Had that been her or me? Alvara snapped the journal shut. "Art is the deepest language ever created. It seems Pan hid stories of you in imagery. Clever way to hide it, but why would he do such a thing if there are written entries filling the rest of this journal?" she asked softly.

I shrugged, having no idea.

Alvara turned to Alice with a proud smile. "I am so proud of your gift, child. I am glad I got to see you use it for the first time. What a wonderful, wonderful gift for a wonderful, wonderful child," she whispered, wrapping her daughter up in a tight hug.

But something about Alvara's demeanor made me feel like she was sad.

I turned to Gunnar. "We can't carry all of these with us, and the amount of magic we used out there had to draw attention to this place. We need to leave."

Gunnar nodded. "Can you send them back to the Sanctorum?"

I sighed, thinking about it. I didn't want to risk losing my grip on Wylde by stepping back over to Chateau Falco. "I'm exhausted, man. I don't know—"

"I will do it," Talon said, scooping up the stack of journals from the desk.

I gripped his shoulder, handing over Pan's horn and his pipes. "These, too," I whispered.

Talon nodded sadly, staring down at them for a moment. Then he closed his eyes, and was gone a moment later.

He returned after a minute and dusted off his paws. "No one was there. I hid them in one of the rooms no one uses."

I stared at him. "I, um, didn't know you could so easily hop back and forth, Talon."

He cocked his head at me. "You just step out," he said, frowning. "I've seen you do it before."

I turned my back on him, muttering under my breath. It wasn't as easy as just *stepping out*. I'd had to use a decent amount of power to travel back and forth. I didn't just *step out*. I put some honest work into it.

Maybe this was what it felt like to not be a wizard and watch someone fling a fireball from thin air. I didn't like it.

"Let's get out of here. I don't want to be anywhere near this place if someone comes asking about a noise complaint."

26

We traveled quickly away from the torn-up scene at the cave, and I had the feeling that I might not ever return. That—other than the Macallan and a buried doodle drawn by the runaway Knight—the place held nothing for me. Not with Pan gone.

Time...

Maybe the knight had been shocked at how long he had been asleep. How much time had passed. I wasn't about to spend the day digging up all the rubble. I could always come back later when I had my Fae magic. Maybe I could even snap my finger and a bunch of fairies could go dig it up for me. I grunted at the whimsical wish.

We made good time with Talon scouting our path ahead and Gunnar sniffing—watching—our rear. And after a few hours, Alvara walked up beside me. Alice was skipping ahead of us, picking occasional flowers, and generally *oohing* and *aahing* at the scenery.

"I forgot to give this to Talon before he took your journals home," Alvara said, holding out the journal she had been clutching in the cave. "And since we were in a hurry to leave, I didn't bring it back up." I reached out for it but didn't close my fingers around it.

"Maybe Alice wants to read some Manling Tales. Or help decipher the images," I suggested.

Alvara smiled faintly before nodding her head and tucking it into her satchel. "She would...enjoy that."

"How long until we reach the Seer?" I asked, glancing up at the sky. It was overcast, and I didn't really have a reason for looking up other than habit. Days and nights in Fae were wholly different from the human realm. One moment it was day, and in the blink of an eye it could suddenly be night. No judging time by the passing of the sun, here. At least, I didn't know how to do so.

Alvara tapped her lips. "From the cave, I would guess six hours, but it has been a long time since I relied upon my feet, so I'm not sure how close that is. Close enough for you, I imagine."

I nodded. We'd been walking for about two hours already. That didn't sound like a long time, but knowing that in Fae, an hour could be the equivalent of a day back home, it still made my shoulders itch. But there was nothing for it. The sooner we found—or didn't find—the Seer, the sooner I could send them home and focus on my Fae magic. Except...I no longer had a cave to live in.

How was a man supposed to hermit without a creepy cave?

I still held a tentative grip on my Fae magic, refusing to let go. I'd had no sudden understanding of the meaning of life, heard no whisper of a nearby tree, and the ribbons of energy that I knew danced around me still went mostly unseen. Sometimes, out of the corner of my eye, I thought I saw something, but it was always gone when I turned to look directly.

Other than that faint clicking sensation in Pan's cavern, the only difference had been it was slightly easier to maintain my grip on the conduit. And the peripheral vision thing. Unless that just meant I suffered some kind of concussion from my fight with Pan.

Surprisingly, I felt no pain from any of that. And seeing the carnage we had caused, all the destruction...I felt a little concerned. Had that been Wylde protecting me?

Or something else? This Catalyst thing, perhaps. Although it had never protected my body from harm before.

To be honest, I wasn't entirely sure what to expect from my reconnection with the Fae magic. I had already merged with Wylde once and had thought that would be the end of it. But it seemed there was now some kind of block between us. The best way I could think to describe it was that we were standing on opposite sides of a glass wall, and were both pressing our palms against it, not making contact. The glass was a little clearer than before, but we still couldn't touch—or merge.

Nothing could really come of it.

Whatever Pan had done to Force me had only resulted in me being able to feel the alien power, not actually do anything with it. Which was even more frustrating than not sensing it at all. How did one make sure they continued to hold a strand of hair between two fingers on a windy day? If you relaxed your fingers to check that you still held it, the wind would blow the hair away.

So, I figuratively continued pressing my fingers together as tightly as possible, hoping I hadn't dropped it hours ago.

"You are using an awful lot of focus to do an awful lot of nothing," Alvara commented, not making eye contact.

I turned to her, narrowing my eyes. "I wish I knew someone who knew a little bit about Fae magic, but all I've found is a grouchy mom."

She arched a very cool eyebrow at me.

I finally sighed. "I'm sorry. Just...a little raw around the edges after..." I waved a hand back the way we had come. Where Pan had died.

She nodded at my apology. "I am also a little raw around the edges," she admitted. "It is unsettling, and terrifying, to be back in Fae." She was staring at Alice who seemed to be reading a piece of folded paper she'd pulled from her backpack. "I'm sorry about Pan."

I nodded in thanks. I'd told them the full story earlier, so they didn't think I was a murdering psychopath. I gave them a very vanilla version of events, of course. We had argued, Pan had chosen to use some magic to teach me a lesson, and part of the cliff had fallen, taking him along with it. All true, in a sickening, tabloid newspaper kind of way.

Luckily, the messages in Pan's cave corroborated my story.

Or this would have been a very lonely walk after they all ran away screaming.

"Any advice would be much appreciated," I told Alvara. "I don't even know if I'm succeeding. I'm just trying not to let go of what I feel."

She sniffed primly. "Well, you're succeeding. But you look like you're trying to flex every muscle in your body to lift a teacup. It's ridiculous."

I chuckled, despite myself. "I can't even see if I'm holding the teacup, but I don't want to risk dropping it."

"See..." Alvara said, repeating the word I had used. But her eyes were locked onto Alice.

"Hold the phone," I said suddenly. "Do you think she can help me see what I'm doing? Like she helped me see that image in the journal? Whatever she did the first time helped relieve some of the strain I'm feeling."

Alvara pursed her lips nervously, thinking. "Let me take a stab at you, first. She's never taught anyone, and I don't want her to lead you down the wrong path. She hardly knows what she's doing with the gift she only discovered a few hours ago. Asking her to teach what she thinks she knows could be disastrous to you both."

I thought about that and finally nodded. It was a fair point. "When Pan died..." I began, carefully composing my voice, "he was trying to Force me to touch my Fae magic through the apparent block I've got in place." She gave me an alarmed look, picking up on exactly what I meant when I used the word *Force*. "It helped a little, but now all I can do is barely hold onto it. I'm scared to let it go for fear of losing it and having to start all over again. Do you know how to Force me further?"

Alvara was now staring at me incredulously. "He Forced you?" she sputtered, sounding horrified. "That could have leveled that whole damned mountain on our heads! And you're asking me to Force you to... what, be *Forcier*?" she hissed in a high-pitched shriek, waggling her hands above her head at the made-up word, as if quite genuinely astonished by my level of ignorance.

I saw Alice's shoulders tense and she almost ripped the paper in her hands in half. She quickly picked up her pace to escape the mom-blast-radius.

"I don't sound like that," I mumbled defensively. "My voice is much lower. More authoritative. Suave—"

"You sound like a buffoon. Say it, and I will consider helping you. If I can't trust the thoughts you let cross from one ear to another, I refuse to help you compound your delusions."

I narrowed my eyes and kicked a rock. "Fine. I sounded like a buffoon," I muttered.

Alvara continued shaking her head, muttering under her breath.

I hadn't used the word *Forcier*, but she made a good point. Intentions were not always the most important thing. Sometimes, they could be the most dangerous of things.

"Forcing is incredibly dangerous," she began.

I nodded. "My parents made me do it often as a child. I only recently learned of the dangers."

She missed a step and cursed under her breath. "Well, you are the Catalyst. Not a man for half-measures. It would make sense, in an entirely insane kind of way."

Finally, she went on in a lecturing tone. "You must Sense the things you want to Sense. Hear the things you want to Hear. See the things you want to See. But you mustn't try too hard. In that way lies *un-sensing*..." she went on for a few minutes, basically repeating herself in different ways, making me feel like I had shown up to a hippie festival of some kind to learn about the cosmic powers of crystals that they sold in their gift shop for thirty-five dollars a pop.

It was ultimately unhelpful for any kind of quick understanding.

"Some can use their senses better than others. The passing of time, for example. Oracles can float the rivers of time to sometimes understand the things that they see."

I had perked up at mention of the word *time*, but she was speaking generally.

"Seeing can manifest in any number of ways. Like Alice, for example. She seems able to see deeper meanings in things. When she saw Falco, I thought it had been a fluke. Then she Saw Gunnar's Wild Side before he had shifted, which was when I first seriously considered she may have a gift. Then she deciphered Pan's journal." I nodded, following along, but not seeing any immediate benefit in kicking Mordred's ass with my eyeball power.

"Those in battle may be able to see attacks sooner than others," Alvara continued. "Those with magic may be able to see the elements dancing around them—"

"That one," I interrupted. "That's definitely one of my thingies. I've done that before this whole Fae magic constipation issue."

She narrowed her eyes at my simplistic definition and vulgar use of descriptors.

Imagine asking a preacher where you could buy one of those *addition symbol* necklaces.

That's the look I got. She was silent for a very long time after that, lifting a hand to silence me every time I tried to speak.

"I think you need to contemplate what I've said so far," she finally said in a tone that let me know it was not a suggestion, and that our lesson was finished. "I don't know how to Force someone anyway, and the way you're talking is making me very nervous."

She sped up to go walk with Alice, handing her the journal, and I heard Gunnar burst out laughing behind me as if he'd been holding it in for quite some time.

I hadn't realized he was walking so close.

I gave him an overhead, double-finger salute without turning around.

Everyone's a critic.

27

I t turned out that we were much closer than Alvara's initial guess. We were soon walking through a forest of pale, yellow trees—the bark peeling off like paper, and the vibrant blue leaves above making me feel like we were swimming underwater.

Alvara had made no move to resume my lesson, and Gunnar was now carrying Alice on his shoulders again, chatting with Talon—who had given up scouting since we were close enough that we didn't want to spook the Seer if she was, in fact, home—and still alive.

I had spent my solitary confinement from Alvara's lessons thinking about what to do next.

Because if this Seer was not here, I needed to find a way to figure out my Fae magic fast, so I could repair the Bifröst.

Because at any moment, Alex and Grimm could return with their sack of rainbow guts, and I would need to figure out a way to repair it with the magic. Or else.

There was also the opportunity to spy on Mordred in Camelot. See what the little prick was up to. Maybe I had more time than I thought to deal with him. It was almost as if I had really killed him at Fight Club, having heard nothing from him other than that our meeting had been rescheduled from the original day after Fight Night to three weeks later.

And when I had left on this trip, I'd had about two weeks on the clock.

I still hadn't seen any creatures on our walk, and it was beginning to truly bother me. No random insects trying to kill me. No pixie patrols. Nothing. Like the land was holding its breath. Yet no sign of a reason why it was holding its breath. Alvara had once told me she heard of vast armies moving about in Fae. And here we were, all by our lonesome.

Which, in the few experiences I could remember in the last year, was extremely rare.

Maybe Mordred was more injured than he let on, and the Land of the Fae was holding its breath in hopes the problem would take care of itself.

I would need to get a closer look to see for myself. Maybe it would be a quick assassination if he was recovering.

If the Seer was a bust, I was sending Alvara and Alice back home, whether they wanted to or not. Alice could sit at Chateau Falco and transcribe the doodles from the journal. Hell, with the time-slippage, I could return a few hours later to find that she was finished transcribing all of them. Voila! Fae magic restored, my blockage gone, and memories returned.

I really doubted that things would play out that simply, but since I was left pretty much alone on our walk, my imagination had gone a little stir-crazy. It could have also had to do with the fact that whether I could sense it or not, I knew I was straining to hold onto that sliver of Wylde.

Like pinching a piece of paper between your fingers.

For. Three. Hours.

Sounds easy, right? Try it. Your fingers start to spasm, go numb, and you can't tell if you're still squeezing them together or not. Before you know it, whoopsies. Paper falls.

To counter that risk, I was very actively using a lot of mental energy to maintain that grip.

To flex while squeezing my teacup, as Alvara had told me.

I even tried her suggestion about being one with my environment. *Seeing. Hearing. Smelling.* I was entirely sure I was losing my grip on my sanity by the time I spotted the large mountain through a gap in the trees. From the cave, I hadn't noticed it, but it had materialized on our walk. With the sky being overcast, it had taken me a bit of squinting to realize it really was a mountain rather than just a trick of the fog on the higher slopes, looking like a cloud.

Odin had told me to find a mountain to repair the Bifröst. Somewhere high.

But now that I saw it through the trees—a little clearer than it had been earlier—I suddenly began to have doubts. How long would it take me to scale a fucking mountain? Hopefully, I would have Grimm by then. I could make Alex walk while I sat my royal tushy down on my royal unicorn, thank you very much.

I was very antsy to see Alex again. I felt naked without my satchel, but more importantly, I needed the two Keys inside it.

Maybe one of them had the answers to fixing the Bifröst. Other than Odin casually mentioning this—which wasn't necessarily trustworthy—I was rolling on the basic default hypothesis that my parents were behind everything. That way I could no longer be surprised when I found they had their hands in yet another god's pie. I'd had enough surprises lately.

If the Bifröst needed repairing, they had probably prepared for it.

They had known I would come to Fae after all, and that I would need to be Forced by Pan. They'd even convinced him to kill himself for it. I took a deep breath, burying that thought. I had to be cold. Heartless. Or I would break down.

In addition to Pan and his decision to commit suicide, Odin had also worked for my parents, and had mentioned Forcing as a solution—to repairing the Bifröst.

This little pickle tickles that little pickle, and Bob's your uncle—my parents were to blame.

They had given me the Keys, going out of their way to actually give me support, for once.

It essentially summed up as, *these are important. You'll need these important things to do other important things later, at some important time. Oh, and you might be the Catalyst. That's important.*

"Why are you talking like that?" Alice asked, frowning at me worriedly.

I jumped with a manly bellow, not having realized I'd been speaking out loud. Definitely not that I'd been mockingly vocalizing my parents' cryptic help. Or that anyone had even been near me.

"Um..."

She waited patiently, but I had no explanation to offer that would even remotely redeem me.

"So, you're not busy?" she asked.

I shook my head, glad for the change of topic. "No. Why?"

"My mom said you looked like you were busy, and not to bother you while you were busy. I ran out of ribbons to tie in Gunnar's hair, so asked him to let me down. I don't think he knows about the ribbons yet, so don't tell him," she said, holding a finger to her lips and giggling. I nodded back, unable to keep back my own smile. "Then I asked Talon if I could hold his spear, but he was eating some kind of seed that smelled really bad and he hissed at me before running away. I tried talking to my mom, but she wanted to go pick some berries, and told me I couldn't have any. Then I came over here and you were talking to yourself."

Wow. Gunnar had been right about Alice. I was beginning to see that kids really were all about the oversharing thing. "No, I'm not busy," I finally said, impressed by her recollection of events. I was one-hundred percent sure that Talon had found some Fae catnip pods. I remembered Yulemas and how Fae catnip pods might be an excellent gift for him. Even if it was me enabling his drug habit. "What's up?" I asked the little detective.

She held up the page I had seen her reading earlier. I had thought it was a coloring page from home, but my skin suddenly prickled when I realized it was a crude drawing, as if sketched with charcoal or some other rudimentary implement.

"Where did you get this?" I asked in a whisper.

She shrugged. "I found it in the cave before you shouted at it and crumbled it all down."

I didn't correct her about the shouting power she had just attributed to me. Because I was too shocked to realize she had accidentally picked up the drawing the Knight had left behind. The one Pan had mentioned.

It was...I had no idea what it was. It looked like a large sun with many rays shooting out from the center. It was a very basic drawing, something a toddler could have duplicated.

She noticed my attention. "See?" she asked, slowly walking backwards. Caught off guard by her sudden motion, I stared at the page. "No!" she folded the page and then brandished it at me warningly. "Don't *look*. *See!*" And she opened it again.

I took a breath and didn't try as hard. Rather than staring, I let my eyes relax as I glanced in the direction of the page. Kind of like those visual puzzles where an image could suddenly pop out of a pink blur. Something shifted, and I held up a finger for her to stop. She did, and it flickered away like a blown-out candle.

"Damn it," I muttered, trying to move back and forth until I saw it again.

Alice sighed, folding the page again. "It's no use. If you kind of see it, and then it goes away, you have to wait a while to get it out of your head. Otherwise you try too hard and ruin it."

I studied the child, cocking my head in surprise. "I think you might just be a better teacher than your mother."

She nodded primly. "Of course I am."

I grinned at her lack of humility. "My Lady," I said, taking a bow.

She dipped her head graciously. "Why are the Queens so scared of you? You're a little mad, but you're not scary."

Part of me registered the thought that a little blonde girl named Alice had just told me I was a little mad while we traipsed about a strange land, reminding me of Lewis Carroll's fabled story. But Alice had a serious look on her face, and she had asked a very serious question. One I didn't feel equipped to answer with her mother absent.

"Oh, that was just a misunderstanding. We had an argument."

Alice grew very still. "Like you had an argument with Pan?" she asked, slicing right to the bone without meaning to. There was no judgment in those innocent little eyes. "My mother and father once had an argument. Then I never saw him again."

And I suddenly wanted to curl up into a ball and die. My white lie had just snowballed into—

Another thought suddenly hit me. I had just lied to a child. About something very important. Something that could put her in danger just for being near me. Because if the Fae Queens did go hunting for me, they would find Alice—a banished Fae—and likely execute her. But since she was with *me*, they would most *definitely* execute her.

Off with her head, and all of that.

I had just done what I hated my parents for. Lying about a significant thing.

I knelt down in front of Alice and held out my hands. She straightened her shirt and set the paper down. "I do," she said solemnly.

My face turned scarlet from jawline to hairline. "No—"

She burst out in giggles. "I was just joking you!" she teased, laughing entirely too hard.

I narrowed my eyes. "Enough of that, you," I growled playfully. "Listen up. I'm about to learn you."

"You can't *learn* someone," she argued, laughing.

"And you can't *joke* someone either," I teased right back, grinning victoriously.

Her laughter cut off. "Oh, my. Are you for serious?" she asked.

"I'm for *real*. But I'm also serious. I am not *for serious*," I said, smiling wider.

"Oh, bother."

"Now," I said, letting my smile slip away. "This is important. I'm going to teach you how to lie. And how to spot a lie."

Her eyes suddenly glittered with excitement. "Yes, please," she breathed eagerly.

"This isn't foolproof, but people have a thing called a tell—something that gives them away when they are nervous. Or lying. Sometimes, they look to the left the moment before they lie. Maybe their nose twitches. Or their shoulders tense. Basically, you should *see* people when you talk to them," I told her, deciding to use a word tied to her new affinity. "Learn their normal facial gestures, so that whenever you see them do something different than usual—their tell—you can almost bet your life they are lying to you. Always look people in the eyes when you talk to them, and they are more likely to let slip a tell. Eye contact makes people nervous."

She nodded studiously, considering my words. I waited patiently, wondering just how clever this little girl might be since she obviously had a gift for seeing.

She blinked suddenly. "The Queens. You lied about the Queens."

I smiled proudly, inwardly stunned she had picked up on it so fast. But to hear how good she was at observing people, and then her gift with images, I had hoped for such a response.

"I'm sorry about that, but yes. I spoke without thinking and wanted to tell you something that wouldn't scare you. The truth is, the Queens tried to attack me over a misunderstanding. And I reacted. I defended my friends and killed a lot of the Queens' soldiers. It was one of the first times I used this," I said, indicating the Hammer at my belt, remembering how I had funneled my Fae magic through it to sow mayhem against the might of the Fairy Queens. It had knocked me out, afterwards. There were consequences to dishing out that much magic, even when using a tool to control it. And Odin wanted me to use even *more* magic to repair the Bifrost. I focused back on Alice. "It was one of the first times I let them see what I could do with my Fae magic. Many, many died. The Queens themselves almost died."

Her eyes were wide as she slowly nodded. "You told me the truth," she murmured. "You didn't show any tells," she explained, touching my cheek in a specific spot.

I decided right then and there that I was never going to play poker with Alice. Not ever. I had no idea what tell she had picked up on, but now I felt self-conscious about it. "Yes. I told you the truth. And I'll try to always tell you the truth from here on out. Very rarely do you need to tell a lie. Only in circumstances where the truth will directly get someone you care about harmed."

"What do you mean?" she asked, frowning.

"If the Queens showed up and demanded to know where Gunnar was so they could kill him, I would lie to them, because they just said their immediate intent was to kill Gunnar."

"What if they threaten to hurt you if you don't give them what they want?"

I sighed, giving her a sad smile. "That's when things get complicated, and you find out what you're made of," I said tiredly, thinking back on all the liars I had met—some for good, some for bad.

She was silent for a time, and I realized the others had covered quite the distance between us as we stopped to talk. I looked down at her. "Can you give me a piggyback ride?" I asked.

She squealed, and then sprinted away as fast as her little two legs could carry her. "Only if you can catch me, Manling!"

I grinned and gave chase.

My heart felt significantly lighter for both telling her the truth and for chasing after a child who could hardly breathe she was giggling so hard.

There was just something about abandoning your pride that felt good at times.

Dealing with mothers who were angry at you for oversharing with their daughters on the other hand...well, that was for later. Right now...

"Fe, fi, fo, fum! I am the Manling, you better run!" I roared, chasing her down.

Talon flinched so violently at my shout that he hurled his pod of Fae catnip up into the air, his eyes about as dilated as I had ever seen them. Gunnar was grinning from ear-to-ear, and Alice screeched at the top of her lungs as she fled.

And I felt a stronger click between Wylde and me, making me smile wider.

lvara had soon picked up on our game, and was now carrying Alice on her back, laughing as she spun in circles every other step. Her lips were stained red from the berries she had apparently found, but she didn't seem to notice, so I didn't point it out.

I did lean over to Talon, though. "What kind of berries did she eat?"

Talon glanced over. "Um, I don't know. I was...busy."

I rolled my eyes. He had been getting stoned on Fae catnip. Even now, he was fastidiously cleaning his paws as if they were filthy. They weren't. And seeing a cat tug on his inches-long claws with fangs that could pierce almost entirely through my wrist...well, his grooming habits left a lot to be desired.

Alvara was about as happy as I had ever seen her. No more of her strange trepidation. "Maybe she found some kind of catnip, too..." I suggested to Talon.

He stopped tugging on a ridiculously sharp claw long enough to shrug. "I've never heard of such a berry." Then he went back to cleaning as we walked.

Not long after, Alvara suddenly stopped laughing, looking about the woods as if surprised. She set Alice down and waved at me, motioning me closer. Talon and I instantly jogged over, wondering if something was wrong. Gunnar, too, began scanning our surroundings for a threat, sniffing at the air warily.

"We are close," Alvara told me. "The Seer is a very private person. I should go ahead so she doesn't flee in fear."

I hesitated, thinking about it. "I really don't want to split up, and what if Pan was right? She might not be here."

Alvara waved a hand. "Nonsense. I've known her for as long as I can remember. She's here. I know it." She sounded uncannily certain. "Just keep Alice with you and come knock on the door in five minutes. That should be enough time for me to calm her down."

I shot Talon a questioning look and he shrugged. "I don't sense any nearby danger," he suggested. "Nor do I sense any nearby presence but us. I don't think she is here."

Alvara swatted him on the nose, earning a stunned look from Talon as his ears tucked back instinctively. "Don't meddle in my affairs, Talon," she chastised him. Alice looked just as surprised as the rest of us, but to be fair, she had spent much of the last leg of our walk psychoanalyzing each of us, staring directly into our eyes for long stretches as she asked all sorts of strange questions, trying to learn our tells. I had created a monster.

Meaning, she had been studying us so closely that I had lost count of the number of times she tripped while walking. So, seeing her mother suddenly swat at Talon's face was entirely shocking for the obvious reasons —he was liable to rip your face off on instinct—but also because seeing anyone suddenly strike another person in a civil conversation was strange.

What had been in those damned berries? It was almost as if she had a slight alcohol buzz. No wonder she hadn't wanted to share with Alice.

Before any of us could react, Alvara was striding down the path and around a corner in the thick trees where a small, almost invisible path veered off the main road.

I cursed, then winced at Alice. "Sorry."

Then we were all following to get a glimpse of the Seer's house, but not close enough so as to risk ruining Alvara's plan. I glanced around the bend to see Alvara striding down the end of an overgrown path with an old house at the end.

I shared a long look with Gunnar. He snorted. "Fixer upper," he said sarcastically.

I agreed with him but didn't voice it with Alice standing beside us. No need to concern her, but it looked like the Seer had been gone for a good long while.

We leaned back out of sight and waited for five excruciating minutes, and I began to wonder if Alvara had been right. Then I stepped onto the hidden path and began calmly walking towards the house. No use marching and making it look like an invasion—even if Alvara had succeeded and warned the Seer ahead of time.

As unlikely as it seemed, the fact that Alvara hadn't returned kind of lent credit to her claim.

The Seer was in. Walk-ins welcome.

The trees cleared around the house, giving me a clear view of the mountain in the distance. I strolled up to the house, which looked well-built and sturdy, if a little neglected in recent years. My shoulders were tense for some reason, so I scanned the area. The yard was overgrown and uncared for, but I didn't see anything sinister. Perhaps it was all for show—to make people assume she wasn't home. Because being a Seer probably attracted all sorts of unwanted requests. People seeking to hear their fortunes, and more often than not, being unhappy with the answers.

Seeing no danger, I resolved to knock on the door.

But it suddenly banged open and Alvara hurried out, holding her fist at her side as if carrying something, even though I couldn't see anything. She grabbed my hand and tugged me down the steps, hurrying from the house.

"Someone's been here, rummaging through my things. I think they know," she whispered, skidding to a stop in the yard and staring at me with terrified eyes.

29

I stared back at her, my shoulders suddenly twitching. "What do you mean, rummaging through your things?" I asked, confused by both her panic and her comment.

"*I* am the Seer, Wylde. Although it's more accurate to say I am a Hearer. She is a Seer," Alvara snapped impatiently, pointing at Alice. "But I didn't anticipate that before coming here. She never showed any of the signs. Perhaps bringing her here was a mistake. It fully woke her gift. You need to get out of here, all of you!" She was flinching and jerking her eyes at even the slightest change of wind from the brush or trees, no matter how innocent, holding out her fist.

"What do you mean, you are the Seer? You could have told me that hours ago!"

"I didn't want to waste my time answering a hundred asinine questions on our walk here. On my last walk..." She cut off abruptly, staring at Alice.

"It's okay, mother. I can see," the little girl whispered. "I understand," she said miserably.

Alvara let out a helpless sob and then wrapped her daughter in a desperate hug. After a few moments, she urgently guided Alice well away from her. Alice didn't take offense, seeming to understand. She backed right the hell away, actually. Alvara locked eyes with me, and I could see they were extremely dilated.

"The berries! What were those berries?" I demanded, shaking her shoulders angrily.

"I knew the moment I entered Fae that I was going to die. If I had known so before I made our deal, I might have..." she let out another whimper, blinking rapidly at Alice. "I would have been better," she whispered, her face contorting with agony. "Please forgive me, my sweet."

"Oh, mama," Alice gasped helplessly, physically shaking as she broke down in ugly tears.

I shook Alvara again, my own eyes misting up at the tide of emotions but not understanding why. "What do you mean, Alvara?" I begged.

She composed herself with a nod. "I heard it in the trees, in the grass, and on the wind. It is my gift—to Hear. The Land of Fae whispered to me of my death, but by then it was too late to change anything. I knew this story was not a happily ever after. Not for me. But...by fulfilling our bargain, perhaps it could be a happily ever after for Alice..." she sobbed. "I help you, you help my daughter—keep her safe after I'm gone." Alvara whimpered, holding out her closed fist like she was handing me a bag. I had forgotten all about it. I heard a faint tinkling of chains below her fist but saw nothing. "Take it and run. I didn't think it would happen this fast, which is why I took the berries. To give you time to run."

Poison. The berries had been poison.

"This can only be passed from one hand to another in death, and I do not know how to read it. Then again, I *Hear* things, and it is hard to Hear a book. Perhaps you need a Seer," she whispered, smiling sadly at her daughter.

I reached out a hand to accept the unseen item and get us the hell out of here. Then her words hit me. "Wait. It can only be passed in death?"

"Yes. I always knew I would need to deliver it one day, just like my husband delivered it to me. It is fitting that we share the same fate."

I noticed she was sweating, and her lips were still stained with berry juice. "Why would you do all this, Alvara? You have a daughter!" I hissed. Alice let out a squeak that made me wince with shame.

"And if the Catalyst doesn't read this book...there will be no world where my daughter will ever be safe," she said, looking me right in the eyes.

I backed up a step, shaking my head. "That's insane. You didn't have to eat the berries!"

"It's not the berries that kill her," Alice whispered, in probably the most forlorn and terrified voice I'd ever heard, making me suddenly very uncertain of the forest around us.

Alvara nodded. "The berries dull the pain, but they are also a poison. It let me control the time enough to give you this, first," she said, holding out her arm. "Sometimes a parent must shoulder a heavy burden to keep their children safe, no matter how horrifying it may seem at the time. I'm sure your parents knew something of this." She held out the closed fist, shaking it, and despite seeing nothing, I could tell she held something with weight.

Gunnar growled. "Something is wrong..." he said, scanning the trees. "We are not alone."

Talon hissed, facing the opposite side of the forest. "I don't see anything, but I think he's right..." he snarled. "We need to leave. Now."

Gunnar abruptly roared and Alvara gasped, but I had been too busy staring at her hand to see what had happened. I looked up at Alvara to see a wicked dagger buried in her chest. She dropped whatever it was that she had been holding and fell to her knees. I saw the grass flatten beneath the unseen item, but Alice suddenly snatched it up, backing away from her mother, shaking her head in horror, unable to look away, her eyes as wide as saucers.

She looked hysterical as she continued backing up into the brush.

I began running towards her, ready to scoop her up and get her clear of whoever had thrown the dagger. "Alice! We need to get out of—"

A portal appeared behind her, and a gauntleted hand grabbed her by her ponytail.

She was shrieking and clawing, swinging and screaming against the armored hand, dropping the paper with the crude sun symbol from her pocket in the process. I heard a very familiar laughter from within the portal. I dove for her, shouting, but the attacker yanked her backwards.

"MAMAAAAAA!" She screamed from the bottom of her soul.

And the portal winked out right before my eyes, her desperate plea shredding my heart to golden ribbons, just like those tied into Gunnar's fur. I cursed and swore just as Talon and Gunnar yowled and howled.

"MORDRED!" I roared, my ears throbbing as I panted, swatting at the ground and trying desperately to find the invisible object Alice had been holding, wondering if she had dropped it like she had the drawing. I shoved the drawing into my pocket, promising myself I would give it back to Alice when I ripped Mordred's scalp off. Taking a little girl? There was a special place in Hell for people like that.

And since I was the Guide to Hell, I knew just how to get there.

I didn't find the invisible book anywhere and cursed. Alice must have still been holding it when she'd been abducted. One thing I knew for certain—Mordred was behind it. I would recognize that laugh anywhere. Now he had the invisible Good Book of Catalyst-ism that was supposed to help me understand my curse.

Alvara had claimed someone had been in her home, rummaging through her things, and Mordred had just kidnapped Alice.

Had...he wanted the book? Or just to piss in my cereal?

Alvara choked, and I gasped to realize she was still alive. I scrambled over to her, lifting up her head and trying to ease her pain. I shook my head angrily. "Why, Alvara? Why?"

She coughed, smiling even though she was in agonizing pain from the long dagger in her chest. "Save...Alice." And then she lifted a weak finger to point behind us. I heard a sound, but Gunnar and Talon were already on top of it, snarling and growling. Alvara let out a tired sigh, and then died, dropping her hand.

I snarled as I spun to face the new threat along with my two best friends.

I blinked incredulously, wondering if I had been bumped on the head. Because I was staring at what appeared to be my first Knight of the Round Table.

And I was very glad Alice wasn't standing beside me as I formed a ball of molten flame over my palm. Because this next part *really* would have ruined her concept of happily ever after.

I hurled it as hard as I could at the Black Knight's pretty little breastplate.

30

I had made sure not to accidentally release my tentative grip on my Fae magic as I tapped into Old Faithful—my wizard's magic. I was a veritable beast when I actually let myself cut loose with my wizard's gift. I knew how to use it as easily as breathing. Simply put, it was solid, dependable, and rarely let me down—

My fire splashed over the Black Knight like a cool summer breeze. He didn't even seem to acknowledge it. The droplets of fire struck his armor and any exposed flesh like water on a hot griddle, rolling off instantly.

"Umm...he's warded against wizard's magic, guys," I said lamely. "In case you missed that."

Gunnar extended his claws, snarling at the steadily approaching Black Knight who had seemed to step out of thin air ten paces away. He was a big son of a bitch, and his armor only made him more imposing. "Why did he attack us? Didn't you and Pan save him? Or is this a different one?"

"How the hell should I know? I never actually met him. He ran away from the cave before we got there, remember? Unless Mordred found his brothers and freed them, this has to be him."

"Hand over the book or the child will die," he said in a calm, low voice, walking our way.

Had...Alice lied to him? Pretended not to have it and using its invisible bag to her advantage? Or was it really lying in the brush somewhere and I had missed it?

"Return the child and we will only stuff one of your own gauntlets up your ass," Gunnar snarled, snapping his teeth loudly.

Talon coughed his agreement, a throaty yowl bubbling up from his lips as he crouched, ears tucked back, and eyes narrowed. "Fuck this guy."

The Black Knight didn't respond, and he didn't slow down, his heavy boots thumping into the earth and leaving tendrils of smoke with each step—grass and flowers beneath his iron boots withered.

Iron. Holy shit. I hadn't considered that. Iron was poison to Fae, and this motherfucker was stomping around without concern—an armored virus, a cancer.

The Knight finally halted a few paces away from us and lifted his Medieval visor, reminding me of a modern-day policeman lifting his aviator sunglasses at a traffic stop. He had iron gray eyes and aged skin, but that was all I could make out. Those eyes were resolute and steadfast. "None shall stand between me and my duty to King Mordred."

Wait, what?

Gunnar didn't bother with questions.

He closed the distance and clawed the Black Knight across the chest. An explosion of white sparks marked the contact between Gunnar's quartz-like claws and the iron armor, shredding it to—

But the armor did not shred. And it did not scratch. The Knight didn't even stumble at the physical force of the blow. Though it did knock his visor closed with a metallic *clang*.

I had seen Gunnar knock people's heads off with a casual backhanded slap.

I stared at the strange wet symbol that looked to have been recently painted on the Knight's chest. It was one of the same runes I had seen on the Round Table when I had spoken each Knight's name, but it had been inverted, and I couldn't immediately recall which Knight it had belonged to.

The Knight glanced down at his chest curiously.

I caught a faint fluttering motion from the corner of my eye and saw one of the golden ribbons on Gunnar's neck come loose, twirling up into the air. The Knight absently brushed at his chest, and I caught a long, golden hair stuck between the plates of his knuckle. A strand of Alice's hair. Time seemed to slow in my mind.

This son-of-a-bitch Knight was helping Mordred—kidnapping Alice for him—and he had murdered Alvara, Alice's mother.

Alice had met her Knight...

And was now an orphan.

This was supposed to be one of the good guys. That inverted rune had changed him. I could almost see distorted waves of power emanating from it, but I couldn't quite focus on them.

I was *looking*, not *seeing*, as Alice had tried to teach me. *You're trying too hard...*

If I could just relax and—

"For Avalon," the Black Knight growled, snapping me out of my daze. And then he stabbed Gunnar through the heart before Gunnar had even fully recoiled from his attack. The blow lifted the seven-foot-tall werewolf off his feet a few inches.

My blood froze to ice in disbelief. Gunnar dropped to the ground as the Knight yanked his sword back. My best friend's white fur was covered in blood, and he stared up at me with one eye, looking desperate and stunned. "Name my pups—" but he cut off with a violent, bloody cough, and his head flopped to the side, lifelessly.

I heard a high-pitched keening sound in my ears, and my vision began to tunnel, framing Gunnar's lifeless, bloody body in vibrant detail. A blue leaf fluttered onto his wound, covering it from view. I waited for him to swat it away...

But he didn't. He would never swat anything ever again. Would never meet his pups. Wouldn't get to name them...

I began panting, unable to turn away as I stared at my dead friend. My brain quite literally couldn't process anything as I stared at a strand of his bloody saliva settling on one of Alice's golden ribbons.

Something clicked inside of me...

But it wasn't enough to save Gunnar. Wasn't even enough to let me touch my Fae magic.

My world flashed white, and I had no conscious control of what I did next. Every single drop of wizard's magic I could grasp suddenly ripped out of me in one concussive blast of lava that splashed the Knight like a tidal wave. I collapsed to my knees, entirely spent, struggling to breathe or even hold myself up as my arms violently shook in protest.

I managed to see the result of my outburst splash over the Black Knight. Like earlier, it had no effect, simply bouncing off of him. He turned to look at me with his cold iron helmet, but all I saw were shadows behind those narrow slits where his eyes should have been.

I couldn't even look my best friend's killer in the eyes.

Something about his posture told me he did not find joy in the task ahead, but more like a man committed to do a job he had agreed to do.

The ground around him hissed and smoked, covered in my lava, and I desperately hoped that at least the heat would cook him alive inside his iron suit. He flicked a bit off of his pauldrons, grunting in annoyance.

I tried desperately to call upon my Fae magic, but I couldn't. In fact, I was surprised to learn that I had managed to maintain my grip on it at all. Thanks to whatever Alice had done on our walk, and the several clicking sensations I had felt, my grip was now stronger, requiring less focus to maintain. But it was still useless.

Despite being unable to do anything with the Fae Magic, I could at least sense it. The air veritably hummed with raw power, begging to be used, but it was all smoke and lights to me—ephemeral. Being able to see it more clearly and not use it only made everything worse. So close, yet so far away...

It felt like Wylde was screaming something at me, but I couldn't hear anything through the high-pitched buzzing still filling my ears. And I almost vomited when I realized my hand rested in a puddle of Gunnar's blood.

*Name the pups...*his blank stare taunted me. Name them what? How was I supposed to go on without my best friend?

Talon startled me by diving in front of me, stabbing his spear straight at the Knight's face, managing to knock the Knight back.

I shook my head, realizing that it would do no one any good if I just gave up right now. Too many people needed me—Alice, Alex, Gunnar's pups...and dozens more.

I was about to attempt climbing to my feet when Talon fell on top of me, knocking me back down. A sudden burst of adrenaline made me scramble, wanting to help him back up so we could fight or flee, but I only succeeded in rolling him onto his back.

The Knight's sword had gored directly through his heart before Talon had knocked him back.

"Tal..." I whispered his childhood nickname, shaking him desperately. "I'll get you some Fae catnip for Yulemas. I promise!" I rasped, hardly able to see through my tears.

My jostling of him knocked loose a single Fae catnip seed from his belt —a seed he must have smuggled from the pod he had been getting into during our walk.

I began shaking him harder, growing angry. "You can't just die like this, Tal! I'll let you open the presents early! Just...please don't die, Tal...You're my last real friend..."

But Tal's eyes were already glazing over, denying me the chance to hear his last words. The buzzing sound in my ears instantly intensified, modifying into a scream of words repeated over and over again.

Ohmygodohmygodohmygod...

Followed by an echoing, creaking, rushing sound. Like ocean waves in a sea cavern. As I stared into Talon's glazed eyes, memories began hammering me like a drum. The roaring in the caves of my ears grew louder—loud enough for my vision to waver—and I realized it didn't sound like waves.

It sounded like a wild, savage, primitive man mourning his two brothers—the only family he had left.

And more visions began to flicker across my mind. Snapshots of childhood, moving as rapidly as leaves in a windstorm, zipping back and forth across my mind, to the song of a man screaming from the very depths of his soul.

Something was happening...

But the sound and sensations abruptly ceased as I saw the Black Knight climb to his feet, seeming none the worse for wear.

I had been so close! What had that been?

The Black Knight looked at me warily, as if having sensed me doing something, and then he relaxed, shaking off his gauntlets and wiping his sword on a black cloth tied at his waist. Then he began walking towards me.

I tried scooting backwards, thinking frantically, but bumped into Gunnar's body and recoiled in horror. Like with the fight against Thor, I had no physical strength left to try using my Hammer—not that it would have done me any good—and I didn't dare risk using my Horseman's Mask when it was already broken. I couldn't even climb to my feet, I was so shaken. I had almost felt something with my Fae Magic, but it had sputtered out upon seeing the Knight stand back up.

At the understanding that this man was practically invincible to our attacks.

The knight dipped his head at Talon's dead body. "Well met, warrior." Then he looked down at me, his black armor glinting against the overcast sky. A fluttering piece of paper caught his eyes and he stomped on it by reflex. He glanced down and grunted. "You have my sketch from the cave," he said, turning back to look at me.

I yanked it out from under his boot, not having realized I'd dropped it. The Knight made no move to stop me.

"No matter. You will see the real Stonehenge soon enough, because King Mordred requests your presence there." I stared up at him, gripping the paper in my fingers. He had drawn a crude depiction of Stonehenge in Pan's cave? I had thought it was a sun.

"Mordred claims you have two items that belong to him. I will take you to retrieve them from wherever you have hidden them." He was talking about Excalibur and the Round Table. "Come peacefully, or there will be trouble."

Peacefully. I had once known the meaning of that word. But it was long forgotten, now.

"Is that why you took the child?" I demanded.

He didn't answer for a few moments, as if debating how much to share. "Mordred did not want you to obtain a book. He didn't believe I could capture or defeat you, so I was sent to destroy the book. When I killed the woman, I saw the child dive for the book, so I took her. But she did not have it either, so I returned." He continued staring down at me. "Now, she is leverage for your cooperation."

"I would rather die," I whispered, staring over at Talon and Gunnar, knowing I had nothing left up my sleeve. Even if I could have used my

Hammer, I had no faith in its ability to harm him. Mordred had juiced him up somehow. Turned a Good Knight into a Knightmare.

He wasn't even breathing heavily.

"Then the little girl shall die," the Black Knight said in a toneless voice. "And you will still be taken to Stonehenge."

"What the fuck is *wrong* with you?" I whispered. "People tell stories about King Arthur's Knights! They call you heroes!"

The Knight lowered his sword, looking mildly ashamed for the first time. "Arthur is dead, and Mordred is the last of the Pendragon bloodline. I have no say in the matter. I fled a cave in search of my brothers, and Mordred found me. Gave me a new purpose—an oath sworn by blood."

I looked sharply at the inverted rune on his armor, my mind slowly whirring to life. Blood oath. Did he mean a Blood Debt? Where the Knight had to obey? It sure sounded like it.

It was also confirmation that this was the Knight I had inadvertently saved.

That Pan had nursed back to health.

Only so he could come back and kill my two best friends.

"It is time," The Black Knight said, sheathing his sword and holding out his large, gauntleted fist. "You have no more protectors, and the child's life depends on your cooperation."

A sudden bolt of lightning struck down from the overcast sky, even though the white clouds held no rain. The unseen blast of lightning shattered a tree fifty feet away, and we both turned to see hundreds of blue leaves drifting to the ground. Nothing else moved, and the woods grew as silent as a tomb.

I slowly looked back at the Black Knight—who had settled his gauntleted hand back on the hilt of his sword—still glaring at the source of the explosion. He finally turned back to me to find me smiling at him.

"You forgot about my unicorn," I said with a slow, malevolent smile.

31

The Black Knight suddenly reached out to grab me with his gauntleted fist, finished with asking nicely, I guessed. A Gateway erupted beside us, and a demon of a man struck the Knight in a flying tackle, wrapping his arms around the Knight's armored waist.

Alex! Godsdamned Alex! Like a Knight in shining...well, Under Armour.

Because he wore a spandex *Under Armour* muscle shirt—the *fabulous* edition.

And he was liberally coated with rainbow spatter. Like, *everywhere.* Knowing that it was actually rainbow blood and guts made it turn from humorous to nauseating. He was covered in gore from killing rainbows around the world. That was a lot of pissed-off leprechauns and broken-hearted children.

The Knight grunted in annoyance but didn't appear fazed by the blow.

However, despite appearances, Alex hadn't actually been trying to tackle him. In fact, he had already rotated to hug him from behind. Unfortunately, the Knight was slow on the uptake as he swung his gloved fists down to where Alex's head had just been pressed against his abdomen.

Ultimately, I watched as the Black Knight double hammer-fisted himself in the nuts with his Avalonian Gauntlets of Injustice. He made a very satisfying keening whine as his knees buckled.

Like he was trying out for the WWE, Alex arched his back and straightened his legs in an improvised belly-to-back suplex move, hoisting the Knight up off his feet and then backwards towards the ground in an attempt to break his neck. The Knight instinctively flung up his hands to protect his head and break his fall, but...

Grimm—also entirely covered with gore from every color of the rainbow—abruptly tagged himself into the wrestling ring, turning the fight into the Tag Team to end all Tag Teams.

Alex's Knight-Breaker Suplex became a Unicorn Pinwheel as Alex adjusted course, as if he had intended it all along, and slammed the Black Knight onto Grimm's impaler-bone, hanging him out to cry—which the Knight definitely did. The barbed horn ripped straight through the knight's armor like a knife through butter, unlike how Gunnar's claws and Talon's spear had failed to leave a mark.

Grimm snarled at the Knight dangling from his forehead. "Feel the colors of pain, meatsack!"

Alex released him, and then glanced back at me to make sure I was alright. I gave him a weak thumbs up. Then his eyes settled on Talon and he gasped. Then upon Gunnar and he froze.

His hands fell loosely to his sides as he jerkily shook his head back and forth in denial.

Despite the glistening tears in his eyes, I watched as a deep, inner fury was born, and a flicker of fear rushed over me at the potential ramifications...

"No, no, NO!" Alex abruptly roared, his knuckles cracking as he clenched his fists. "He was going to be a father! A boy needs his father!"

My ears actually popped at the volume of his sudden shout. He rounded on the Knight—who was still struggling upside down on Grimm's horn, somehow not yet dead. Mordred had warned me about the Knights, and I had known they were deadly, but everyone had undersold these tin cans. This was just ridiculous. How was he still alive?

Alex apparently wanted to develop a hypothesis to answer that question.

He walked up and kicked the Knight's helmet off his head, but since he was still facing the wrong way, I couldn't see his face. Alex then began pummeling the upside-down Knight's back with the meat of his fists, hammering him further and further down Grimm's barbed horn. The Knight gasped and wheezed and cried out for every inch Alex gave him.

Heh.

But Grimm didn't let Alex have all the fun. Every time Alex slammed his fists down, the Knight slid a little bit closer to Grimm's snapping teeth. Alex then began kicking the Knight in the back of the head again and again, as if to help Grimm get that bite he was craving. Alex was screaming and panting incoherently—a mindless blood rage—the entire time.

I couldn't yet stand, but I don't think I would have even if I could. This prick had killed Talon and Gunnar for no other reason than that they were in the way.

Grimm finally flung his head and sent the Knight flying into a tree trunk and that stopped him cold. You know, since he hit the tree teeth-first.

"It's not working," Grimm snarled to Alex. "Let me have a go at him." And he pawed at the ground with a hoof, emitting embers and sparks, even though we were on dirt and dead grass.

Indeed, the Knight was sitting back up, spitting out a bloody tooth. What the fuck? He had close-cropped, iron-gray hair to match his eyes, and a hard, cinder-block face. And he didn't even seem to have a headache. But he didn't immediately get up, either.

"I will kill him," Alex swore in a low tone. "I will destroy him," he added, his shoulders rising and falling rapidly as he clenched his knuckles at his sides.

I briefly wondered why Alex hadn't already experienced a change—the Land of the Fae bringing out his Wild Side like it did for everyone else who came here. Because with his current storm of rage, it was going to happen any second. And he was already scary as hell. What would his Wild Side be like? And I was in no position to contain him. We needed to get out of here. As far away from this Knight as possible.

"You don't have the power, Alex," I whispered, tears spilling down my cheeks. "You're not really even hurting him."

Alex had turned to stare at me, a helpless look on his face, when something beside Grimm caught his eye. He stiffened, staring down at my Darling and Dear satchel that had fallen to the ground at some point in their fight with the Knight. I almost let out a sob of relief to see they hadn't lost it, but that sob died away when I saw that something had fallen out of my bag.

Which...was impossible. Things literally couldn't fall out of my bag. At least no important things. Random mundane things, sure, but never anything that I wanted to be kept safe.

Like...the Hand of God, for example.

Yet there it was.

The glass pyramid sat atop a few blue leaves, looking like an unwrapped Yulemas present. And Alex claimed the present for himself before I could do anything to stop him.

He flicked the tip of the pyramid up, revealing a cap that I hadn't known could be flipped up like that anymore, and promptly dumped the contents—powdered stone of great significance—over his head. The dust swirled around him, clinging to every square inch of his body in a very unnatural way. Then I watched it slowly sink *into* his skin, and my heart rate spiked in alarm.

I lost my ever-loving shit. "What that *hell* are you doing?!" I shouted at him, both furious and terrified of the repercussions.

He gently set down the now-empty glass pyramid and met my eyes. "I will not let this go unavenged, no matter what it costs me. Gunnar's children need to know their father's murderer paid for his crimes. I will pay this price. Calvin and Makayla Randulf will have their justice."

Those words stopped me cold. And I felt another clicking sensation in my mind, this one significantly louder. But it wasn't as important as what Alex had just said. Nothing was as important as what Alex had just said.

"Calvin and Makayla..." I whispered, spotting a golden ribbon that had fallen loose and was now sitting at my side.

Alex glanced at me, frowning. "Gunnar didn't tell you?" he asked. "They want to name the twins after your parents."

I opened my mouth to say something, but nothing came out. I picked up the ribbon, wrapping it around my finger absently. Something to distract my thoughts. "Oh..." I finally said. I turned to stare at Gunnar, sniffling. "I am godfather to...Calvin and Makayla," I said woodenly, testing it out on my tongue. "Gunnar...didn't have time to tell me that." I said, thinking back on his last words. The sentence he never completed. *Name the pups...Calvin and Makayla.*

"I thought you knew," Alex murmured, sounding embarrassed.

I shook my head numbly. Then I heard the Knight standing up, spitting out more blood.

I shook my head harder, snapping myself out of it. I turned to Alex with my best dad glare. "You can't just become a Maker, Alex!" I said, indicating the now-empty Hand of God. And probably not by dumping the freaking dust on his skin, either. There were rituals and shit to observe. None of this reckless, experimental—

Then my words hit me. One actually could *just become* a Maker. My parents had done exactly that by experimenting on me right before they died. And another very strange thought crawled up into my noggin. Had... my parents made me a Maker as...a test run. For this moment? They had told me that Alex was vital to me somehow.

Except they had also told me Talon was vital, and he was now dead at my feet.

And that Carl was vital, but he had gone back home for an indeterminate length of time.

But...Alex was best friends with Ruin—an untethered Beast. Technically, it could work.

The three of us had entirely forgotten about the Black Knight, but we sure noticed him suddenly swinging his sword at Alex in a powerful, overhead swing, like he was wielding an executioner's axe. His mouth was wide open as the blade began to fall from over his head, and his numerous missing teeth made his mouth resemble a can-opener.

Not again, I thought to myself, and I flung my hand out at the Knight to protect my son, begging for any scrap of power my body could draw out.

I felt power suddenly rip out of me, and I gasped. My Fae magic! But it didn't go towards the Knight, blasting him back to Camelot like I would have preferred.

It connected with the dust coating Alex—the Hand of God—and I saw his skin suddenly change, turning into rough iron. Alex had flung up his hand to catch the blade in his open palm, and the sword struck it with a piercing *clang*, bending at a ninety-degree angle.

I grunted, not having intended anything of the sort, and knowing I couldn't have done so if I had tried.

"Sweet," Grimm commented, seeming to smile. "Think this is his Wild Side or was it that magic cocaine?" he asked, lowering his horn for me to grab and hoist myself back to my feet.

"I have no idea, man," I whispered, grunting as I pulled myself to my feet and leaned on my unicorn like a badass fairy godfather. Too bad I didn't have a cigar.

Alex head-butted the Knight in a whip-quick blur and yanked the bent sword out of his grip. The Knight snarled, swinging a fist at Alex's unprotected face. Alex calmly leaned to the side and sliced off the offending hand.

"For Calvin," Alex growled.

The Knight gasped in disbelief, reaching out to grasp his stump with the other hand.

But Alex was faster, and cut that hand off, too.

"For Makayla," he added, sounding calmer.

The Knight stumbled backwards, staring down at his missing hands in horror, likely wondering how he could cauterize them before he bled out.

Alex inspected the bent sword in his fist, likely considering how it had so easily cut through the Knight's armor when nothing else—except Grimm's horn—had been as successful. Instead of tossing it, he kept it.

I placed a hand on his shoulder before he decided to punish the Knight further. "That will do. A handless Knight is hardly a threat. And I think sending him back to Mordred looking like this will buy us some time."

Alex nodded obediently and stepped aside.

The Knight was staring at us, looking stunned to have suffered such an epic defeat from a boy with no armor and no weapon, when he had defeated two massive furred warriors with single blows.

I stared down at my two best friends, grimacing at one of those golden ribbons, now covered in Gunnar's blood. I still had one wrapped around my finger. I looked back up at the Knight and spoke in a low growl. "Give Mordred a message. Tell him we will meet him at Stonehenge soon after the Rainbow King takes over the skies. But not to *give* him anything. To destroy him."

The Knight gave a jerking nod and touched his bloody stump to the inverted rune on his breastplate with a sickening squelch. Then he simply winked out of view.

I narrowed my eyes at that. It was probably something I was going to have to look out for if we ran into any more Knights. They could Travel, somehow.

32

I turned to see Alex shaking his hand. The iron-like skin flaked off like dried mud and he flexed his fingers experimentally. "Thanks."

I grunted. "It was all I could manage. If you two hadn't gotten here when you did..." I was silent for a few moments. Then I caught them up to speed with my day—all the dirty details. Alex had been especially horrified to hear about Alice. Judging by the look on his face, I wondered what else he might have decided to cut off the Knight if he had known about that a few minutes ago.

Once he had calmed down, we all stared down at Gunnar and Talon, thinking sad, dark thoughts.

My eyes kept latching onto the golden ribbons, and it made my soul want to just burn away to ashes. Alice was out there in Mordred's clutches —probably terrified out of her mind after witnessing her mother's death only moments before. Whether she had the apparently invisible book Alvara had tried to give me or not, I was going to go save her.

In fact, I realized I wasn't even concerned about the book. It could burn for all I cared. As long as I saved Alice—the last remaining member of the party I had taken to Fae—it was worth it. Otherwise, this had all been a complete failure. I needed to save the little detective.

Because the world was a brighter place with her in it.

To save Alice, I had a job to do. Repair the Bifröst. And Alex probably wasn't going to like my plan for that.

Mordred had somehow brainwashed the Knight with a Blood Debt, forcing him to hunt me down and bring me to Stonehenge with Excalibur and the Round Table neatly gift-wrapped for the new King of Camelot. Which meant Mordred had learned some things about me—to know I had been heading to the Seer's house meant the Knight had been spying on me, probably with that Traveling ability we had seen.

Mordred obviously wanted me alive, though, or the Knight would have killed me like he had my friends. He wanted me at Stonehenge—the same place the Knight had been doodling on the paper now folded up in my pocket.

I thought about it for a few moments, grew aggravated, and decided I no longer cared why.

They wanted me at Stonehenge? I'd go to Stonehenge, nab the girl, and kill everyone who looked at me sideways.

"We...have the rainbows," Alex said, staring down at Gunnar and Talon's lifeless bodies.

I nodded, absently wondering how exactly that worked. Would I get rainbow guts on my hand every time I reached inside or was it like the other things I stored in there?

But Alex had a point. To save Alice, I needed to first fix the Bifröst—because the Aesir could kick off Ragnarok any moment. Or Thor could pay me another visit. He now had two reasons to hate me. For humiliating him, and then winning the *#1 Son Award* from Odin.

To repair the Bifröst, I needed to get rid of this stupid block. Despite somehow casting my Fae magic at Alex to give him the strength to fight the Knight, I hadn't been able to tap into it a second time. I felt stronger, my senses sharper, but the block was still there.

I studied Alex thoughtfully. Something about him and the Hand of God had let me inadvertently tap into my Fae magic. If that was the only tool I had, it would have to be enough. There was no other option on the table.

"What does Mordred even want with you at Stonehenge?" Alex asked.

"Excalibur is in the Armory, and the Round Table is too big to just carry around on your back."

My eyes widened, and I shoved my hand into my satchel desperately. I finally found the small glass vial and let out a breath of relief. What if it had broken? I held it up to Alex. "Ichor from the Round Table," I told him.

He nodded knowingly. "Just like what you lured Mordred with at the Dueling Grounds." I nodded. "He probably wants a bit more than a vial. And you already baited him with that once."

I grunted. "It's all I brought," I told him, not wanting to explain that the rest was inside the War Hammer. Not after I had seen him dump the Hand of God all over himself. He might go find a rubber hose to siphon the ichor from the Hammer if I turned around to take a leak.

"Alex?" I asked, shoving the vial into my Fendi satchel.

"Yes?" he answered, sounding as if he knew what was coming just by my tone.

"We need to talk about that stupid thing you did. With my magic pyramid," I clarified, brandishing it at him.

"Yeah, I got caught up in the—"

"I think I can do you one better," I interrupted, with a faint smile.

He frowned, narrowing his eyes suspiciously. "Oh?"

I told him my idea. Grimm let out a long whistle.

Alex ran a hand through his hair. "You sure? What if it, I don't know, burns me alive or something?"

I shrugged. "Life's about new experiences. And you brought this on yourself," I reminded him. "When you played with my toys without asking permission."

He let out a breath. "Okay. That's fair."

Grimm shook his head at the two of us. "You're both insane."

We ignored the unicorn.

With that matter settled, I glanced over at my Darling and Dear satchel on the ground. It was high-time I consolidated my bags and took back the magic one. Something about wearing it just made me feel better, and Alex had proven he wasn't responsible enough to hold it.

The only reason I hadn't berated him about it was because...maybe he had been right. Things didn't just fall out of my satchel. And the Hand of

God had worked on him—at the very least, it had worked as some kind of focal point for my Fae magic—when not much else had helped so far, despite all those pleasant *clicking* sensations getting my hopes up.

Alex stepped in front of me, his palm resting against my chest. "Let me put this stuff in your satchel, Nate. That's not important right now, and I can easily do it. You should...probably say goodbye to Gunnar and Talon," he said, his voice cracking at the end. He lowered his eyes, and I saw that they were bloodshot.

I wanted to argue...

Except he was right. I'd been avoiding looking at them. I felt too raw. It didn't actually even feel real. How could it? Their deaths had been so swift, when I was used to *them* being the swift executioners. If they had died during some long, drawn-out battle, I would have been able to process it easier, but this...

It was going to take me a while. I handed Alex my Fendi satchel, feeling like I had just handed him a barbell that had been hanging on my shoulders. He scooped up the Knight's bent sword—for obvious reasons, the Knight had been unable to pick it up to take with him when he fled—and shoved it into the Darling and Dear satchel.

He noticed my attention. "Could come in handy," he said with a shrug. Then he stopped. "Heh. Handy..." then he shook his head clear of the macabre thought, resuming his work.

I shared a long look with Grimm. "You're a bad influence on him."

"Whatever you say, Fairy Godfather."

I took three deep breaths, and then finally looked at my two childhood friends. I stared at them, letting memories roll over me until I felt raw. I don't know how long I sat there, but Alex stepped up beside me at one point and carefully set the Darling and Dear satchel down by my side. I wiped at my face and glanced at the logo on my satchel. What were the odds that I would meet the crazy bastards at that bar when drinking with Anubis—

I froze, my breath catching. *Anubis.*

Thanks to Charon, he owed me two get out of Hell free cards...Two *come back to life*, cards.

Could...I use them to bring Gunnar and Talon back to life? I'd intended them for my parents, but the more I thought about it, I wasn't sure I wanted them back. Not because I hated them or anything, but...

I'd made my own family with Gunnar and Talon. Hell, with Pan dead, I was Talon's *only* family. And Gunnar was about to have a family of his own —a little Calvin and Makayla of his own—named after the two who had given him a new home as a child.

If I brought my parents back, I knew I would quickly grow to hate them, because I would always see the loss of Gunnar and Talon when I looked at them. And they would resent me for not choosing Gunnar, especially when they saw Ashley carting little Calvin and Makayla off to preschool without their father.

But bringing back my two best friends...

I wouldn't have that feeling of regret, because my parents had died a long time ago.

Could the solution really be that simple? Had Anubis really meant I could use them like this? The only problem was that I hadn't fulfilled my part of the bargain yet.

And there was always the risk that bringing back the dead was a mistake. What if they came back...different? I knew you needed to keep bodies cold, like those cryogenic—

I looked up at Alex sharply, making him flinch. I made my decision. "We need to bring them with us," I rasped, smiling crookedly as I pointed to the mountain in the distance. The probably very *cold* mountain. "I think I might have a way to bring them back."

Grimm neighed uncomfortably, and Alex grimaced. "Nate...are you sure about this? I'm still trying to process their deaths, too, but bringing them back...it sounds like a really bad idea."

"Never quit never quitting," I told him confidently. "Cheat like a bastard to win like a king."

He nodded uncertainly. "Okay. Do you have a change of clothes in your bag? I checked and couldn't find one," he admitted.

I studied him pensively before nodding. "Sure. Let me just check."

I shoved my hand inside, verifying that the three unclaimed Horsemen Masks, the Hourglass, and the Hand of God were all inside. I masked my relief, glad that Alex hadn't managed to nick anything else from my nuclear storehouse. I pulled out a pair of jeans and a plain tee.

"Here," I said, throwing the clothes at him. Then I turned to Grimm. "Time to earn your pay," I told him.

He glanced at the four bodies and snorted. "It's going to take two trips..." he said, grimacing.

I nodded. "Take me and Talon, first. Alex can go with Gunnar."

33

As I sat atop the mountain, surrounded by snow, staring out at the Land of Fae surrounding me...I felt entirely alone. I had set Talon beside me, but that only made it worse. Alex and Grimm would be back with Gunnar soon.

But right now, I was entirely alone, and facing a seemingly insurmountable problem.

Fix my Fae magic so I could fix the Bifröst.

As I sat there, thinking hard about any possible options, I realized I was going about it all wrong. I took a deep breath and...I let go of everything. The stress. The blame. The anger. The guilt.

I decided I was done *thinking*. I no longer cared about the problems of the past, my stupid legend, who had lied to this person or that person.

No more pity. No more patience. No more excuses.

It was time to look forward and focus on what mattered, not the things I couldn't change.

It was time to roll my sleeves up. If not now, with my two best friends dead and a little girl kidnapped, when *was* it time?

As I made this decision, I felt something loosen inside of me. An easing. I felt a sudden surge of energy begin to fuel me. I noticed I wasn't alone anymore, but I didn't turn to look. I took a deep breath, staring out at the tapestry before me—the Land of the Fae. Two Ravens circled the peak of the mountain, cawing loudly at me. "What's a nice guy like you doing on a mountain like this?" I asked the Wanderer.

Odin grunted. "Wanted to see you in action," he admitted. "You've got all the ingredients; all you need now is the courage."

I nodded absently, focusing on my breathing. "Stay out of my way...Dean."

I sensed him stiffen at the choice of names. Possibly an olive branch. Possibly.

A moment later, he was gone. At least as far as I could tell. But I was confident he was nearby, watching. It wasn't every day a Bifröst was born.

Grimm landed lightly a few paces away and Alex awkwardly wrestled Gunnar down, doing his best to not drop him or bump his head on a rock. I didn't get up to help him, staring straight ahead and breathing in and out, relaxing my body. I mustn't try too hard.

Alice had taught me that.

Alex set Gunnar on the other side of me from Talon.

I pointed a finger about ten paces away from me. "Sit," I told him softly.

Once he was seated, I finally turned to my two best friends, lying dead beside me. I stared at Gunnar and Talon and let my raw anguish wash over me.

I thought about Pan's unconditional love. His sacrifice.

I thought about Alice, all alone, and terrified. How she had helped me remember to laugh and play, even when things seemed dark after Pan's death.

How I had taught her to lie...

How she had promised me we would find our happily ever after. And how a Knight—a noble character she had been excited to meet—had ruined her happily ever after, flipping the script and murdering her mother right before her eyes. And then he had kidnapped her.

If a Good Knight could turn bad...becoming a knightmare...

Maybe it was time I let the world see what lengths a Wylde boy would go to in order to save a princess.

As these emotions swirled within me, I realized I was panting. I was squeezing fistfuls of snow in my hand, but it didn't melt in my palms.

I glanced down to see that it wasn't snow, but rocks from within the frozen earth. I had squeezed them to powder with my fists. I opened them, letting the dust drift away in the swirling wind atop my mountain. Something about it looked familiar, but since I had decided not to think, I dismissed the stray thought.

That's when I realized I could feel Wylde humming softly in the depths of my soul, drawn out by my raw emotions. My lack of thought.

Star light, star bright, it's okay, I'll be alright... I smiled, letting the melody wash over me.

I thought about Alice telling me I tried too hard, and let my mind relax even further. I set one hand on Talon and the other on Gunnar and tried to remember them as they had been. Their fur tickled my fingers, and I felt tears dripping from my eyes.

Wind began to swirl around us, faster and faster, screaming in the peaks and crevices, falling snowflakes biting into my neck. But I ignored that.

Rather than try to pull Wylde out, I chose to sink down deep within myself.

As above, so below.

And I felt Wylde grasp onto my figurative hand, squeezing.

Because I think I finally understood. There wasn't anything to pull out. Wylde was Nate. Nate was Wylde. I had been trying too hard. Thinking too much. Looking, not seeing. Analyzing, not feeling. Accusing, not accepting.

Pan had Forced me to tap into my Fae magic during our fight, and then he had shocked me with his death.

Then Alice had carefully swept up the shards, showing me how to laugh and play again. And with a single act, Alvara had taught me what parenting truly meant—to make the tough decisions in order to give your child everything they might need to one day make the world a better place. No matter the cost to the parent. Even if the child might not understand for a very long time.

And then Talon and Gunnar had died to protect me, shattering my emotions all over again. Undying loyalty in action.

I had been considering my Fae magic problem like I was rebuilding a house to its former glory. But what if my problem was a little like repairing the Bifröst? Take a bunch of broken pieces, shake them up in a magic sack, and then cast them out into the universe with a ridiculously overpowered blast of magic and hope for the best?

Although I had been broken down, I had grown stronger for it—like a broken bone that had healed back together, stronger around the fracture than anywhere else.

Those breaks were an improvement. I didn't want to simply go back to what I had once been—two separate individuals. Because I wasn't just Wylde. And I wasn't just Nate.

Both of us had *lived*. We had both progressed far beyond who we had once been. We had experienced new things, tasted new pains, loved new loves...

What was the use in living in the past?

We had changed, and so...

I gripped Wylde's hand in a gentle, loving embrace, and then I let him go, refusing to continue being one half of a whole. I rose back up from the depths of my being and let out a figurative breath. And then I waited.

Instead of the familiar clicking sensation, the wall between us shattered, and I felt Wylde let out a deep breath as he slowly filled all the little cracks and holes in my soul. It wasn't a tidal wave of childhood memory. It was a faith of sorts. An acceptance. Because it wasn't about studying all the individual Lego pieces of our two different pasts. Those would be remembered, or they wouldn't.

It was about what beauty we could create with a hodge-podge of random blocks.

Ordo ab chao. Order from chaos.

The only question that mattered was what we wanted to build next.

I took a deep breath, feeling more full—more complete—than I had ever felt before.

My fingers unclenched from the furred bodies beside me, and I lifted my arms towards the sky, smiling as I let my eyes focus on Grimm and then Alex. Night had apparently fallen because the sky was now pitch black.

Grimm and Alex were staring at my hands with wide eyes. I looked up to see that I was holding star light in either fist. I turned back to meet their eyes.

"Let's make a fucking rainbow, boys."

34

I set the star light to either side of me, so I could see better. Then I reached inside the satchel at my feet and began pulling out rainbow guts, humming to myself absently as I worked.

Star light, star bright...

Not wanting to get my hands dirty, I made the rainbow guts inside the satchel begin arranging themselves into something more like a bolt of cloth. I waited a few moments, still humming absently, and then I grabbed one end and pulled it out of the satchel. I was careful not to pull too fast because it took a bit of time for eighty-one dead rainbows—I had counted—to get their act together and join forces. I didn't want it to rip, of course.

That wouldn't do at all.

I reached out and scooped up one of the balls of starlight. Then I massaged it into the new rainbow like I was kneading dough.

The rainbow began to smolder beneath my knuckles, but I continued kneading, feeling sweat pop up across my brow. After a few more moments, the rainbow burst into flame.

I let out a sigh, shaking out my fingers tiredly.

I looked over at Alex and smiled. He was staring at me with wide eyes, muttering in disbelief. "Family," I told him. He nodded, looking determined to make me proud, despite his fear. Good. He would need that for what came next.

I focused on the Maker Dust around him—within him—and grabbed at it like I was catching a fish in a stream with my bare hands. Alex gasped, arching his back, and a surge of power flowed into me. I watched him clinically, making sure I wasn't borrowing too much power too fast. But he was strong—a quality ingredient. After a few moments, he began to relax and, content he wouldn't pass out on me, I set the flow from him to me into a constant, steady drip.

A small cloud flickering with red power drifted up the mountain path and I smiled.

"I'm glad you could join us, Ruin," I said.

He bobbed up and down, slowing beside me to inspect my work with the ever-burning rainbow. "I felt my family calling me. That they needed help," he said, glancing from me to Alex, gauging the flow of power between us and nodding his approval.

"Do you mind?" I asked. "I could use a little bit more of the red," I said, indicating the rainbow in my lap. "One bolt should do."

"Sure," he said, studying me in surprise but asking no questions.

"Why don't you just throw it at me and I'll catch it," I said. "It's hard to throw in the middle of all this," I explained, still pulling out more of the rainbow from my satchel.

"Okay." He drifted back a few paces. "On the count of three," he said. He began bobbing up and down as he counted out loud, giving me something to See rather than just Hear.

How considerate of him.

"One...two...three!"

The sizzling bolt of red lightning shot out of him with a deafening crack, and I flung up a hand to quickly catch it and slam it into the rainbow. It crackled and zapped as it shot down the entire length of the rainbow within my satchel.

I let out a tired, shaky sigh and looked back up at Ruin. "Thanks. I think we're ready." I jerked my chin upwards. "Fifty feet up, I need you to just remain in place," I told him. "Grimm's going to run through you with the rainbow. I need you to juice it up with everything you have."

"I'm going to do *what*?" Grimm asked incredulously.

Ruin nodded obediently and drifted up into the sky as indicated.

"Grimm, take this end in your mouth."

When he didn't respond, I looked up.

"You did *not* just say that to me," he said in disbelief.

"Alex is wearying fast," I told him sternly. "Let's save the dick jokes for later, eh?"

He trotted over, studying me. "So, it *is* still you," he said, leaning low to bite down on the end of the rainbow I held out.

I nodded absently, reaching deeper into the satchel, yanking out fistfuls of the new crackling, burning rainbow, and dumping it into a heaping pile beside me. I reached out for the other ball of star light, sweating harder now. I took a deep breath, checked on Alex—who was weaving back and forth ever so slightly now—and then slammed the star light down onto the rainbow, relieving some of the strain on Alex. I let out a shudder, wiping at my forehead with my sleeve.

Then I turned to my unicorn, ignoring the stunned look on his face. "Okay, I need you to fly through Ruin as fast as you can," I told him.

He grimaced distastefully but nodded. He didn't need to speak for me to know what he was thinking. And it had nothing to do with magic or Grammarie. I was asking him to make the biggest rainbow in the world.

Any other time I would have laughed. But Alex wasn't looking too good.

"Hurry," I told him.

He didn't bother replying, simply sweeping up into the sky a good distance from Ruin, the stream of sizzling rainbow trailing behind him like a ribbon, illuminating the snowy mountain with color for the first time.

Without further prodding, Grimm sprinted at Ruin in a blur, the rainbow now whipping and cracking behind him like a cloak. I continued hurling fistfuls of rainbow from the satchel as fast as I could, keeping one eye on the sky so I could witness the birth of the new Bifröst.

Grimm struck Ruin with a thunderous boom and then burst out the other side, the Bifröst screaming loud enough to make the mountain tremble as the size, flames, and lightning quadrupled. I'd made it a little faster than the old Bifröst. Because if you weren't going to improve something, why even attempt it, right?

Grimm zipped out of sight, tugging the Bifröst behind him in a blur.

I was panting as I reached the end of the rainbow and managed to let it go before it was yanked out of my hand. I looked up, shaking with exhaustion, and stared as the end of the Bifröst passed through Ruin to the sound of a sonic boom.

Sparkles exploded across the sky and the Bifröst let out one final birthing cry, confirming it had been a successful delivery. Ruin drifted to the ground like a leaf falling from a tree, swaying back and forth in exhaustion, as well.

I very carefully dialed down the connection between Alex and me, keeping an eye on him to make sure he was handling the decrease in flow without harmful effect. I gauged it by watching his breathing, making sure it was slow and steady until I turned it off completely.

He promptly passed out, but Ruin caught him at the last moment.

I let out a breath of relief as Ruin carried Alex away, and I very carefully released my own power. I leaned back with a tired smile and focused on my breathing. I had forgotten to tell Grimm how long he needed to carry the Bifröst, but it would eventually snap tight on his end and force him to let go. Or it would disappear entirely from his mouth, making it pretty clear his job was done.

A cloaked silhouette approached, looming over me and I smiled up at him.

"Suck on that," I told him tiredly.

He continued to stare at me, his face shadowed from view. "Do you have any idea how...incredible that was?" he asked, sounding disturbed.

"I thought the *suck on that* comment was pretty clear."

He continued staring down at me and finally shook his head. Then he sat down beside me and I got a better glimpse of his face. It was Dean, not Odin. I laced my fingers across my chest and looked back up at the stars, smiling proudly.

"Is he a Tiny God, now?" I asked, thinking about Alex and Ruin.

Dean shook his head. "He's something, but he hasn't bonded Ruin, if that's what you mean. He could, but he hasn't. Being a Tiny God just means you can dominate a soul. It doesn't necessarily have to be a Beast."

I looked over at him, arching a brow. "Oh?"

Grimm abruptly landed beside us with the force of a meteor, baring his teeth at Dean. "Fixed your fucking rainbow, candy-ass Cyclops," he snarled. Then he turned his back on the Allfather and trotted away.

I risked a look over at Dean to find him frowning. "That would have been funnier if I had been in my proper form," he suggested drily.

I chuckled, surprised by his sense of humor. Both Dean and Odin had dry senses of humor. "I need you to bring Anubis up here. I've got some work to do tonight."

Dean arched a brow at me. "You do, do you?" he said flatly.

"It would be much appreciated. I'm quite tired."

Silence answered me. I glanced over to find that Dean had left, so I turned back to the sky, and decided to count the stars. Part of me wished I could specifically recall the exact steps I had taken to birth the new Bifröst, but I was pretty sure I would pass out if I attempted it. The thing about Fae magic—at least in my case—was that it was instinctual.

No cookbook or measurements to map out. I let the thought go. Maybe someday.

It would soon be time to go to Stonehenge. No matter what Anubis decided.

Even though I didn't have enough Fae magic left to even lift a feather.

But I did have a War Hammer. And it wanted to kiss Mordred right on the lips.

35

Alex had woken, tired, but none the worse for wear after I'd used him to repair the Bifröst. He and Ruin had gone for a walk, leaving me to my thoughts.

I had been inspecting the now-empty Hand of God curiously, considering Odin's comments about Tiny Gods. I'd taken out the three Horseman Masks, going over my list of names with a fine-toothed comb.

I stared at the War Hammer, hefting it in my fist, thinking. It was still pregnant with ichor and begging to be used. But that was dangerous. It could give Mordred exactly what he wanted—the ichor within. Then again, he had seen the War Hammer several times and hadn't been remotely concerned about it, so when he saw me holding it again he might dismiss it out of sheer familiarity, potentially giving me an opportunity to take him out.

I set the Hammer down with a sigh and my gaze drifted over the Knight's sketch in a perfunctory manner, my thoughts drifting to Anubis' tardiness. But I froze as the sketch sprang to life—awoken by my casual glance—revealing something much more than a crude depiction of Stonehenge or what I had taken to presume was a sun.

I blinked rapidly, surprised at what I saw. Familiar Runes marked ten of the columns—matching those I had seen on the actual Round Table in Chateau Falco.

Then I noticed something else and my eyes widened in disbelief. That...how had no one ever noticed *that* before? I wondered if Mordred knew, decided it was best to assume that he did, and I jumped to my feet, shoving everything into my satchel.

Anubis appeared as I was packing, not looking pleased at my summons. But he was here.

I turned to him, setting my satchel down. I dipped my head respectfully and told him what I wanted. "As long as they come back as themselves, not some deranged zombie or anything," I clarified.

Anubis snorted. "That only happens in the movies. They might be a little disoriented for a few days. A little emotional or passionate, but that's it.

"What do you mean, passionate?" I asked, frowning in concern.

He thought about it for a few moments. "Instead of saying gosh darn it, they will curse really loudly." He saw the dubious look on my face and rolled his eyes. "You're already dangerous enough, Temple. I'm not going to give you two super-powered zombies with anger management issues to put on your team. It will be like they missed a night of sleep. Nothing more."

"Promise me."

"I promise," he said, rolling his eyes. At my nod, he glanced over at the bodies of Gunnar and Talon behind me, considering my request. "You haven't completed your task yet, by the way," he reminded me.

"Then let's talk loan terms."

He thought about it for a few moments. Then he gave me an easy shrug. "Okay. You can have your two souls early—with the commitment that Mordred dies within one year and is returned to me. If you fail, their souls—and yours—are returned to me."

"Two years," I said.

He narrowed his eyes. "Having doubts already? I've already got you bent over a barrel."

"No doubts. Two years for two souls sounds fair," I said, lowering my eyes so he knew I wasn't being disrespectful. "If I had it my way, I would finish it tonight, but I have other commitments that could complicate my timetable," I explained, lifting the coin around my throat for him to see.

My Horseman's Mask.

Anubis finally nodded. "Deal." Then he simply reached into his pocket and pulled out two balls of light. He held them over Gunnar and Talon and I suddenly grew very nervous, my heart pounding.

This was it.

He released the orbs and I watched them settle into each of my friends.

A few moments later, they gasped and woke, blinking rapidly.

I fell to my knees, overcome with emotion.

Anubis spoke in a calm, measured voice. "Hear me, Gunnar. Hear me, Talon."

They sat up, looking very surprised.

"You died. Nate Temple brought you back to life. Gave you a second chance..." and I watched as Anubis knelt beside each of them, comforting them and answering their questions like the kindest of doctors.

I had never seen him act like that, but minute by minute, I saw my friends calm down, and as I looked into their eyes...

There wasn't even a hint of doubt that they were back. Because their three combined eyes were full of tears as they smiled back at me. It had worked.

"Calvin and Makayla, eh?" I asked Gunnar.

He nodded excitedly. "Alex told you..."

"I did what—"

Alex froze, staring in disbelief at the afterparty we were throwing.

Talon hissed at him dramatically and Alex actually jumped.

Talon burst out laughing, his tail flicking back and forth as he climbed to his feet, stretching his paws overhead. Then he looked at me and grinned. "I need some catnip, Wylde. Something to perk me up."

Tears fell down my cheeks as I reached into my pocket and handed him his stash, unable to speak. He walked up and glanced down at it. Then he swatted it out of my hand and wrapped me up in a tight hug. "Thank you, Wylde," he whispered.

I squeezed him back as tightly as I could. "Don't mention it, Tal."

Soon Gunnar was shoving Talon away and swallowing me with his massive upper body. "Thank you for giving me the chance to meet my kids. You just became godfather of the year."

I pulled back, laughing. "That's fairy godfather to you," I told him sternly.

His eye widened. "You...got your powers back?" he whispered, gripping my shoulder.

Talon grabbed my other shoulder. "You remember?"

"I got my powers and I remember enough. The important parts, anyway."

"And he repaired the Bifröst," Dean said from behind me, sounding proud. Like stern-father proud, not parks and rec participation trophy proud. It was a reserved pride rather than the overexuberant cheerleader.

Alex and Grimm went to congratulate Talon and Gunnar, so I turned to face Dean. I stared him in the eyes and dipped my head at his compliment.

"What's next?" he asked me, and I felt everyone lean close to hear my response.

I smiled.

36

We stepped out of Fae as a group, appearing outside Stonehenge and fanning out to make sure we weren't surrounded. I had my Darling and Dear satchel across my chest and the War Hammer at my hip, ready for whatever Mordred had planned. Through the damp, foggy air, a light flickered from within the center of the ring of standing stones. I released the Gateway behind me with a sigh of relief, stepping clear of any puddles. It had rained recently, which wouldn't make a fight any easier.

But Mordred was here. Next step was to find Alice.

Because if he hadn't brought Alice with him, I was going to skin him alive, strip-by-strip, until he talked. To use a child as leverage was truly unforgivable to me. Preying on those weaker than you to obtain what you wanted? Not today.

I idly wondered if Mordred had brought his right-hand man.

Well, *no-hand* man, technically.

Gunnar and Talon had stared at Alex in disbelief when I told them what Alex had done to their murderer. It was that same look of respect I was now used to seeing everyone give Alex—spiced with a healthy pinch of fear. They hadn't laughed about it until I elaborated on the exact details of the fight—how Alex had essentially made the Black Knight his bitch.

Gunnar and Talon wanted to finish off what Alex had started, and I didn't blame them one bit.

I stared towards the prehistoric monument, remembering the picnic I'd once had here with Callie Penrose. We had sat right there in the center on a night much like this one. The cynical part of me wondered if that, too, had been some cosmic machination dictated by my parents, but I shrugged off the paranoia. Regardless, I had returned. And this time, I wasn't sure Stonehenge would survive. Not after the hidden message I had seen in the Black Knight's sketch...

Even though I hadn't quite wrapped my head around what it literally meant, the implications were profound. The fabled Knights of the Round Table were buried here. As was King Arthur Pendragon. Or at least major clues leading to their final resting places were hidden somewhere within the ancient ring of standing stones. It was time to find out why Mordred wanted me here—after I saved Alice.

According to plan, Gunnar and Talon nodded at me before silently slipping into the shadows like ghosts, despite the numerous puddles and wet mud. Grimm neighed loudly, announcing our arrival so as not to startle Mordred. It was important for him to know Grimm was here. I could possibly use that. Tell Mordred that we could both get something we wanted—he could hand over Alice, and I could send her away on Grimm.

Leaving Alex and me to square off against Mordred and his Black Knight.

Because Talon would have already tossed a pebble our way if he had encountered unfair odds within the center—or outside—of Stonehenge. That was one reason he and Gunnar had slipped off on their own—to scout the area. I waited a few more moments just to be sure. Then I let out a breath, rolling my shoulders. So far so good.

Grimm stayed where he was, knowing his approach would only send Mordred into attack mode. Simply knowing that Grimm was lurking outside the safety of Stonehenge would be enough to give Mordred pause, and hopefully get him to agree to hand over the child.

I took a deep breath, shared a look with Alex, and then we made our way through the puddles over to Stonehenge proper, walking past the tall standing stones. Each was over ten-feet tall and their very presence made me feel like I had stepped back in time. Because they had stood erect for at least four thousand years, silent observers of mankind's history.

We entered the ring to find Alice with her hands tied behind her back near one of the standing stones. She wasn't chained to the ground, but she also seemed determined to stay in one place, her eyes wide with fear. Mordred and the Black Knight stood perhaps ten feet away from her, watching us approach. I was careful to avoid eye contact with her, lest I lose my control—which Mordred was likely counting on.

I halted near the center and glanced back at Alex, who had his hands clasped behind his back in a respectful manner. "Hey. Remember that guy?" I asked him, pointing at the Black Knight.

Alex squinted. "He looks vaguely familiar…" Alex then unclasped his hands from behind his back to scratch his head with the finger of his large gauntlet. His other arm hung at his side, accessorized with a matching gauntlet. "But I can't put my finger on it with that helmet in the way," he finally said, lowering his armored hand.

I shrugged, turning back to the Black Knight, who had tensed rigidly upon seeing Alex wearing his gauntlets. "He's got a point, but I remember you," I assured him. "The rune on your chivalrous pecs gives you away, you naughty minx," I said, pointing at his breastplate.

The Black Knight didn't react further than that initial flinch.

"Are you sure it's the same rune?" Mordred asked, sounding amused. I turned to see he was indicating our surroundings. I followed his finger to see runes painted on many of the standing stones around us. The same ones indicated in the Knight's sketch—except painted red and inverted, just like the one on the Black Knight's chest.

That answered one question, even though it wasn't all that surprising. Mordred knew about the Knights. Hell, the Black Knight had probably told him.

But what was Mordred's ultimate game plan? If he knew about the Knights, what did he need from me? I was fairly certain I knew the answer, but I wasn't sure how the Ichor would help him. Had he marked the relevant standing stones so that he knew where to dig?

Instead of reacting, I turned back to the Black Knight, studying the rune on his chest. Then I nodded. "I'm sure it's him. He left his gloves at my party. And look at that," I said, pointing at his stumps. "He isn't wearing his hands. Kind of a dead giveaway."

On cue, Alex removed the gauntlets and tossed them onto the ground. "You're welcome."

I turned back to the Black Knight and whispered loudly across the clearing, as if only he could hear me. "Did you give him my message?" I asked using my right hand to conceal that my left finger was pointing at Mordred.

The Knight nodded stiffly. His stumps didn't clench, obviously, but his forearms flexed in a sad attempt at intimidation.

I gave him a thumbs up. "Thanks for giving me a hand with that."

"I see you finally learned how to make a rainbow," Mordred said calmly, changing the topic.

I nodded. "Mine was *way* bigger than yours," I told him, chuckling. "You know, I've really missed you, Mo. Hug it out? It might just be our last chance."

"Did you bring the Ichor?" he asked, ignoring my comment.

I shoved my hands into my pockets, searching in a dramatic display. I was surprised to feel a small stone inside one pocket, but I didn't react as I palmed it and withdrew my hands. "Damn. I *knew* I had forgotten something," I told Mordred. "Do I need to go back and get it, or can we just get this over with now?"

He...smirked.

I felt my pulse quicken, wondering what the hell that reaction had meant.

The stone between my fingers was sharp and smooth, and I suddenly recalled what it was. Not a stone, a diamond. The one Pan had made on the cliff before he fell. I recalled his last lesson, commanding me to *feel the rock.*

As Mordred continued to stare at me with that victorious smile, I followed Pan's advice, reaching out to the standing stones with a bare sliver —all I could currently handle after repairing the Bifröst—of my Fae magic. I almost gasped in disbelief at what I found.

The Knights weren't buried beneath the standing stones...

They were fucking *inside* them, encased in the stone like they were coffins.

It was a bizarre distortion of the sword in the stone myth. The Knights in the Stonehenge.

And with the red runes splashed onto their make-shift coffins...I was pretty sure Mordred had already figured that out.

37

I thought desperately, trying to find a way to mitigate whatever Mordred had planned.

"My unicorn is out there," I said, gesturing behind me. "What do you say we solve each other's problem. You give me the child, and my unicorn takes her far away. She has nothing to do with...whatever this is," I said, hiding my knowledge about the Knights.

"What a great idea," Mordred said, gesturing for us to go ahead. I narrowed my eyes warily and Mordred smiled. "Please take her away. You would be doing me a great service. I want nothing to do with babysitting a child. My Knight took certain...liberties with that decision." Mordred pointedly glanced down at the Black Knight's stumps. "I believe he learned two very valuable lessons for his mistake."

Without waiting for my approval, Alex advanced towards Alice, keeping a ready eye on the Black Knight and Mordred. I slipped the diamond into my pocket and rested my hand close to the War Hammer, ready for anything.

Alice was staring at Alex with bloodshot eyes, shaking nervously at the strange turn of events—from captivity to freedom with not a drop of blood spilled. I agreed with her, not trusting this peaceful turn of events one bit.

Something was wrong. First, Mordred hadn't cared about the Ichor. Now, he didn't care about the girl. What was he playing at?

My breath began to pull faster as I waited for the answer to manifest—my shoulders rigid as I watched for even the slightest motion that might signal an attack. Mordred dipped his head toward Alex, making my hackles rise. Did he actually have a splinter of chivalry deep inside of him? Alex didn't bother untying Alice—he simply brushed a thumb down her cheek and smiled reassuringly. Then he gently pushed her behind him to cover her retreat, keeping his eyes on the Black Knight as he followed her, walking backwards.

"Sorry about your friends," the Black Knight abruptly said with a horrible lisp, followed by a harsh chuckle. The lisp caught me by surprise for a moment until I remembered Alex had removed many of his teeth in their first encounter.

Alex paused, cocking his head at the Knight in confusion. Then he glanced over at me, silently asking if I understood the Knight's comment. I shrugged, discreetly tapping my fingers two times atop my War Hammer— a prearranged signal.

Alex turned back to the Knight and shrugged. "Sorry for what?" he asked, resuming his backwards walk.

The Black Knight used his stump to lift his visor, revealing a gap-toothed grin. "Sorry for putting them down like the animals they were."

"Oh, *that*," Alex said, waving a hand dismissively. "That has nothing to do with me. If you feel guilty, you can always apologize to them," he said, a smile creeping over his cheeks as he pointed behind the Black Knight.

He flinched, turning just as Gunnar and Talon struck him like linebackers—from two different sides and two different heights. Gunnar went for the legs and Talon went for the face, knocking off the Black Knight's helmet with a piercing screech. The double impact sounded like it had snapped the Knight's legs in half.

"Get her out of here!" I shouted at Alex, drawing the War Hammer in my fist.

Mordred had instantly jumped clear, his lips pulling back into a snarl. "How..." he demanded, staring at Talon and Gunnar incredulously. They had the Knight face-down in the dirt and Gunnar was beating the living hell out of him, snarling so hard it was more like a coughing bark. Talon was slicing away at his armor in a meticulous fashion. Then I saw him yank a plate free and hurl it behind him. They were stripping him of his armor.

I turned back to Mordred. "How many swipes does it take to get to the center of a Knightsie Roll Pop?" I asked, smiling faintly,

Mordred obviously didn't get the reference. "My Knight told me they were dead," he snarled.

"Pffft," I said, waving my free hand dismissively. "Only a little. They're fine, now. See?" The Black Knight was now trying desperately to stump-punch his foes, but they wouldn't even let him get away with that as they ripped off more plates of armor, faster and faster.

Mordred studied me, looking apprehensive for the first time, which made me feel a whole lot better. I'd finally done something to disturb his plans. "Anubis," he cursed.

Gunnar leaned down and suddenly bit off the Black Knight's head, bringing a brittle silence back to the clearing.

I dusted off my hands dramatically. "That looked familiar," I commented, smiling at Mordred.

Because Gunnar had done the exact same thing to Mordred at Fight Club.

Gunnar spat the head out in Mordred's direction and we all watched it roll in front of him. Mordred visibly calmed himself, taking several deep breaths. "It is of no consequence," he finally said. "I have more Knights. Let me introduce you to my Court."

And the runed standing stones around us exploded in a sandstorm of prehistoric grit.

I flung up a hand, casting out a spherical shield so I didn't choke to death on the sudden cloud. I hoped Gunnar and Talon had leapt clear of the explosion...

38

When the sound died down, I dropped my shield and ran blindly through the cloud of dust to find Talon and Gunnar slumped together in a muddy pile. I checked that they were still breathing and let out a sigh of relief. I nudged them with my foot, but they didn't stir. They weren't getting up anytime soon, knocked unconscious from the blast.

Luckily, I had been standing in the center of the ring. I was doubly glad that I had bargained for Alice when I had, otherwise her tiny, fragile body would have been obliterated by the explosion.

The dust hung in the air, merging with the fog to create a thick mist, slow to settle as it hung in the air. And through that mist, an armored figure suddenly emerged not ten paces away. I hurriedly began walking backwards, towards the center of the ring, not sure if he was friend or foe, and knowing there were more where he came from. His armor looked bright and polished despite his hibernation, but I watched in horror as it began to grow darker, and a blood rune on his breastplate began to grow brighter.

Soon, ten more stumbling knights stood around me, all of them clad in pristine armor and armed with deadly medieval weapons of some sort or another. But their armor was also growing steadily darker in direct proportion to the brightening red runes on their chests.

"Fight it!" I snapped at one of them, panicking.

He spun suddenly, lifting his visor in my direction. Those green eyes looked surprised to see someone other than a Knight present. "Only a Pendragon could break this sorcery!"

I groaned inwardly as I watched him resort to scratching at the rune on his armor. It didn't smudge in the slightest. Since it was growing brighter with each passing second, it merely looked like he was polishing it.

And I suddenly understood what Mordred had done. He had set this whole reawakening up, so he would win either way. Because in addition to this curse that bound the Knights to him against their will, he was also a Pendragon—Arthur's illegitimate son.

Everyone turned as Mordred began to laugh.

The Knight I had spoken to rounded on Mordred, settling his gauntlet on the hilt of the sword at his hip. "What is the meaning of this, Mordred?" he demanded in a defiant growl.

Mordred was saved from responding as the ground began to rumble. Everyone pivoted to see a coffin slowly shimmer into existence in the exact center of the ring, rising from the mist not three paces away from me. The coffin was made entirely of glass and decorated with golden runes that made the hair on the back of my neck stand on end. Runes that looked suspiciously similar to the ones I had seen in the Ichor from the Round Table.

Like the Ichor currently filling my War Hammer. But...did I dare throw my freaking Hammer at King Arthur's coffin while surrounded by his Knights of the Round Table? That sounded like a good way to get impaled a dozen times. Instead, I pointed desperately at the coffin, shouting. "Your King needs you! Arthur Pendragon needs you! Fight this!"

The Knights turned to stare at the coffin—their posture hopeful and expectant. But the coffin didn't open. No handsome King appeared to save the day. It just hovered above the ground, looking pretty. While the Knights' armor continued to turn darker and darker.

All too soon, the area flashed red and all the Knights fell to their knees, groaning.

Then, as if in a stupor, they began to chant, the words seemingly pulled out from them. I didn't bother paying attention to specifics, because it sounded like an age-old oath to serve their king with blind trust and devotion. Mordred smiled down at them adoringly, holding his hands open at his sides to accept their praise with kingly grace.

Yeah. Screw that. One Black Knight had been bad enough. But to have close to a dozen of them running around doing Mordred's bidding? Not on my watch.

I hurled the War Hammer at Mordred with all the magic at my disposal, even feeling a bit of my Fae magic leaking into the throw. If I could kill Mordred, maybe I could break the curse he had used on the Knights. My Hammer struck Mordred right in the chest and sent him flying into a broken standing stone with a pleasant crunching sound.

I panted, a slow smile creeping over my face. I did it. I had killed—

The Knights continued chanting as if nothing had happened, swearing their allegiance to the dead guy on the rock.

And I watched in disbelief as Mordred climbed to his feet, dusted off his shirt, and then frowned down at the War Hammer. "That packed more punch than I had expected," he said, shaking his head.

Then he shrugged and looked back up at me, flashing me a wink.

"Mordred *Pendragon*, at your service. Thank you for not bringing the Ichor, Nate. I knew that if I told you to bring it you would leave it behind. It would have made things complicated—"

Glug, glug, glug.

We both turned to see Alex suddenly standing a few paces away from Mordred, chugging golden liquid from a glass vial. "Ahh," he said, tossing it down and wiping a sleeve across his mouth. "That's better. What did I miss?"

I shoved a hand into my Darling and Dear satchel, frowning in utter disbelief to find the vial of Ichor missing. When the hell had the little thief stolen the vial of Ichor? Then I remembered who had offered to repack my satchel in Fae and I cursed. But why had he stolen it?

Before anyone could speak, the runes on the coffin abruptly flared and the lid sprang open, making me jump since it was right beside me. Golden smoke rose up from within, and I gasped in disbelief. It hovered in the air, condensing into a stunning golden cloud of chivalry, nobility, and overall goodness—King Arthur's soul.

I could practically feel its warm rays of benevolence—

It suddenly zipped towards Alex like an arrow fired from a bow, knocking him down to the ground like a harpoon.

Mordred screamed.

I screamed.

We all screamed for the real King.

The Knights finished their chant and rose to their feet, their armor now entirely black. Whatever Alex had done to turn the tide, it had been too late. Dousing himself with the Hand of God must have made him susceptible to King Arthur's spirit. Add in the Ichor he had just consumed and...

A king had been born. Or a poor bastard had been harpooned by a King's spirit.

But assuming this was a beneficial development, what did that mean? Was Alex now actually Arthur? Or maybe Arthur's spirit really had decided to kill Alex for daring to drink the Ichor. The Ichor I had thought was *Merlin's* blood. Had the Ichor in fact belonged to Arthur instead? Pandora had implied that the Ichor was a piece of Excalibur—the Blood. Maybe another of the missing pieces was inside the coffin! I could grab it and then Shadow Walk Alex, Gunnar, and Talon back to Chateau Falco, re-forge Excalibur, and then return to face Mordred another day with a Pendragon of my own. King Freaking Alex.

I was already peering over the lip of the coffin; my subconscious mind having made the decision for me. But the coffin was entirely empty. I dropped down directly into a puddle to find the possessed Knights all facing me, looking like they had a strong opinion on me grave-robbing their old boss's final resting place.

The Knights slowly lowered gauntlets to hilts, preparing to teach me a lesson. I hadn't even been able to handle one of these clowns on my own, let alone close to a dozen! Maybe I could—

One of the Knights suddenly shouted out as he pointed away from me. They instantly lost interest in me and turned to see what had alarmed their fellow Knight, and we all saw Alex climbing back to his feet. Alex shook his head, looking as if he was shrugging off a good punch to the chin. Mordred noticed our attention and rounded on him with a territorial snarl, lifting his arms to destroy the new threat to his throne.

"Alex!" I screamed.

And I hurled the golden Mask at him.

Earlier tonight, while sitting atop the mountain, surveying all of Fae, I had realized that I'd already come to at least one decision regarding the Horseman Masks.

I wanted to ask Alex if he would join me as the Horseman of Justice. Especially after seeing his reaction to Gunnar's death...

He had proven himself numerous other times as well, and I believed he would fit this particular Mask well. I'd had other candidates in mind for consideration, but after seeing him against Thor and then the Black Knight...

He had kind of skipped the try-out requirement.

Of course, the actual decision to slap it on his rosy cheeks was entirely up to him, but Mordred was about to throw everything he had at Alex, and beggars couldn't be choosers.

Alex saw the golden Mask hurtling at him and dove to catch it, grasping onto it the moment before Mordred unleashed a ball of green light.

Mordred's blow scorched across Alex's side instead of striking him full on, and I saw blood fly as he landed and rolled awkwardly into a large puddle.

Alex didn't get back up. He didn't even stir.

I had a clear view of the Horseman's Mask, and the light spray of blood across its face from it dragging over his wound as he tumbled through the mud.

I waited, silently urging him to get up, begging King Arthur's spirit to give him a boost of energy. Mordred grunted satisfactorily and turned to face me and his Knights.

"Now, where were we," he growled, his eyes locking onto me. "Oh, that's right. You were going to take me to where the rest of the Ichor is," he snarled. "So I can destroy it for—"

The Knights shouted out, interrupting Mordred as Alex suddenly jumped to his feet and began sprinting behind Mordred's back, clutching his wounded side with one hand and the Mask of Justice with the other.

Mordred swore, and began flinging bolts of power at Alex, but Alex dove behind a block of stone, rolling to his knees out of Mordred's immediate sight. I watched as he stared down at the Mask in his hand, and I saw him hesitate.

He needed time.

I began hurling bolts of lightning at Mordred and the Knights as fast as I possibly could, anything to keep them distracted long enough for Alex to make his decision. I flung the bolts blindly, panting and snarling, not even caring if any struck true or not. In fact, it was better if they simply struck all around my targets chaotically, confusing the hell out of everyone.

Because if Alex donned that Mask, all the bad guys would be toast in about ten seconds.

If my own Mask hadn't been cracked, I would have slapped it on before even walking into this cursed place.

As I continued throwing bolt after bolt, I saw Alex reach down for something in front of him that I hadn't noticed a moment ago.

My War Hammer sat in the mud, handle pointed up into the air. And it was glowing brighter than I had ever seen. The Ichor I had hidden within was responding to the Ichor now flowing in Alex's veins. As his hand neared, the glow increased until it was almost blinding.

His hand wrapped around the handle and it lashed out with golden tendrils of lightning that seemed to anchor the Hammer down into the mud. I stared incredulously as Alex tugged on the handle as if trying to dislodge the lightning anchors in time to save his life from Mordred.

The stone mallet remained firmly rooted in the ground, but that handle...

It just kept on rising as Alex continued to pull—now standing to his feet for more leverage as he dropped the Horseman Mask and used both hands to pull the Hammer from the ground, gritting his teeth in determination. But as he pulled...

A stunning sword slowly unsheathed from the stone, inch-by-glorious-inch.

The blade finally came free with an echoing chime that seemed to rise up into the sky. The golden arcs of electricity that had been holding the stone anchored to the ground abruptly snapped back up into the sword, crackling across the surface for a few seconds before fizzling out.

I flinched as the coffin beside me suddenly let out a hissing sound and sank back down into the ground. We all just kind of stood there for a second, gawking incredulously at the dude with the sword in his hand.

How in the world...

My War Hammer had been...*Excalibur*? The godsdamned Sword in the Stone?

The stone mallet crumpled into dust, and Alex finally lifted his eyes to stare at Mordred with a very broad smile.

"Daddy's found his sword..." he said.

"Excalibur," Mordred rasped in disbelief, his face paling. Then he abruptly Shadow Walked his ass out of Stonehenge. One by one, the Knights winked out of view as well, following their boss like lemmings.

I shook my head incredulously, staring at Alex. No, at *Arthur*.

"Dude..." I said, pointing at Excalibur. "You broke my War Hammer."

Alex blinked a few times and then let out a sigh. "I guess I did. Sorry."

"Are you kidding me? Don't say *sorry*. This was better than any other outcome I expected after those Knights started changing colors."

Alex sat down on a rock, staring down at the gleaming blade. "It's not complete. I think it's still missing a piece," he said, sounding troubled. "I don't understand—"

I cleared my throat, cutting him off. "Pandora said it was in the Armory, right?" I asked, thinking out loud. Alex nodded adamantly, as if I had just proven his point. I shook my head. "She said that when *you* were in the Armory. And when the *War Hammer* was in the Armory," I said, growing excited as my mind raced down the rabbit-hole.

Alex blinked rapidly. "Why...why didn't she just tell us? Tell me?" he added, sounding betrayed.

I smiled in understanding. I'd been through a lot of lies recently, and I had a budding understanding on the matter.

"I think she did tell you, just in her own way." He grunted, not buying it. "The whole hot tub thing," I explained, nodding as the pieces kicked into place in my mind. "Like the Lady of the Lake. She said she needed to give you something, remember?"

Alex's cheeks flushed red. "She, um, gave me quite a lot in the hot tub. Several times, in fact."

And, kids, that's what happens when you open Pandora's Box, I thought to myself.

I rolled my eyes at his joke, but he wasn't laughing. Okay. Puppy love. I sighed. "In addition to the *piece* she gave you in the hot tub," I said drily, "I think she gave you one of Excalibur's pieces in the hot tub. Like a ritual." I thought about it. "The Soul or the Name. One of those two."

Because the Blade was obviously the War Hammer he had stolen from me. I'd get over that one day. Maybe.

The Blood—which Alex also stole from me—was the ichor from the Round Table—whether belonging to Merlin or Arthur, I wasn't quite sure yet. Sometimes the easiest answer wasn't the right answer when it came to magic. And several sources of mine had seemed to strongly believe that the Ichor had been Merlin's blood.

The Power was probably the Hand of God Alex had used—giving him the ability to harness King Arthur's spirit, rather than a Beast. Just like Odin had said atop the mountain. Even then, he was giving me answers. I found myself wondering how many other answers I had been given without knowing it, but I quickly cut off that train of thought to focus back on Alex.

All things considered, that left only the Name and the Soul as possibilities for remaining pieces for what Pandora had given him. Or, I was wrong, and Pandora had just let him check out her box. Pun definitely intended.

I looked at Alex, realizing that he still looked depressed. Someone he obviously cared quite a bit about had lied to him.

He scooped up the Horseman Mask from the ground, smiling at it.

"I was going to ask you about that before Mordred almost killed you, in case you were wondering. You've earned it," I said carefully, gauging his reaction.

Alex looked down at it for a long moment, and then finally shook his head gently. He held it out to me. "It means a lot, Nate. More than you will ever know...but I think I have a different job to do," he said, glancing back to where Mordred had last been seen.

"And what job is that?" I asked, taking back the Mask, ignoring my feeling of disappointment, but understanding his decision at the same time.

A slow smile crept over his face, and he began to chuckle. Soon, it was a great, booming laugh, loud enough to wake Gunnar and Talon. They glanced up sharply, staring over at us. I waved at them and then turned back to Alex.

"Well?" I pressed, wondering what had made him laugh. Mordred wasn't really one to laugh at, no matter what kind of sword Alex now wielded.

"Mordred has the Knights," Alex said, looking up at me. "Maybe I should get some of my own..." He risked a glance at Gunnar and Talon. "Can you think of anyone who might be a good fit? Or know where I can find a big table?"

I smiled, my mind suddenly racing at the prospect. To have a new breed of Knights of the Round Table at Chateau Falco...

Partnered up with my new breed of Horsemen...

"Yeah, I can come up with a few names. But I have first right of refusal on recruiting sociopaths," I said sternly. "Or I won't share my table."

Alex grinned. "I can live with that. You only need three Riders. I think I'm going to need a few more Knights than that..." he said, his smile returning. "And mine probably won't be sociopaths."

I thought about my parents as I stared up at the stars. About their tapestry of deceit, as Pan had called it.

Maybe it *was* kind of beautiful...

Grimm landed softly beside me and a spindly creature suddenly leapt off his back to hit me like a four-legged octopus. Alice screeched loud enough to shatter my eardrums, and then began planting kisses all over my cheeks. Then she squeezed me in a chokehold, burying her head into my neck.

There was something about a kid hugging you...they wrapped around you like a Band-Aid. Maybe they were a little like Band-Aids. To cover up the owies in your soul.

I was just thankful she was alive.

"We found our happily ever after!" she said, finally pulling back to stare at me with her bright blue eyes. "I *told* you we would. Even if it went all topsy-turvy on us."

I smiled, refusing to set her down. I'd needed that hug.

Grimm trotted over to Gunnar and Talon, who still looked too dazed to risk upward mobility. And I smiled at Alex, a silent thanks for saving her. He smiled back.

"Happily ever after," I mused. "Yeah, we found it, Alice. And look," I said, turning her to face Alex. "A real King. Let me introduce you to my good friend, Arthur Pendragon."

Alex rolled his eyes at my choice of name.

Alice slapped my shoulder reproachfully. "That's not an Arthur, that's an Alex," she said, frowning down at him doubtfully. Then she cocked her head suddenly, staring at him in a dazed, distant fashion. "Oh, you're right. He's both!" she whispered, sounding startled.

Alex looked relieved to hear her confirmation, but a little uneasy to have that wisdom come from a small child.

"Looks like we found our dragon and our knights," I told her. "Even if they did switch roles. The dragon saved us from the knights."

She nodded sagely. "I like that ending better," she said with a sad smile, thinking of her mother.

"Me, too, Alice. Me, too..."

It looked like Chateau Falco was going to need to host a career fair soon.

But first, hot chocolate and marshmallows...

And maybe some Yulemas planning...

Nate Temple returns in KNIGHTMARE. Get your copy online today!
http://www.shaynesilvers.com/l/545396

Turn the page to read a sample of **UNCHAINED** *- Feathers and Fire Series Book 1, or* **BUY ONLINE (FREE with Kindle Unlimited subscription).** *Callie Penrose is a wizard in Kansas City, MO who hunts monsters for the Vatican. She meets Nate Temple, and things devolve from there...*

(Note: Callie appears in the TempleVerse after Nate's book 6, TINY GODS...Full chronology of all books in the TempleVerse shown on the 'Books by Shayne Silvers' page)

TEASER: KNIGHTMARE (TEMPLE #12)

I sat atop my mountain, idly regarding the countless miles upon miles of sprawling land far, far below me: from calm, secluded ponds to bioluminescent forests; from turbulent seas of boiling sands to frigid, fingernail-splintering tundras; from oceans of molten stone to fields of glass reeds, and even a monochromatic island with a white mansion, white walls, white *everything*.

But that was long gone now. I'd introduced it to color. And destruction.

Every inch of this savagely breathtaking world was inhabited by multifarious hordes of nefarious, exotic, and alien creatures that could have only been birthed from the darkest depths of a god's nightmare—all majestically malicious and insatiably malcontent.

The less frightening they appeared, the more horrifying they likely were.

And most lucky souls would never discover that the ecosystem, let alone the organisms within, even existed, unless they had their heads firmly tethered in the clouds, wasting away their days by reading strange, fantastical—allegedly fictional—scribbles that had been scratched into dismembered, prehistoric titans known as trees by mad men and women living out their days in voluntary solitary confinement.

Readers of mythology and fairy tales were the only beings with forewarning of the dangers—and beauties—that the world truly had to offer. Because those gullible souls had technically earned a PhD in Faeology and had a survival guide built into their subconscious mind.

For the non-readers, or readers of more mundane genres, ignorance was bliss—they just didn't know that the joke was on them.

Because the Land of the Fae was very real.

And it had been my new home for...a while now. I'd claimed this mountain for myself—Mount Wylde. My neighbors were succubi sprites, feral fairies, conscious elementals, pitiless goblins, kings, queens, talking trees...

Except none of them dared visit me atop my mountain. They'd tried—in the beginning.

I had dissuaded them. Violently.

I knew that much, but I had trouble recalling any specific altercations. I was fairly certain that I had first come here to recover from a mental malady; some days that thought was nothing more than a vague reverie, leading me to question whether it was fact or fiction.

Because I knew that I had been *born* here.

However...

I had strange dreams of another place—an entirely different world where every moment didn't revolve around the mastery of my instincts, dominance, and power. A different life where I wore a disguise and a different name. A life where visiting the Land of the Fae had been an objective, not an odyssey.

Which story was true? Was my mountain in Fae a *new* home or my *true* home?

Was I Wylde, or someone else?

Maybe *this* was my mental malady—not knowing which life had been real.

One thing I knew for certain—emotions were dangerous for me to entertain, let alone try to control. And dwelling too long on thoughts of that other life threatened to suffocate me with emotions I normally avoided.

Even *acknowledging* this now—that dream of a different life—I felt a storm brewing deep within me, a violent hurricane threatening to rise to the surface of my mind and annihilate everything within one hundred paces. I rolled my shoulders irritably, shaking off the sensation—and the tempting dream—with a shudder.

Instead, I focused on the currents of power curling through the very air as I took a calm, measured breath. The constant ebbs and flows of power were ingrained into every facet of the Land of the Fae—the trees, the creatures, the air, the water. And I could manipulate it, make it dance to my desire.

Life *lived* here, birthed and strengthened by the constant battle of give or take, do or die, kill or be killed.

Any existence that was less chaotic seemed pointless to me. In nature, stagnation was decay, and growth—movement—was life.

What was the point in any other method of living? A life of sedentary suicide? No. Death feasted on the unambitious, those content with the crumbs of mediocrity rather than scavenging for the slightest morsel of self-betterment—in any scope whatsoever.

Those who chose to never challenge and improve *any* aspect of their lives for the better were no different than lambs led to a slaughter.

Power was the answer. The more power one attained, the longer they lived. Power was the key to happiness, and happiness was the art of living.

A sudden burst of wind rustled my hair, whipping up cyclones of snow and grit as it screamed loud enough to send most creatures hissing and fleeing back into their hiding places.

Without moving a muscle, I stopped it.

The wind immediately fell flat, squashed down as if it had only existed in my imagination. It may as well have. I grunted dismissively, the simple flex of power helping to reestablish my sense of self, banishing those errant thoughts of some other paler reality.

Reality *was* my imagination.

Existence was granted only by my approval.

Because on this mountain, I'd found power. I had reclaimed my power here. I wasn't sure where I had lost it, or how, but I'd found it again—like I'd momentarily lost my shadow only to find it had simply been obscured by another larger shadow beside me.

I settled my palm across the staff resting across my lap. *Shadow,* I thought to myself, feeling uncomfortable for some reason. I squeezed the shaft hard enough for part of it to crack and crumble over my knuckles. With no outward movement, I instinctively grasped the dust and reforged it into the very fabric, the very essence, of the staff.

Then I settled it back across my lap, forcing my pulse down to forty beats per minute.

I tried to remain in that zone, knowing that it kept my mind—and thoughts—devoid of all but the most relevant of concerns. That was the lowest pulse rate I'd been able to attain.

Then again, I'd grown bored with attempting to lower it any further.

I'd grown bored with almost every activity or momentary hobby in my time here, as a matter of fact.

My education was advancing, but not at the pace I desired, and thinking of it made me angry, impatient, and bitter. I quickly forced my pulse to slow again, refusing to let my emotions take hold—only danger awaited me on that path.

I needed new adventures, new skills to learn—before I turned into yet another lamb.

I sensed movement to my right and almost flinched in surprise, having forgotten that I wasn't currently alone. My winged unicorn—alicorn, technically—had glanced over at me as if having read my thoughts on boredom. "Never you, Grimm," I murmured, not meeting his gaze. "I'll never be bored with you."

Grimm snorted softly before returning to his meal—a faint wisp of a rainbow, this time. It had been a while since we'd seen any truly vibrant rainbows—as if they knew a rainbow killer now occupied the once solitary mountain.

I could have simply *made* a rainbow for him, but he'd argued that me doing so took all the fun out of killing them. Like breeding cows or sheep and calling their slaughter a *hunt*.

Which made sense.

Domestication was weakness.

Still, the diluted diet—and poor company—made him antsy, hungry, and...cautious.

There had been other visitors, but I couldn't recall them staying for any measurable length of time. One had stayed by my side, but she was a mentor of sorts, a wielder of great powers that I was still struggling to learn —an elusive, fickle branch of power dissimilar to my other methods of wielding power.

But I cared about those visitors. Some of them...

Didn't I?

I risked a glance at Grimm. Yes. I cared about him. If I looked closely enough, I would notice the wings of black smoke sprouting from his back, but they would only become visible to others when he consciously chose to unfurl them. Usually, when it was too late to save themselves from instant death.

It was hard for anyone to hide magic from me now, though. Not after my time on this mountain. *My* mountain. Magic...spoke to me. Sang to me. It was simply a part of me.

I glanced down again, unimpressed by the thousands upon thousands of feet of open air between me and the base of my mountain.

My world.

I sighed wearily.

Maybe someone else wanted it. I was running out of entertainment, and stagnation was a very tempting suggestion at times—even though it meant certain death.

Because all of Fae stretched out before me—all the magic, monsters, stories, fables, and legends told over campfires for hundreds and thousands of years. They were down there, living, drinking, eating, fucking...

And I couldn't seem to remember why I cared about such things.

Like being concerned with the daily schedule of an ant colony.

The metaphor caused a weak bubble of a memory—a rarity for me, lately—to slip past my defenses. I focused on it, curious.

And it slowly began to clarify in my mind's eye. I remembered that the Fae Queens—Summer and Winter—had both sent armies to the base of my mountain, allowing a single messenger to travel to the peak to demand an explanation of my intentions.

And I'd thrown each of them off the cliff—right here, in fact—without uttering a single word, and without my pulse climbing higher than forty-one beats per minute.

Summer's representative had flown further, but Winter's had hit a tent full of fellow soldiers, so it had been a wash, really.

They hadn't sent anyone else since, and had soon departed, leaving me in peace. No. That wasn't right...

I absently scratched at my beard, frowning. "Hey, Grimm?"

He jolted in surprise, not accustomed to hearing me talk twice in less than an hour. He quickly regained his composure and glanced over at me, licking rainbow-colored blood from his lips. The snow beneath his meal was liberally painted in matching splashes of color. His nostrils flared, and his black feathers rose briefly—the red orbs on the tips glinting wetly in the pale sunlight—before the long feathers fell back down to rest against his flesh.

"Yeah?" he asked guardedly.

"Didn't the Queens send more messengers after the first two?"

Grimm studied me thoughtfully for a few long moments before finally nodding. "Yes. They brought written messages the second time, fearing their voices might offend you."

I frowned, shaking my head. I vaguely recalled the exchange. "What did they say again?"

He paused long enough for me to glance back at him. "You didn't read them," he replied cautiously. "You said you didn't care what ants had to say, request, or demand, and that it was better for them if you didn't read anything they'd sent..."

Ants.

That was what had jogged my memory. I nodded absently, shifting slightly in the snow, still only recalling the topic as if it had been a foggy dream from my childhood.

"You want to read them?" he asked, interrupting my thoughts. "I kept them. In case you changed your mind later."

I considered it for about ten seconds before finally shrugging. "Sure." Because I could think of absolutely nothing else more interesting to do at the moment. It was marginally better than stagnation.

"Alice put them inside your satchel," he said, jerking his chin to my right. "I'd offer to grab them, but I don't have thumbs," he said dryly. I turned to see the white-scaled leather satchel beside me, and I frowned, feeling a momentary flash of alarm.

Something about that leather was dangerous. I'd heard numerous people say so, but I couldn't recall any of their faces, or any of their actual warnings. I shook off the thought, reaching my hand into the satchel. Almost instantly, I felt two folded papers. I pulled them out, frowning down at the wax seals of the thick parchments.

One was a blue snowflake.

The other was a golden flower.

I felt a sudden wave of anxiety, but I didn't know why. It wasn't like I was afraid of the Fae Queens, but...some instinct was screaming at me in a muffled voice.

I set the folded letters in my lap, choosing to regain my composure before opening them. I glanced over at Grimm. "Where is Alice?"

Grimm arched an eyebrow at me. "Well, she was sketching over on that rock a few hours ago. Then she suddenly decided to go pick elderberries."

My shoulders tensed of their own accord, something about his answer making me uncomfortable. I couldn't place why, but it felt similar to the danger I had felt from my satchel. "Why did you say *suddenly*?"

Grimm studied me suspiciously. I stared right back, having no idea what I had done that might be construed as suspicious.

He sighed. "Dude. You randomly decided to start taking your clothes off—without giving us a word of warning." He jerked his chin to my other side where I noticed a pile of old clothes sitting in the snow. "You hadn't even pulled your shirt over your head before she noticed and ran away as fast as she could. She tossed her sketchbook into the igloo, snatched up her basket, and then ran that way," he explained jerking his chin behind me.

I frowned, looking over my shoulder at the igloo pressed up against the wall of the mountain—our little home. I saw Alice's sketchbook on the ground, halfway into the doorway, corroborating Grimm's story.

I glanced down to see that he was right about another thing. I was definitely naked. Luckily, the letters from the queens concealed most of my dangerous bits.

"You don't remember any of that either?" he asked, sounding mildly concerned.

Instead of answering, I focused on the letters, scratching at the stubble on my chin with two fingers. "You should probably go check on her. I'll put some pants on," I said woodenly.

He didn't move for a few moments, but I pretended not to notice, turning each letter over as if inspecting them for magical traps. The truth was, I vaguely remembered doing exactly as Grimm said. But only *after* he'd mentioned it. Part of me found nothing wrong with my decision to strip down to my skin, but I was beginning to sense an altogether different voice in my head. It was muffled and distant, but it carried a lot of emotional baggage with it. And that voice was growing louder, and closer to the forefront of my thoughts with each passing second.

"Go. Get. Alice!" I snapped. I had to consciously focus on my words, feeling a sudden migraine coming on—a splitting tension in the base of my skull that threatened to knock me unconscious. And it had all started with that abstract voice.

My tone must have given Grimm cause for alarm, because he was already galloping away from me as fast as he could.

I let out a shuddering breath, relieved to have relative privacy, even if only for a few moments. Long enough to work out this problem in my mind.

"What the hell is happening to me, and where is that voice coming from?" I whispered out loud. And I realized I sounded afraid.

Turn the page to read a sample of <u>UNCHAINED</u> - Feathers and Fire Series Book 1, or **BUY ONLINE (FREE with Kindle Unlimited subscription)**. Callie Penrose is a wizard in Kansas City, MO who hunts monsters for the Vatican. She meets Nate Temple, and things devolve from there...

(Note: Callie appears in the TempleVerse after Nate's book 6, TINY GODS...Full chronology of all books in the TempleVerse shown on the 'Books by Shayne Silvers' page)

TRY: UNCHAINED (FEATHERS AND FIRE #1)

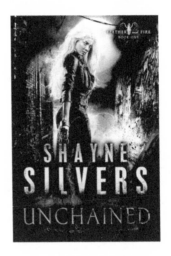

The rain pelted my hair, plastering loose strands of it to my forehead as I panted, eyes darting from tree to tree, terrified of each shifting branch, splash of water, and whistle of wind slipping through the nightscape around us. But... I was somewhat *excited*, too.

Somewhat.

"Easy, girl. All will be well," the big man creeping just ahead of me, murmured.

"You said we were going to get ice cream!" I hissed at him, failing to compose myself, but careful to keep my voice low and my eyes alert. "I'm not ready for this!" I had been trained to fight, with my hands, with weapons, and with my magic. But I had never taken an active role in a hunt before. I'd always been the getaway driver for my mentor.

The man grunted, grey eyes scanning the trees as he slipped through the tall grass. "And did we not get ice cream before coming here? Because I think I see some in your hair."

"You know what I mean, Roland. You tricked me." I checked the tips of my loose hair, saw nothing, and scowled at his back.

"The Lord does not give us a greater burden than we can shoulder."

I muttered dark things under my breath, wiping the water from my eyes. Again. My new shirt was going to be ruined. Silk never fared well in the rain. My choice of shoes wasn't much better. Boots, yes, but distressed, *fashionable* boots. Not work boots designed for the rain and mud. Definitely not monster hunting boots for our evening excursion through one of Kansas City's wooded parks. I realized I was forcibly distracting myself, keeping my mind busy with mundane thoughts to avoid my very real anxiety. Because whenever I grew nervous, an imagined nightmare always—

A church looming before me. Rain pouring down. Night sky and a glowing moon overhead. I was all alone. Crying on the cold, stone steps, an infant in a cardboard box—

I forced the nightmare away, breathing heavily. "You know I hate it when you talk like that," I whispered to him, trying to regain my composure. I wasn't angry with him, but was growing increasingly uncomfortable with our situation after my brief flashback of fear.

"Doesn't mean it shouldn't be said," he said kindly. "I think we're close. Be alert. Remember your training. Banish your fears. I am here. And the Lord is here. He always is."

So, he had noticed my sudden anxiety. "Maybe I should just go back to the car. I know I've trained, but I really don't think—"

A shape of fur, fangs, and claws launched from the shadows towards me, cutting off my words as it snarled, thirsty for my blood.

And my nightmare slipped back into my thoughts like a veiled assassin, a wraith hoping to hold me still for the monster to eat. I froze, unable to move. Twin sticks of power abruptly erupted into being in my clenched fists, but my fear swamped me with that stupid nightmare, the sticks held at my side, useless to save me.

Right before the beast's claws reached me, it grunted as something batted it from the air, sending it flying sideways. It struck a tree with another grunt and an angry whine of pain.

I fell to my knees right into a puddle, arms shaking, breathing fast.

My sticks crackled in the rain like live cattle prods, except their entire length was the electrical section — at least to anyone other than me. I could hold them without pain.

Magic was a part of me, coursing through my veins whether I wanted it or not, and Roland had spent many years teaching me how to master it. But I had never been able to fully master the nightmare inside me, and in moments of fear, it always won, overriding my training.

The fact that I had resorted to weapons — like the ones he had trained me with — rather than a burst of flame, was startling. It was good in the fact that my body's reflexes knew enough to call up a defense even without my direct command, but bad in the fact that it was the worst form of defense for the situation presented. I could have very easily done as Roland did, and hurt it from a distance. But I hadn't. Because of my stupid block.

Roland placed a calloused palm on my shoulder, and I flinched. "Easy, see? I am here." But he did frown at my choice of weapons, the reprimand silent but loud in my mind. I let out a shaky breath, forcing my fear back down. It was all in my head, but still, it wasn't easy. Fear could be like that.

I focused on Roland's implied lesson. Close combat weapons — even magically-powered ones — were for last resorts. I averted my eyes in very real shame. I knew these things. He didn't even need to tell me them. But when that damned nightmare caught hold of me, all my training went out the window. It haunted me like a shadow, waiting for moments just like this, as if trying to kill me. A form of psychological suicide? But it was why I constantly refused to join Roland on his hunts. He knew about it. And although he was trying to help me overcome that fear, he never pressed too hard.

Rain continued to sizzle as it struck my batons. I didn't let them go, using them as a totem to build my confidence back up. I slowly lifted my eyes to nod at him as I climbed back to my feet.

That's when I saw the second set of eyes in the shadows, right before they flew out of the darkness towards Roland's back. I threw one of my batons and missed, but that pretty much let Roland know that an unfriendly was behind him. Either that or I had just failed to murder my mentor at point-blank range. He whirled to confront the monster, expecting another aerial assault as he unleashed a ball of fire that splashed over the tree at chest height, washing the trunk in blue flames. But this monster was tricky. It hadn't planned on tackling Roland, but had merely jumped out of the darkness to get closer, no doubt learning from its fallen comrade, who still lay unmoving against the tree behind me.

His coat shone like midnight clouds with hints of lightning flashing in the depths of thick, wiry fur. The coat of dew dotting his fur reflected the moonlight, giving him a faint sheen as if covered in fresh oil. He was tall, easily hip height at the shoulder, and barrel chested, his rump much leaner than the rest of his body. He — I assumed male from the long, thick mane around his neck — had a very long snout, much longer and wider than any werewolf I had ever seen. Amazingly, and beyond my control, I realized he was beautiful.

But most of the natural world's lethal hunters were beautiful.

He landed in a wet puddle a pace in front of Roland, juked to the right, and then to the left, racing past the big man, biting into his hamstrings on his way by.

A wash of anger rolled over me at seeing my mentor injured, dousing my fear, and I swung my baton down as hard as I could. It struck the beast in the rump as it tried to dart back to cover — a typical wolf tactic. My blow singed his hair and shattered bone. The creature collapsed into a puddle of mud with a yelp, instinctively snapping his jaws over his shoulder to bite whatever had hit him.

I let him. But mostly out of dumb luck as I heard Roland hiss in pain, falling to the ground.

The monster's jaws clamped around my baton, and there was an immediate explosion of teeth and blood that sent him flying several feet away into the tall brush, yipping, screaming, and staggering. Before he slipped out of sight, I noticed that his lower jaw was simply *gone*, from the contact of his saliva on my electrified magical batons. Then he managed to limp into the woods with more pitiful yowls, but I had no mind to chase him.

Roland — that titan of a man, my mentor — was hurt. I could smell copper in the air, and knew we had to get out of here. Fast. Because we had anticipated only one of the monsters. But there had been two of them, and they hadn't been the run-of-the-mill werewolves we had been warned about. If there were two, perhaps there were more. And they were evidently the prehistoric cousin of any werewolf I had ever seen or read about.

Roland hissed again as he stared down at his leg, growling with both pain and anger. My eyes darted back to the first monster, wary of another attack. It *almost* looked like a werewolf, but bigger. Much bigger. He didn't move, but I saw he was breathing. He had a notch in his right ear and a jagged scar on his long snout. Part of me wanted to go over to him and torture him. Slowly. Use his pain to finally drown my nightmare, my fear. The fear that had caused Roland's injury. My lack of inner-strength had not only put me in danger, but had hurt my mentor, my friend.

I shivered, forcing the thought away. That was *cold*. Not me. Sure, I was no stranger to fighting, but that had always been in a ring. Practicing. Sparring. Never life or death.

But I suddenly realized something very dark about myself in the chill, rainy night. Although I was terrified, I felt a deep ocean of anger manifest inside me, wanting only to dispense justice as I saw fit. To use that rage to battle my own demons. As if feeding one would starve the other, reminding me of the Cherokee Indian Legend Roland had once told me.

An old Cherokee man was teaching his grandson about life. "*A fight is going on inside me,*" *he told the boy.* "*It is a terrible fight between two wolves. One is evil* — *he is anger, envy, sorrow, regret, greed, arrogance, self-pity, guilt, resentment, inferiority, lies, false pride, superiority, and ego.*" *After a few moments to make sure he had the boy's undivided attention, he continued.*

"*The other wolf is good* — *he is joy, peace, love, hope, serenity, humility, kindness, benevolence, empathy, generosity, truth, compassion, and faith. The same fight is going on inside of you, boy, and inside of every other person, too.*"

The grandson thought about this for a few minutes before replying. "*Which wolf will win?*"

The old Cherokee man simply said, "*The one you feed, boy. The one you feed...*"

And I felt like feeding one of my wolves today, by killing this one...

Get the full book ONLINE! http://www.shaynesilvers.com/l/38952

Turn the page to read a sample of **WHISKEY GINGER** *- Phantom Queen Diaries Book 1, or* **BUY ONLINE.** *Quinn MacKenna is a black magic arms dealer from Boston, and her bark is almost as bad as her bite.*

TRY: WHISKEY GINGER (PHANTOM QUEEN DIARIES # 1)

The pasty guitarist hunched forward, thrust a rolled-up wad of paper deep into one nostril, and snorted a line of blood crystals —frozen hemoglobin that I'd smuggled over in a refrigerated canister—with the uncanny grace of a drug addict. He sat back, fangs gleaming, and pawed at his nose. "That's some bodacious shit. Hey, bros," he said, glancing at his fellow band members, "come hit this shit before it melts."

He fetched one of the backstage passes hanging nearby, pried the plastic badge from its lanyard, and used it to split up the crystals, murmuring something in an accent that reminded me of California. Not *the* California, but you know, Cali-foh-nia—the land of beaches, babes, and bros. I retrieved a toothpick from my pocket and punched it through its thin wrapper. "So," I asked no one in particular, "now that ye have the product, who's payin'?"

Another band member stepped out of the shadows to my left, and I don't mean that figuratively, either—the fucker literally stepped out of the shadows. I scowled at him, but hid my surprise, nonchalantly rolling the toothpick from one side of my mouth to the other.

The rest of the band gathered around the dressing room table, following the guitarist's lead by preparing their own snorting utensils—tattered magazine covers, mostly. Typically, you'd do this sort of thing with a dollar-bill, maybe even a Benjamin if you were flush. But fangers like this lot couldn't touch cash directly—in God We Trust and all that. Of course, I didn't really understand why sucking blood the old-fashioned way had suddenly gone out of style. More of a rush, maybe?

"It lasts longer," the vampire next to me explained, catching my mildly curious expression. "It's especially good for shows and stuff. Makes us look, like, less—"

"Creepy?" I offered, my Irish brogue lilting just enough to make it a question.

"Pale," he finished, frowning.

I shrugged. "Listen, I've got places to be," I said, holding out my hand.

"I'm sure you do," he replied, smiling. "Tell you what, why don't you, like, hang around for a bit? Once that wears off," he dipped his head toward the bloody powder smeared across the table's surface, "we may need a pick-me-up." He rested his hand on my arm and our gazes locked.

I blinked, realized what he was trying to pull, and rolled my eyes. His widened in surprise, then shock as I yanked out my toothpick and shoved it through his hand.

"Motherfuck—"

"I want what we agreed on," I declared. "Now. No tricks."

The rest of the band saw what happened and rose faster than I could blink. They circled me, their grins feral...they might have even seemed intimidating if it weren't for the fact that they each had a case of the sniffles —I had to work extra hard not to think about what it felt like to have someone else's blood dripping down my nasal cavity.

I held up a hand.

"Can I ask ye gentlemen a question before we get started?" I asked. "Do ye even *have* what I asked for?"

Two of the band members exchanged looks and shrugged. The guitarist, however, glanced back towards the dressing room, where a brown paper bag sat next to a case full of makeup. He caught me looking and bared his teeth, his fangs stretching until it looked like it would be uncomfortable for him to close his mouth without piercing his own lip.

"Follow-up question," I said, eyeing the vampire I'd stabbed as he gingerly withdrew the toothpick from his hand and flung it across the room with a snarl. "Do ye do each other's make-up? Since, ye know, ye can't use mirrors?"

I was genuinely curious.

The guitarist grunted. "Mike, we have to go on soon."

"Wait a minute. Mike?" I turned to the snarling vampire with a frown. "What happened to *The Vampire Prospero*?" I glanced at the numerous fliers in the dressing room, most of which depicted the band members wading through blood, with Mike in the lead, each one titled *The Vampire Prospero* in *Rocky Horror Picture Show* font. Come to think of it...Mike did look a little like Tim Curry in all that leather and lace.

I was about to comment on the resemblance when Mike spoke up, "Alright, change of plans, bros. We're gonna drain this bitch before the show. We'll look totally—"

"Creepy?" I offered, again.

"Kill her."

Get the full book ONLINE! http://www.shaynesilvers.com/l/206897

(Note: Full chronology of all books in the TempleVerse shown on the 'BOOKS BY SHAYNE SILVERS' page.)

MAKE A DIFFERENCE

Reviews are the most powerful tools in my arsenal when it comes to getting attention for my books. Much as I'd like to, I don't have the financial muscle of a New York publisher.

But I do have something much more powerful and effective than that, and it's something that those publishers would kill to get their hands on.

A committed and loyal bunch of readers.

Honest reviews of my books help bring them to the attention of other readers.

If you've enjoyed this book, I would be very grateful if you could spend just five minutes leaving a review on my book's Amazon page.

Thank you very much in advance.

ACKNOWLEDGMENTS

Team Temple and the Den of Freaks on Facebook have become family to me. I couldn't do it without die-hard readers like them.

I would also like to thank you, the reader. I hope you enjoyed reading *LEGEND* as much as I enjoyed writing it. Be sure to check out the two crossover series in the Temple Verse: The **Feathers and Fire Series** and the **Phantom Queen Diaries.**

And last, but definitely not least, I thank my wife, Lexy. Without your support, none of this would have been possible.

ABOUT SHAYNE SILVERS

Shayne is a man of mystery and power, whose power is exceeded only by his mystery...

He currently writes the Amazon Bestselling **Nate Temple** Series, which features a foul-mouthed wizard from St. Louis. He rides a bloodthirsty unicorn, drinks with Achilles, and is pals with the Four Horsemen.

He also writes the Amazon Bestselling **Feathers and Fire** Series—a second series in the TempleVerse. The story follows a rookie spell-slinger named Callie Penrose who works for the Vatican in Kansas City. Her problem? Hell seems to know more about her past than she does.

He coauthors **The Phantom Queen Diaries**—a third series set in The TempleVerse—with Cameron O'Connell. The story follows Quinn MacKenna, a mouthy black magic arms dealer in Boston. All she wants? A round-trip ticket to the Fae realm...and maybe a drink on the house.

He also writes the **Shade of Devil Series**, which tells the story of Sorin Ambrogio—the world's FIRST vampire. He was put into a magical slumber by a Native American Medicine Man when the Americas were first discovered by Europeans. Sorin wakes up after five-hundred years to learn that his protege, Dracula, stole his reputation and that no one has ever even heard of Sorin Ambrogio. The streets of New York City will run with blood as Sorin reclaims his legend.

Shayne holds two high-ranking black belts, and can be found writing in a coffee shop, cackling madly into his computer screen while pounding shots of espresso. He's hard at work on the newest books in the TempleVerse—You can find updates on new releases or chronological reading order on the next page, his website, or any of his social media accounts. <u>Follow him online for all sorts of groovy goodies, giveaways, and new release updates:</u>

Get Down with Shayne Online
www.shaynesilvers.com
info@shaynesilvers.com

facebook.com/shaynesilversfanpage
amazon.com/author/shaynesilvers
bookbub.com/profile/shayne-silvers
instagram.com/shaynesilversofficial
twitter.com/shaynesilvers
goodreads.com/ShayneSilvers

BOOKS BY SHAYNE SILVERS

CHRONOLOGY: All stories in the TempleVerse are shown in chronological order on the following pages

NATE TEMPLE SERIES
(Main series in the TempleVerse)
by Shayne Silvers

FAIRY TALE - FREE prequel novella #0 for my subscribers

OBSIDIAN SON

BLOOD DEBTS

GRIMM

SILVER TONGUE

BEAST MASTER

BEERLYMPIAN (Novella #5.5 in the 'LAST CALL' anthology)

TINY GODS

DADDY DUTY (Novella #6.5)

WILD SIDE

WAR HAMMER

NINE SOULS

HORSEMAN

LEGEND

KNIGHTMARE

ASCENSION

CARNAGE

SAVAGE

FEATHERS AND FIRE SERIES

(Also set in the TempleVerse)

by Shayne Silvers

UNCHAINED

RAGE

WHISPERS

ANGEL'S ROAR

MOTHERLUCKER (Novella #4.5 in the 'LAST CALL' anthology)

SINNER

BLACK SHEEP

GODLESS

ANGHELLIC

TRINITY

HALO BREAKER

PHANTOM QUEEN DIARIES

(Also set in the TempleVerse)

by Cameron O'Connell & Shayne Silvers

COLLINS (Prequel novella #0 in the 'LAST CALL' anthology)

WHISKEY GINGER

COSMOPOLITAN

OLD FASHIONED

MOTHERLUCKER (Novella #2.5 in the 'LAST CALL' anthology)

DARK AND STORMY

MOSCOW MULE

WITCHES BREW

SALTY DOG

SEA BREEZE

HURRICANE

BRIMSTONE KISS

MOONSHINE

CHRONOLOGICAL ORDER: TEMPLE VERSE

FAIRY TALE (TEMPLE PREQUEL)

OBSIDIAN SON (TEMPLE 1)

BLOOD DEBTS (TEMPLE 2)

GRIMM (TEMPLE 3)

SILVER TONGUE (TEMPLE 4)

BEAST MASTER (TEMPLE 5)

BEERLYMPIAN (TEMPLE 5.5)

TINY GODS (TEMPLE 6)

DADDY DUTY (TEMPLE NOVELLA 6.5)

UNCHAINED (FEATHERS...1)

RAGE (FEATHERS...2)

WILD SIDE (TEMPLE 7)

WAR HAMMER (TEMPLE 8)

WHISPERS (FEATHERS...3)

COLLINS (PHANTOM 0)

WHISKEY GINGER (PHANTOM...1)

NINE SOULS (TEMPLE 9)

COSMOPOLITAN (PHANTOM...2)

ANGEL'S ROAR (FEATHERS...4)

MOTHERLUCKER (FEATHERS 4.5, PHANTOM 3.5)

OLD FASHIONED (PHANTOM...3)

HORSEMAN (TEMPLE 10)

DARK AND STORMY (PHANTOM...4)

MOSCOW MULE (PHANTOM...5)

SINNER (FEATHERS...5)

WITCHES BREW (PHANTOM...6)

LEGEND (TEMPLE...11)

SALTY DOG (PHANTOM...7)

BLACK SHEEP (FEATHERS...6)

GODLESS (FEATHERS...7)

KNIGHTMARE (TEMPLE 12)

ASCENSION (TEMPLE 13)

SEA BREEZE (PHANTOM...8)

HURRICANE (PHANTOM...9)

BRIMSTONE KISS (PHANTOM...10)

ANGHELLIC (FEATHERS...8)

CARNAGE (TEMPLE 14)

MOONSHINE (PHANTOM...11)

TRINITY (FEATHERS...9)

SAVAGE (TEMPLE...15)

HALO BREAKER (FEATHERS...10)

SHADE OF DEVIL SERIES

(Not part of the TempleVerse)

by Shayne Silvers

DEVIL'S DREAM

DEVIL'S CRY

DEVIL'S BLOOD

DEVIL'S DUE (coming 2021...)

Made in the USA
Las Vegas, NV
02 April 2022

46769686R00146